BLOODY TRAILS

A WESTERN DOUBLE

BOB HERZBERG

Bloody Trails: A Western Double
Paperback Edition

Wolfpack Publishing
1707 E. Diana Street
Tampa, FL 33610

www.wolfpackpublishing.com

Paperback ISBN 979-8-89567-832-9
Ebook ISBN 979-8-89567-831-2

To Colleen,
The Angel who was always there for me

BLOODY TRAILS

KRAINERS' CABIN

ONE

The noise of the brush was loud in the natural silence of the forest as the man in overalls frantically shoved bush branches out of his way so he could plunge forward unimpeded. Unfortunately, the sound carried, and his pursuer was immediately alerted to his location.

The sun was gradually going down and the winds from the Ouachita Mountains were picking up, gaining speed as they blew through the forest. But as Herm Bartlett kept moving, as sweat soaked his clothes and formed on his forehead despite the winds, his anxiety increased as he realized his wife was still in their kitchen, lying on the cracked wooden floor, her head caked with blood.

His long legs made a frantic path through the foliage as the man chasing him closed the gap. He could even hear the big man coming nearer with a swing of his pursuer's legs covering four, maybe five good strides as he moved fast on Bartlett's trail.

As the farmer ran, the tears long suppressed were

coming to the surface. He wondered, as he ran through the woods ducking branches and skirting tree trunks, whether he was indeed a coward. He had left his beloved wife of twenty-three years back there to die. He didn't fight them and he didn't sacrifice himself to their attack, he just upped and ran. And not only his beloved Sarah, but little Angela as well. She was left there, sitting innocently at the long table, blinking her baby-blue eyes at what was happening and failing to understand what was going on until it was too late. But when her mother was bludgeoned like a mad dog, she screamed. She screamed and screamed as if there would be no end to it. Herm still heard it when he was already a hundred yards from the cabin. It would haunt her father's dreams for the rest of his natural life—that is, if he still had one left after this chase.

It's a rare person who doesn't trip and fall when forced to run and not prepared for it. So Herm fell heavily, face-forward onto the broken twigs beneath a plush cottonwood. He grunted in pain and then, raising his head an inch off the ground, hardly noticed the blood streaming down his busted lip.

Then he heard the sudden loud swish of a branch being thrown aside and shot up from the ground in a panic. He traveled a mere twelve feet before the impact hit him on the back of his left shoulder blade. He cried out, the searing pain hitting him as he plowed forward, head down and legs moving fast.

The failed swing had thrown his pursuer off-balance and he stumbled, giving Bartlett a chance to gain some ground, but with each step the farmer's shoulder radiated stabbing pains. Had he had time to consider it, he would've realized that his shoulder was severely dislocated and his ranch shirt was torn and the left strap on his overalls was severed. He tried to gather what few thoughts he had as he ran. Perhaps he could swing around to the wagon, to reach into the boot and bring out the shotgun. To turn the thing on this animal at his heels and let go both barrels at his big ugly head. Then go back to the cabin and gun down the other animals who took his wife and probably murdered his red-haired little girl. He could still see her little blue eyes blinking without comprehension at what was going on just before that hulking thing broke his poor wife's skull.

Herm stumbled again, but he righted himself quickly. He had turned during his run, hoping to angle his way back to the wagon and get to the gun. He kept shoving aside the branches of the thick shrubbery blocking his way, his shoulder shooting darts of fire through him as he did so.

Bartlett was close to the trail now. He could even see the surrounding woods parting and better sunlight in the distance. Then he slowed down and shoved aside the last branches to view the spot he had left their wagon. The sight made him recoil in shock.

There they were: the old man, that awful crone of a wife, and worst of all, that tall, beautiful daughter of theirs, still standing with proud carriage and the narrowed green eyes of a predatory cat, making her presence felt even in this forest of already predatory forest creatures. The old man and woman were quickly —for them anyway—unloading the family's belongings from the wagon and carrying them toward the main house, a one-story frame structure with a sloping roof and worn shutters. The daughter stood there with her arms folded stridently, ordering her parents to get a move on—as if she was a warehouse supervisor prodding lazy workmen to unload freight at a railroad yard.

Still, the horrible reality struck him: In his panicky flight, he had been running in a full circle.

His eyes quickly went down toward the hard-packed ground beneath the wagon and caught a glimpse of Angela's little brown-haired doll—the one he had personally bought the material for so his wife could sew it together and present to her happily squealing little girl for Christmas—these vultures having no use for it.

But the view took too long, the pause dangerous, and now he would reap the consequences. The footfall was right behind him, and Herm had just enough time to see the arm with the hammer raised high and then strike down with awful force. The pain was but a momentary flash before the hammer's claw knocked off his straw hat and plowed a quick path down from the top of his skull. Then, Mose kneeled down to the fallen body and continued the swing of his claw hammer—again and again and again.

The three others at the wagon stopped what they were doing and looked at the bushes where the killing had taken place. Her arms still folded, Clarissa walked over to the spot and saw Mose standing erect with the dripping claw hammer in his big hand.

"It's all right!" she called to them cheerfully. "Mose just butchered another animal, that's all."

Satisfied, they all went back to their "work."

Mose stuck the hammer in his belt and scanned his handiwork. Then he lifted up Bartlett's left foot and turned around.

He then dragged the body across the leaf-covered ground and finally arrived at the cabin. Pulling the body inside, he then slammed the door shut.

In another minute or two, the chopping sounds began...

KATHERINE GELDER SAT on the row of benches in the First Greenwood Presbyterian Church. Her eyes rose up to the rafters of the plywood ceiling, then to the beautiful stained windows (an expense for the town, but Reverend Archwald figured they were worth it), then she looked at the wall on the right, then the one on the left. Then her eyes went to the hefty organ player whose name she didn't know who played beautifully, but was an eyesore to look at.

Her father elbowed her and harshly asked, "Girl, you payin' attention?"

She looked at her Bible and quietly recited the psalms along with everyone else.

Her folks had nicknamed her "Kat." As she sat there and the reverend droned on, her wandering mind went back to six weeks ago, when she and her pa bid farewell to his stepbrother and his family as they embarked on their journey to stay with other kin in Phoenix, before ultimately traveling to sunny California. At dinner that night, despite genuinely liking her step-uncle and his lovely wife, Kat was really fond of little Angela. She was adorable, with her blue eyes, button nose, and red hair peeking out for beneath her little bonnet.

She remembered the way Uncle Herm (or was it

step-uncle Herm?) smiled at his wife, the way he was always attentive to her. He would always have his rough hand on his wife's shoulder, stroking her red hair, affectionately squeezing the already parchment-like skin on her arm through the sleeve of her old faded brown dress. All this love shown while they were all sitting at the dinner table! She wondered then if her own pa would show her—not all that demonstrative stroking and patting—but little things like his concern, respect, encouragement, the quiet affection—*I mean, I am his daughter, right?*

But Sam Gelder wasn't that kind of man. His wife had been gone from their lives for almost a year. He was raising his daughter on his own and he *still* couldn't find any prospects in town who would make a good mother for her. Lord knows, he tried. But she remembered that the women he brought home always liked her handsome dad, but after they had gone upstairs with him, they really seemed to have no further use for him—at least, not for couple days or so anyway.

She knew her father was a handsome man—for a small town like Greenwood anyway. Tall and dark-haired and with sharp blue eyes and a thin nose that reminded her of pictures in her schoolbooks of some Greek god. But Sam Gelder wasn't a Greek god, he was the town marshal. He didn't issue lightning bolts from his hands, he rousted drunks and buffaloed the town's hardcases, not with a scepter but with a Colt. And here she was, in a church whose dictates she didn't understand and whose rituals bored her. Kat was now on the lee side of seventeen; she had a yearning for some old-fashioned adventure, not singing lyrics in a rotting old building (despite the expense of those windows) which didn't appeal to her. But here it was, the summer of 1896, and the small towns of the west were still latched onto their small-town ways. She was hoping the coming twentieth century would be a lot more interesting.

But some things *never* changed. The next morning, after the Bartletts had left, her pa told her that she *used* to look as cute as her little niece—stepniece—and then, compliment over, ordered her to clean the dishes. She resentfully did so, loudly clattering a few plates while she was at it. Stewing, she reminded herself that she was a bit tall and gawky for her age, but her dark-blonde hair, blue eyes, upturned nose, and full lips hadn't hurt in attracting boys. As she had wiped the dishes, Kat spied him still sitting at the table, a whiskey bottle close at hand as he stared at something which wasn't there at the end of the table. A stain on the tablecloth? She doubted it.

Maybe he just didn't want her to grow up. Or maybe he was bitter that he had to work harder to feed her as well as himself.

Or more likely, as she attained womanhood, she reminded him too much of someone he'd lost not too long ago...

Gelder and his daughter went slowly down the boardwalk, not saying a word. Then Kat took her eyes off the walk and looked up to see Deputy Horace Grimes coming toward them. Or rather, he waddled toward them. Idly, Kat guessed that the big deputy might actually be attractive to the opposite sex if he could shed a few dozen pounds.

Grimes stopped before them and, after his huffing and puffing ceased, blurted out that he got a report from that new-fangled box they just installed in the marshal's office.

"Must be something powerful important to get you to move as fast as that," drawled Sam with a smile and a sparkle in his eye. He loved poking fun at his deputy's girth—though he tried (and usually failed) not to be cruel about it.

"Well, this *is* important," Grimes replied. "The Hot Springs Bank has been robbed."

Gelder dropped the smile. Without thinking, he glanced at his daughter, who also looked concerned.

"How long ago?"

"Happened this morning, a few hours ago."

"It's half-past eleven now. How early?"

Grimes exhaled and said, "Must've happened before the sun rose. Front door was unlocked. They just walked right in. Rifled the tellers' cages, then got to the safe."

"The safe? Hasn't that got a timer set for eight forty-five in the morning, if I recall?"

Grimes nodded and said, "Yep. And the man who set the timer set it for three thirty a.m.!"

"What?!"

Grimes nodded and said, "One of the bank officials, little guy named Bates must've been in on it. He didn't show up at the bank the next morning and his place was empty, no clothes, no luggage. But he didn't go far."

"What happened?"

Grimes said, "The posse caught up to Bates somewhere in the Ouachitas. He already had a bullet in the stomach, as well as other places. In fact, he was shot up from this way to next Thursday. The other man must've double-crossed him. The money was all gone. Anyways, Bates *still* held on long enough, believe it or not, to tell us who the other man was. Someone *a lot* more experienced at this kind of job than a mousy bank clerk. Wanted for bank robbery in Texas too. A jasper from the Panhandle named Dirk Johnson."

Gelder pursed his lips and thought about it. "Johnson. Maybe this question is pointless, but did anybody get hurt during the robbery itself?"

Grimes shook his head. "Not a soul. I mean, who was around in the middle of the night?"

Sam gave a little half-smile and said, "That figures. Johnson usually avoids bystanders like the plague. No complications like folks gettin' in the way and then having to shoot anyone. No people, no posses, get an inside man, break in in the middle of the night, and get out clean with no blood on his hands and no rope in his future. The only one he blew away was his 'partner'..."

Grimes agreed. "He's good, all right. The Hot Springs marshal said he might be headin' this way."

"With a whole mountain range in front of 'em?"

"I said he was good. Trail went cold up in those rocks..."

Kat's eyes went from her dad's to the deputy's. Deep down, she tried to hide her excitement. *A real live bank robber headed this way! Nothing ever happened in Greenwood since they dedicated that Civil War cannon in the town square!*

She then blurted out, "Is he really coming this way??"

Grimes smirked at Sam—who didn't smile back—

and said to her, "You don't have to be scared, Button. He probably won't head this way."

Kat didn't say anything, but her face showed fury. *Scared?! And who does this hippopotamus think he's calling Button?!*

Gelder, however, was not as amused by her question as his deputy was.

Quietly, he said, "I'll get back to the jail and call Hot Springs and get more information on this man."

"Oh, something else," said Grimes, just remembering something. "That York woman was back this morning."

Gelder frowned and asked, "And what did she want this time? As if I didn't know."

Grimes nodded and said, "Yep. She still wants to know what we're doin' about apprehending her big brother's killers."

Kat's eyes practically sparkled as she heard all this. She couldn't stop smiling.

Grimes then added, "She also mentioned this family she was after and the disappearances and all—"

Sam cut him off. "Yeah, I've heard her stories already."

"You got to admit, Sam. Some folks around here are gettin' scared. They've heard news from kin in other counties. Like folks were on their way to somewhere and they never get there. Now if this were twenty, maybe even *ten* years ago, I'd say the damn Indians caught 'em as they were heading west and..." He then cut his finger across his throat in a slicing gesture, accompanied by a comical sound meant to convey throat-cutting. Then his eyes suddenly became alert and he glanced uncomfortably at Kat.

Excitement was clearly etched on her face.

She asked, almost hopefully, "Are there really killers around here disappearin' folks?"

Grimes humored her with, "Now why would you want to think such—"

But Sam cut him off. Glaring at Kat, he said harshly, "Now you wipe that stupid smile off your face right now, young lady, or I'll wipe it off for you!"

Kat frowned, both hurt and embarrassed by her father's threat—especially in front of a clown like Grimes.

"Well," said Grimes, himself embarrassed by Sam's threat, "I better get movin'. See ya later."

"Right," said Gelder as they watched the deputy waddle down the street...

As THEY WENT DOWN the boardwalk. Sam said, "I don't know where you get the idea that you can ask things like that. My job is *my* business, you understand? Not yours!"

Kat looked up at him with hurt in her eyes. "But... you're my dad. I...I just want to show my concern for what you're doing. Maybe be able to help you down the way—"

He stopped and looked down at her seriously. "Now listen," he started, and then up came that long index finger to make the usual condescending point to her. "You are not to get involved in my job. Bein' a law dog is for *grown men*, not little girls."

"Little girls!"

He nodded and said, "You keep your mind on

school! Miss Stoutly tells me your grades could be a whole lot better."

"Yes, but I'm not going to go to school forever! I've got to have *something* to do when I leave it."

"You will! You'll be the wife of some nice young man and have a family of your own. You're not going to worry about bank robbers and cattle thieves and folks disappearing. That's *my* job! And the boy you're gonna marry isn't going to be some no-good layabout like Leo Groman!"

"Leo's no layabout! He don't need no schoolin' either! He's got book learnin'!"

"You need someone who moves his behind to put food on the table, not some jasper with *book learnin'*!"

"But, Pa—"

"Not *now*, Kat! I've got to go to the office to get more on this bank robber and the disappear—well, I've got to go to the office. Now go back home!"

She hesitated, a frown on her face.

Gelder said firmly, "I don't want to slap you in public, Kat. But I will if I have to."

Kat looked up at him as tears started to come. But before they could spill out, she turned and ran down the street.

Sam watched her go, swallowing a little as he saw her get to the corner and then vanish around a cluster of people. What made him threaten her like that yet again? Whatever it was, he immediately hated himself for doing it. Was he *that* wound up lately that he would threaten physical harm to his own flesh and blood like that? Not only threaten her, but actually do it—especially when Kat looked a little *too* set in her ways. Something was spooking him lately and he wasn't sure what it was. He tried to relax then, and turned around and headed to his office at the local jail...

KAT WIPED her eyes as she looked down, watching the boardwalk, but hardly noticing the people on them. It was then that she ran headlong into Josie Arnold.

"Oh! I'm sorry, ma'am—Josie!"

Josie held her at arm's length and smiled at her.

She was taller than Kat and had a good seven years on her, with a striking pair of eyes which were both piercing and hypnotic. Kat would always be struck by her charm and presence—as did most everyone else in town, including its men. Josie's pinned-up dark-brown hair shone in the late morning sun as she grinned widely at the younger woman.

Kat asked, "Were you shoppin' for groceries?"

"No, silly! I just came back from the Woodburys. I once again communed with Wilbur..."

Kat looked back up at her and said, "Uh-huh." She figured it was all bunk, but she didn't have the heart to tell Josie her real feelings.

"Anyway," Josie chirped, "what are you doing here this fine Sunday morning?"

Kat frowned and said, "It's my pa."

Josie put her arm around the younger woman's shoulders and walked her down the street. She said, "We-e-el-l-l, you tell your old Auntie Josie about it."

Josie Arnold wasn't really her aunt, but she loved giving herself the title.

"Aw," Kat started hesitantly, "Pa's been chewing me

out again 'cause I looked like I wanted to get involved with his bein' a marshal, that's all."

"We-e-l-l-l, your pa's got troubles of his own. You can't blame yourself all the time."

"Don't I know it. Pa's been wound up about those disappearances."

As she walked her down the street, Josie's face became still for a moment and then she asked, "Disappearances?"

Kat nodded and said, "Oh! You know!"

"Oh yes! I think you told me about it before."

Kat reminded her, "Yes! Folks have been vanishing not far from town. It's like they ride through all these nearby counties, maybe they're on their way west or maybe not, but then it's like, poof, they disappear. Damn odd, ya ask me."

Josie stopped and held her at arm's length again. She looked into her eyes and said, "Now, Button, you shouldn't say those words. They're the words of the Devil."

Kat nodded shyly and replied, "Yes'm." She may have called her Button, but at least she didn't yell at her like Pa. Or raise her hand to her—or actually go through with the slap.

Satisfied, Josie put her arm around her shoulders again and continued their walk.

"Now," she said good-naturedly, "tell me again about these...disappearances."

"Well, I really started hearin' about it maybe a week ago. One night, Pa has Deputy Grimes up at the house and I was supposed to be asleep upstairs."

"But you weren't?"

"No, I wasn't. I kind of lingered on the stairway

steps and heard 'em talking about folks vanishing. It's like they come through the town, load up on supplies for travel, and then ride out. No one's seen or heard of these folks since. Deputy Grimes just told Pa about it again a few minutes ago, and right in front of me too! That's when Pa got angry at me for being interested in it. Strange, these folks just vanishing..."

"Well, how do you know that? Maybe these folks just got to their destinations."

"But that's the thing. The families called or wrote letters to these places and the answers they got is these folks never arrived! You know, they were just passing through and—"

Kat stopped and a scared expression came to her face. Then she turned to Josie and said, "Oh my God! What if the Bartletts disappeared? Lord, that little girl!"

"Little girl?"

"Their red-haired little girl! It was Herman Bartlett, his wife, and their little girl! They left town a few weeks ago heading for California!"

"Now, now," Josie said consolingly. "I'm sure they'll arrive out in California unharmed and your fears will be for nothing."

"But that little girl!"

The older woman could see that the anguish on Kat's face wouldn't go away and tears were in her eyes.

"Ohhh!" Josie said, in a humoring tone, reminding Kat a little of Deputy Grimes. Then she squeezed her shoulders tightly. "You're a good person to feel so concerned about them, but I'm sure nothing's happened to them. Kat, honey, folks have been traveling across the Oklahoma territory or wherever for years on their way out west and nothing's happened to them."

Kat looked up at her through the tears. She said, "As God is my witness, Josie, I want to believe you, but..."

"But what, silly?"

"They were supposed to stop off to be with kin near Phoenix, but they never showed up."

Josie gently pulled Kat out of the way of people on the boardwalk and over to an alley at the side of a building next to a general store.

"How do you know this??"

Kat looked around with some guilt. Then she said, "I've been looking through Pa's desk at the jail. He's got a report on the family from their kin in Arizona. It's been over a month and no word."

Josie said patiently, "It still doesn't mean they 'disappeared.'"

Just thinking about it, Kat couldn't stop herself and the tears started to come.

"My God, that little girl!"

Josie embraced her again.

"Now, Katherine Gelder, you stop that right now!"

"I can't help it! Just thinking about what could've happened to them! That little girl, Angela!"

The older woman's eyes shaded for just a moment, and then she pulled back and gave Kat her handkerchief.

"Here now. Dry those tears. Now, you know your Aunt Josie wouldn't lie to you."

As Kat wiped her eyes, she shook her head.

"I'll bet your pa will hear about them in a week's time. They'll be somewhere in Southern California already set up for farmin'!"

"I...I hope so..."

"Of course it'll be so! Now let's get out of this here alley before folks think we're planning something bad."

Josie led her out onto the boardwalk again. To Kat, Josie wasn't a bad sort, though she *did* get sick of this twenty-four-year-old woman talking to her as if she was six years old.

Then, as Kat looked across the street, she noticed a woman in her thirties coming down the walk, as if she was in a hurry. The woman had on a little hat tied around her soft chin and wore a brown dress that looked like it had been worn for traveling more than going about town. She was tall and her shoulders proud and straight, her green eyes large behind rimless spectacles, and her reddish-brown hair tied in a bun.

Kat said in a harsh whisper, "There she is again!"

"Who, honey?"

"That...that redhead across the way. In the glasses."

Josie turned and looked at the woman moving fast down the opposite walk.

"Well, what about her?"

"She's new in town. Looks like a real cold fish. I seen her come into town a few days ago with nothin' but an old carpetbag. No travelin' companion with her. No husband, no kin. Don't know what her business is, but when she talks to folks, she sounds real cold to them, like snotty. Like she'd just as soon drop dead than speak to *us*!"

Josie also found herself staring at the woman. "Really?"

Kat nodded and said, "Some folks say she's hidin' something. Like maybe she's a criminal or some kind of 'confidence woman.' You know, some young woman some fancy Dan conman brings with him to lure some mark and take their money."

Josie kept staring at her till she finally said, "Huh!"

Kat looked up at her, clearly not expecting that reaction.

Then Josie went back to form and said, "Well, then, if I were you, Button, I'd stay far away from her. Sounds like she's got a snooty nose, and this town doesn't need more folks like that!"

Kat actually smiled at that and said, "I hope that's just it and nothing more."

"What do you mean?"

"I don't know. Maybe she's got something to do with the disappearances."

Josie stared at her friend for a long time then, thinking about this...

Kat soon parted from her and went down the street. She quietly, but firmly, refused Josie's insistence that she accompany her to her next séance, this time with the Ashevilles. It seems that old man Asheville was kicked in the head by his mule a couple weeks ago. The mule was shot dead by his eldest son and his wife wanted to keep in contact with the old man. Josie advertised herself as a conjure woman who could bring her husband back before the grieving widow, if only for a few minutes. Josie made quite a good living at it, never once doubting her own ability. The relatives of these dead folks seemed satisfied, though Kat couldn't figure out for the life of her how her good friend Josie was able to bring back the dead, even for a moment.

Then she looked up again and saw the young woman with the spectacles turn down an alley. Curiously, Kat crossed the street and also went into the alley, keeping a far enough distance so she wouldn't be discovered.

The woman was moving briskly through the alley with determination. Nervously she glanced about her to see if anyone was near. But in that brief moment, when she wasn't facing front, she rammed into a big sweaty example of smelly manhood named Alvin Willis.

"Hey, little lady!" he said loudly.

Willis had just been on his ninth beer and had actually been relieving himself close to the side of the saloon he had exited from.

The woman looked up at him, vainly straightening her glasses.

"You look like you got a burr in your saddle, breezin' through here like your corset's on fire!"

Not answering him, the woman tried to step around him, but he blocked her. Attempting to go around him again, he blocked her again.

"Please!" she said firmly. "Let me pass!"

Kat heard the woman's curt words and guessed that she was from up north.

Just then, Willis put his meaty hands on the woman's shoulders and said, "Not on your life, honey! You look like you needs a man to slow you down some."

The woman pushed against his chest and struggled in his embrace. She smelled his body odor and the beer on his breath and felt like vomiting.

Hidden a few yards back behind two barrels, Kat watched them, wondering if she should interfere.

But then, seeing the woman's black purse as a

barrier between them, Willis pulled it out of her grip and threw it to the side. But when the purse made impact with the building's brick wall, a loud gunshot erupted close to them.

Kat ducked back against a wall when she heard the shot. Then she gingerly peeked out to look at them.

The shot surprised Willis and caused him to release his grip on her waist.

That's when the woman drew out a switchblade knife from a pocket that had purposely been sewn into the waistline of her dress. With an ugly click, she flicked the blade open, its sheen reflected in the few shafts of sunlight which made it into the alley.

Willis saw the purse lying on the alley's floor, a big hole in its corner and gunsmoke coming out of the hole. Then he saw the blade in her hand. He stared at the woman with frightened eyes, turning white as he did so. Even in his drunken, not-very-well-used brain, he realized that this woman could've either shot or stabbed him at any time and easily claimed self-defense. She was not like the usual demure female that he could drunkenly grab at will—this woman had weapons on her and appeared to be ready to use them.

In fact, while Willis was still in something close to shock, the woman quickly went to the purse and picked it up off the ground, nervously looking around to see if others had heard the shot. When she found that no one had shown up at the end of the alley, she purposely turned toward Willis, the still-smoking purse in her left hand and the open knife in her right. From her distance down the alley, Kat could still see the woman planted firmly before Willis, her expression ugly as she glared with hardened eyes at the big man.

Angrily, the woman hissed at him, "Get out of here!"

Willis stared at her, his mouth open, revealing his tobacco-stained teeth. He felt like relieving himself yet again, but instead, backed away from her and awkwardly turned and fled down the other end of the alley, loudly tripping over a garbage can as he did so. Wasting no time, he sprung off the ground and continued his flight to the other end of the alley until he was out of sight.

Kat peeked out long enough to look again at the woman's angry face as she held the knife tightly in her fist. She saw the sheer rage and swallowed at the sight. Then she saw the woman calm down and look around again to make sure she wasn't seen. Quickly, she folded up the knife and put it back into the extra pocket at her waist and made sure the gun was secure in her purse. Then, assuming a prim and proper pose, she continued down the alley, her head held high, her shoulders straight, curtly stepping over the smelly contents of the spilled-over garbage can that had got in Willis's way.

Frightened by what she had witnessed, Kat abandoned her plan to keep following the woman, at least for the present. Instead, she nodded to herself as she came to a final conclusion.

This woman *must* have something to do with the disappearances...

TWO

THEY SAT ON THE FRONT PORCH AND SCANNED THE clearing before them, both spotting the buckboard a quarter mile down the trail.

They heard the chopping noises coming from the cabin loudly echoing in the cool breeze and were hoping the approaching newcomers wouldn't hear them.

Liz Krainer was rocking in her chair, a concerned look on her aging face.

"I hope Mose gets through with that man. Those folks are gettin' close fast."

Gus Krainer replied, "He always finishes on time, Liz. And if they ask questions, we'll say our boy is just choppin wood, that's all."

"Still too close for comfort," she said, then spat on the railing, killing a rather large fly in a split second.

Gus Krainer had been called Gustav in the old country, this being Prussia.

He was formerly a military brat who would follow his father, the general, into the army, entering military school, as did so many other German boys at the time, at age eleven. In 1864, the young soldier found himself joining his fellow Prussians fighting Austrian troops. A young, green soldier from Vienna stabbed him in the left hip with his bayonet and during another skirmish he got a rifle ball in his left shoulder. However, the most distinctive wound he had, the sharp gash across his right hand came from another man in his barracks who accused him of cheating at poker (which was true). Then one day, he and two men had stormed into the home of an Austrian family along the border. The parents and their little boy were shot dead and the three soldiers helped themselves to the eldest daughter, then aged fourteen, as well as her little sister, then aged twelve. Nothing was too good for the Imperial Prussian Army.

Afterward, both girls were shot in the head and tossed down the family's well. The men had looked in vain for food in the cabinets, but the war had made the task of Austrians feeding their families hard. It was only after finding the cupboards empty and no more food on the property that the soldiers realized they had made a horrible mistake. By throwing the bodies of their victims down the well, they had unwittingly poisoned the water.

Enraged, they burned the house to the ground and, cut off from their company, were forced to forage off the parched and battle-scarred land. Lost and hungry, with the elements against them and their proud Imperial

Prussian uniforms reduced to rags, the men were forced to trudge deeper into the forest in an effort to find food. But the ravages of war had taken their toll on the landscape; small creatures who would have provided them sustenance had fled for pastures far away from rifles and cannon fire. With their tempers already frayed, and their hatred against each other reaching a boiling point, it was then that a famished and delirious Gustav took out his bayonet and slashed both his comrades in the throat as they slept. Then, almost as an afterthought, he slowly licked the blood off the blade's flat side. Enjoying the taste, he then looked down at the bodies of the men he had gutted and started to smile.

He had just solved the problem of how he would avoid starvation...

Elizabeth Mueller was the daughter of southern wealth and privilege. At eighteen, her coming marriage to the son of a plantation owner seemed secure, a rich dowry offered to her mother and father, with the nuptials planned just as the Confederate army fired on Fort Sumter. But King and Country—or in this case, Jefferson Davis and the cause of slavery—came first. The frosting had barely dried on the wedding cake before a Yankee shell blew her betrothed into several fragmented body parts flying all over the battlefield at Shiloh. Liz had mourned the loss of her beloved the only way she knew how—she ate. Pastries at first, then pies, then whole meals which would have satisfied all the members of a Daughters of the Confederacy picnic. Formerly attractive to the average male, she was now approaching 270 pounds and her stately walk became a sad waddle. Along with a fatness of face and body, her parents noticed other, more disturbing, symptoms. First she started talking to herself, then it progressed to hearing voices that weren't there, then viciously kicking small objects out of her way, be they stools, cobblestones, or small dogs and cats. These would be accompanied by angry curses at her parents, though for the life of them they couldn't understand why.

Within the space of a year, Liz had gone from the future bride of a rising young southern officer from a good family to a fat and homely girl who talked to people who weren't there and kicked puppies into the stratosphere. To her wealthy parents, she wasn't only an embarrassment, but an outright danger. She had already attacked a female cousin at the dinner table, claiming that the slice of cherry pie she was about to eat, really belonged to *her*. To Liz's parents, something had to be done—and there were places for *that*.

But Fate, or the Muses, or rather a Union shell from a cannon fired by the 5th Massachusetts artillery detail blew up the road ahead of the horse-driven wagon which contained a half a dozen members of that special society called the Mad. The horses were destroyed, the wagon overturned, the asylum's orderlies seated in the front were killed, and besides her schizophrenic comrades—and *unlike* her parents' Negro slaves—she was free. All five women were later captured, but not Liz, for despite her girth, she was still young and agile, an agility mixed with the survival instincts of a whorehouse rat.

During her journey, something else happened: She started to lose weight. After months on the run, she even lost her taste for food—ordinary food, that is. Hiding out for months as Generals Sherman and Sheridan burned crops in the Shenandoah Valley to deprive the Rebs the means to feed their soldiers, Liz was forced to live off anything else that was edible. At first, it was small mammals. Then it progressed to larger ones, *if* she could find and capture them.

Then one day, a young Union soldier, no more than sixteen, with a freckled face and baby-blue eyes, found the abandoned shack she had been living in. A ball had penetrated his ribs and he had barely made it as he crawled through her front door. At first, she cared for the young man and fed him what scraps she could.

But one moonlit night not long after the young man arrived on the small property, as crickets sounded off outside and various flies buzzed around the makeshift dinner table, Liz picked up the soldier's rifle and fired a ball into his head. She was just able to catch the pleading look in the youngster's eyes before the ball made his skull fly apart. Then she put down the rifle against the wall, picked up a pot she had rescued, and went out to the well to get some water to boil on the stove. Afterward, she took out the large knife blade she had with her from a store she had broken into, and got to work.

Then she harked back to the days when she helped her mom baste a Thanksgiving turkey...

LIZ SAT THERE WATCHING the buckboard as it rattled up the road. She leaned over and spat again.

"Gettin' close," said Gus.

It was then that the chopping noises stopped. Mose was through with his work.

"Give them the stale meat," said Gus. "As usual..."

"Can't fatten 'em on that," said Liz, putting aside her pipe.

"It'll be good enough," Gus said. "And if they complain..." He shrugged then and tiredly rose from his chair. He faced the trail and started to put on a patented smile.

"Only two of 'em," said Liz, disappointed.

"Well, what did you expect? An army?"

"No youngins! I likes the young ones." Her eyes got far away when she added, "Tasty..."

THE PRUSSIAN IMPERIAL Army found young Gustav Krainer slowly trudging toward an army campsite, his clothes in tatters and rags. They realized that he had been wandering the countryside for weeks. But then the company commander realized something else about the young soldier's condition—he hadn't lost weight. In fact, he looked pretty well-fed.

Under interrogation (and after being fed with army rations which held no pleasure for him, nor sustenance), Gus told them that the two young men with him deserted—a claim loudly disputed by their families, who could, they said, vouch for the courage of their boys in uniform. It wasn't until six days later, while there was a break in the fighting, that an army patrol made the discovery. As gingerly as they could, they brought the remains of the men back for examination by camp doctors. The bodies were mangled and torn, with exposed bones and cartilage suggesting that the men had been ripped apart by a wild animal. But the bombardments that shook the nearby forests had effectively depopulated the area of bears or other beasts. It was a few days after that when medics discovered the bite marks on the shin bone of one of the dead men. Gus's superiors realized what had happened, but kept quiet about it. They didn't even bring up the issue when they quietly ordered his dismissal from the army. It would not be good for the image of the Prussian military if it was revealed that one of their own was suffering from combat fatigue—much less what Gustav Krainer had done with his time away from the regiment.

And so, to make sure that his affliction remained a secret—and after providing him with enough capital to do so—they had him on a ship headed to the New World, no questions asked. He had little choice: Either go to America or be shot on the trumped-up charge of desertion—which, in their eyes, was better than to be shot for what he was *really* guilty of.

The War Between the States was over. Gustav could now live in a nation in relative peace—unlike the German states—and start a new life. He was given some money, new clothes, a worn valise, and a military detail personally escorted him to the pier and sent him off. His affliction, they realized, was now America's problem.

As for Germany itself, the army command structure and the politicians and crowned heads who lorded over the citizenry hoped to look forward to more days of glorious conquests into the new century and beyond...

THE COUPLE who stopped their buckboard outside the worn log fence looked at the house and the smaller cabin next to it. Gus went out to greet them.

"Howdy!" he said, raising his hand in a slight wave. Gustav has learned much from Americans since his trip from Germany over twenty years ago.

The husband in the front seat looked at him without a word.

The old woman leaned forward and said, "Hello," in a thick accent.

Gus was taken aback. He paused for a moment and then asked curiously, "Are you...Dutch??"

"*Nein*," answered the middle-aged man in the driver's seat.

Forming a smile, the short blonde woman next to him added, "We are Germans!"

Gus almost took a step back.

Then he said to them, "What are you doing here?"

The woman, who seemed to be the friendlier of the two, replied, "We are on our way west. We heard of the California valleys. We hope to farm there."

The husband nodded stonily. Unlike his wife, he had yet to crack a smile.

"Yes!" she added cheerfully. "My husband is Franz Schuler–in this country, he is called 'Frank.' And I am Viktoria–over here they spell it with a 'C'" She glanced sheepishly at her husband as if she had said a major faux pas. He didn't respond to her look.

"So," she cheerily continued, "we have traveled far with all our belongings. And we would like to stay and have a place to sleep before we go on to our..." She finally found the word. "...des-tin-ation!" Then she nodded and smiled with satisfaction.

Gus liked Viktoria right away. He even liked her Bavarian accent (for what else could it be?), as well as her golden-blonde hair under a bonnet, pink rosy cheeks, and charming smile. She so reminded him of the many women he had loved (and left) back in his days as a Prussian officer; always smiling, totally innocent to danger, and without guile of any kind.

It was like leading lambs to the slaughter.

But then, something in him broke. He didn't know if it was homesickness or sentiment or feeling a rare actual concern for another human being, but he was suddenly against the idea of these fellow countrymen getting off their wagon, entering their home and never leaving it.

Franz stared at him again, waiting for the signal to drive the buckboard through the fence and into their barn, unsaddle the horses, and enter the main house for what they hoped would be a good hot meal after their days of travel.

Viktoria, still smiling charmingly, said, "So...if there's no problem, we'd like to get—"

Suddenly, Gus said something to both of them in German, especially Franz. His words were harsh and demanding. Not that he displayed anger toward them—just urgency.

He said, "Get out of here, both of you! It is not safe for you here! Do you understand??"

Franz and Viktoria stared at him.

The old man replied in German: "What is this? What danger is there?"

"Take my word for it!" Gus answered, knowing full

well that neither Liz or Mose—who had now appeared at the cabin's entrance wiping his big, bloody hands on a rag—understood German.

Liz stood on the porch and eyed them with suspicion. *What was Pa jabbering with these people in German for?*

Gus kept up the warning. "Go! Get out of here now!"

Viktoria was now scared, and Franz caught a look in Gus's eye, even under the shadow of his beaten-up slouch hat, that chilled him.

He nodded slightly to Gus, then turned to the horses and shook the reins. They started to move forward.

From the porch, Liz angrily shouted, "Hey!"

As Franz turned the horse back to the trail, Liz went back into the house.

The Schulers were talking to themselves in German as Franz tried to pick up speed.

Viktoria asked, "Better hurry, Franz, this place scares me!"

"Trying to move these nags as fast as I can! They're tired!"

By then, Liz emerged from the house toting a two-barrel shotgun. Effortlessly, she raised it shoulder high and fired. The blast of both barrels was thunderous in the small area.

Franz shot forward off the seat and his body bounced onto the horses, frightening them. It quickly flopped onto the ground beneath them and laid there with several bloody holes in the back.

Viktoria screamed and tried to grab the trailing reins but they were already on the ground beneath the horses. Mose then ran over to the fence, easily leaped over it, and put his massive right hand on the chest of a panicky horse, stopping him from moving any further. Then he reached up and tried to grab Viktoria. She screamed again and backed away, awkwardly backing off the edge of the buckboard and falling heavily to the ground.

With her bonnet now pushed back to the base of her neck and her blonde hair falling down, Viktoria painfully got off the ground.

Mose stepped forward and reached around the horses.

"*Nein!*" she shouted, and tried to push him away.

The shove wasn't much, but it allowed her the time to duck another lunge from him and run into the woods.

Gus looked at the scene with sympathy, but he did nothing.

Pulling the claw hammer out of his waistband, Mose ran into the forest after her. Similarly, Liz went back into the house and fetched more shells for the gun. Then she ran out of the house, past the fence, and strode toward the grove of trees Viktoria had disappeared into. But before she passed Gus, she stopped and glared at him, shaking her head. Then she continued her pursuit.

Viktoria tripped and fell hard on the ground, skinning her right knee. Then she rose quickly and spotted a thick cottonwood a few feet ahead. She made for it and then ducked behind its trunk. She flattened herself and kept quiet, praying that these lunatics would pass her. She ignored the fulsome tears rolling down her cheeks as she thought of Franz...dear, dear Franz, lying in the trail back there with Lord knew how many shotgun pellets in him.

Viktoria didn't dare peek out from behind the tree to see if they were still there. She even tried to stifle the sounds of her excited breathing. Unfortunately, she couldn't do anything about the insects which suddenly crawled up her legs and down the tree's bark and into her hair, including a small spider with spindly legs coming down around her left cheek. She shut her eyes tightly, not even lifting a hand to swat it.

It was several minutes now. Liz and Mose seemed to have turned off and gone further away from her tree, over on the other side of the grove. She wondered if now was a good time to break out of her hiding place and run.

Then, after several moments, while still silently debating this course of action—and while yet another spindly legged arachnid alighted on her right shoulder—she heard Franz speaking to her in German.

"Viktoria! Where are you? Viktoria, help me! I am wounded!"

He sounded like he was just a couple feet away from her. She smiled, a sudden happiness overcoming her. *Maybe he wasn't killed after all!*

"Franz!" she cried.

Viktoria stepped out from behind the tree trunk just as the claw hammer came down. The empty shell that used to be a woman dropped limply to the ground; the insect life helping themselves to her.

Liz ordered, "Get 'er off the ground, Mose! I don't want no damn bugs on my food!"

Mose quickly slid the now-bloody claw hammer back into his weathered belt and bent over. He lifted the body up off the ground, turned back to the cabin, and carried her there.

Gus stood by and watched sadly as she disappeared into the cabin.

Liz said, "Glad you came to your senses. I don't know what got into you or what you said to them, but you forced me to use the shotgun and now Mose has to dig out all the pellets from that man's body!"

Gus answered, "The old man was giving me trouble. Started to talk out o' turn..."

"Yeah?" she said with some skepticism. "Sounded like *you* were giving *him* trouble!"

"Not at all, Liz."

"You sure 'bout that? You weren't gettin' sentimental for these two? They *are* from the old country, after all."

Gus shook his head.

"I told you. The old man was stubborn. Thought we were going to charge him a bundle and was ready to turn around and said he'd go somewhere else. Which, as you can see, he almost did..."

Liz relaxed a little and said, "Well, anyway, you still know enough kraut to fool that blonde. Maybe you should teach me kraut sometime. We got enough of these foreigners comin' around here and I'm gettin' awful tired of trying to figure out their jabberin'..." Then she shot him a withering look. Unsaid was the fact that if she knew German, then she'd be able to translate any private words Gus might say to his former countrymen that she and Mose and Clarissa couldn't understand. It's not that she didn't trust her husband of thirty years, she just understood that sentiment for a person's place of birth is a hard thing to forget.

Making her point, Liz then turned and walked back toward the house, the shotgun under her arm.

"Hey, Mose!" she called. "Clean 'er up first! Not like that sodbuster from Texas! You left him out so long, the maggots got to 'em..."

After Gustav got off the boat somewhere in the recently reopened Charleston harbor, he hefted his carpetbag and made himself scarce. This new country, he realized, was going to be a different kind of battlefield than the one he had fought on. Their recent war was over and all was supposedly calm and peaceful. But he knew—he felt—there was tinderbox beneath the calm, something ready to explode at any moment. Americans, he quickly discovered, never sat still; they were always moving, never at rest, and probably rarely at peace.

So he decided to move as well. And with what little cash he still had in his pockets, he bought a train ticket and headed south. Being a foreigner who knew little English, he avoided conversations, but sometimes found himself listening to people conversing in small packs and he tried to unobtrusively listen in to what they were saying and especially what the words meant.

It was somewhere on the outskirts of Athens, Georgia in the spring of 1866 that he first met her.

It was a general store on the trail to town; two stories of a false front and weathered logs put together strong enough to store supplies and serve the usually weary travelers. It was nightfall, and the old couple that ran the place, Ed and Cora Sims, were headed home after a busy day. However, they left their "girl" to clean up the ground floor and lock up for the night.

Liz was exhausted. She laid the push broom against the counter and wiped the sweat from her forehead. It was a long way since she was the belle of the ball in a land of endless summer breezes, mint julips, magnificent ballroom gowns, clean coaches pulled by the finest blooded stock, grand staircases in mansions that always went up into infinity, vast lands covered with bushels of cotton, and a virtual army of slaves to care for it all. But she couldn't even return to her folks—the ones who had her committed a lifetime ago. They were gone, both dead from broken hearts because their daughter had been reported missing. Or perhaps they had their hearts broken because their world of entitlement and privilege was gone forever, with blue-uniformed troops occupying their hometown.

But now it was a full year after Grant and Lee met at Appomattox. No occupying Union troops terrorized her, but there was no family or friends either. She had killed a soldier in that burned-out cabin during the war and helped herself to him. Months of low wages had helped slim down her weight, but with the hardship her beauty was fading as well. Now she was just "the help" in one establishment after another. Though once in a while, when someone was alone—they could be in the woods, at night in a field, or alone in some barn when no one else was around, the old Madness returned. Their backs were turned, she quietly pulled out a short knife or found a heavy object, and she killed. Not only killed, but ate—as much as she dared to without alerting others to her madness.

Liz was going back to the old glories of the plantation era when big Mose Hardin entered, the bell over the front door ringing loudly in the still of the place.

Liz looked up and said, "I'm closin' up, mister."

Hardin closed the door and stared at her as if she was crazy.

"Closin' up?" he asked in a harsh voice, whiskey-scarred and arrogant. "Listen, girlie, I just rode some miles from Rome and I'm lookin' for provisions. Now, I got a list here—"

"Mister, we're *closed*! Now could you come back tomorrow? We'll open at eight thirty."

"I'm not 'comin' back tomorrow'," he said, making fun of her down-home accent. I'm headed to Arkansas and I ain't wastin any time! You expect me to stick around town just 'cause you've got a broom up your ass and won't do your job! What am I, a piece of dirt?"

Liz stared at him with the same withering look she would later give Gus.

"No. Piece of dirt's too clean compared to you."

The rage on his face was quite real, but instead of doing what was expected of her and whimper and run, she grabbed up the broom next to her.

"No one talks to Mose Hardin like that!" he shouted.

"Always a first time."

Hardin growled, "Bitch, you ain't been raised right..."

He stomped forward, the floor shaking as he walked toward her.

Liz raised the broom and was ready to swing it at him when the bell rang over the front door.

She and Hardin turned to see Gustav standing there taking in the scene.

Angrily, Hardin asked, "Who the hell are you?"

The newcomer blinked at the question, but answered, "My name's Gustav—uh, Gus Krainer. What you doing?"

His English was still not perfect.

"None of your business, white trash," the bigger man hissed.

Gus shut the door, the little bell jiggling as he did so. He stared at the big man with something close to anger. He wasn't sure what "white" meant, but he clearly understood the word "trash."

Planting his feet firmly, Gus glared at him. Then, with all the fury in him, as well as years of honor in one of Prussia's finest military regiments, he said, "Dead drop!"

Hardin looked at him oddly and said, "What??"

Liz didn't know what they were saying, but the man's unusual arrival distracted Hardin long enough. As the big man's back was turned, she quietly laid the broom aside and then reached back over the counter. What she was feeling around for was one of those new double-action revolving guns that Samuel Colt had just put out.

What her hand actually touched was a large claw hammer which Ed Sims had used earlier in the day to yank some rusty nails out of the wall at the other end of the store.

Hardin turned back to her just as she brought out the hammer.

He quickly realized what she was doing, but before his mind reacted to the point that it commanded his big, meaty paw to lift itself up and grab her hand, the hammer's claw buried itself in the top of his skull, knocking his Stetson off.. The pain seared through his head and gushes of blood ran down his bearded, pock-marked face. Fortunately, he didn't cry out when he was struck.

Gus stared at her with widened eyes. "*Gott in himmel!*" he muttered.

Hardin's body hit the swept floor with a loud thud.

Then Liz looked up and shouted at him, "Bar the door!"

"What?!"

Realizing that his English wasn't that good, she shouted, "The door!" and then she pantomimed locking it.

Quickly guessing what she wanted, Gus nodded, obediently went to the door, and then strained to roll a full barrel of molasses in front of it to block anyone from entering.

As he was doing this, Liz looked down on the dead man. He laid there on the wooden floor, bleeding without letup. She just kept staring at him, the urge growing fast within her. She had held off the Madness for something like four months. Not since the sleeping drunk she stabbed to death and then devoured somewhere in Savannah. She licked her lips as she stared at Mose Hardin's corpse.

He was too big to waste.

After an exhausted Gus got through with the heavy barrel and he turned around, he saw the blood on her mouth.

Rising to her feet and wiping her mouth with the back of her hand, she tried not to sound *too* guilty. "It's not what you think! It's just–you see...I've got a problem."

Gus walked forward slowly. Then he stopped and looked down at her.

"I...I won't do it again!" she said. "Honest!"

Gus shook his head and said, "I won't...condemn you. Sometime...you have no choice..."

Liz saw the very real understanding in his eyes and said, "Even the Bible mentions eating the body of Christ."

Gus nodded and said, "Let's hide *this* body."

Liz almost smiled. "I...I can't believe it. You understand?"

Gus nodded.

"Wow."

"I just ask of you one thing."

She knotted her eyebrows and asked suspiciously, "What would that be?"

"I want you to share dinner with me..."

Liz grinned up at him.

She could mop up the blood later...

THREE

Leo Groman was waiting outside the schoolyard fence, tall, gangling, and wearing a pair of wire-rimmed cheaters. He was all of eighteen, and his light brown hair shone in the late afternoon sun and his sharp blue eyes focused on the hand-carved wooden door until it finally swung open and young people ran out of it, usually with cheer.

His classes had ended, but he hung around for a good forty-four minutes to wait for his girlfriend—or at least, he was *hoping* she could be his girlfriend. Kat was someone he had been attracted to since they had met in the first grade and he always had a crush on her. However, when he had run into her and her pa outside of church (which he and his father did not attend) or picnics or town gatherings, he had always felt a chill from her old man. True, Leopold Groman was not what you'd call a rowdy young man; he rarely got into fights, though he was certainly picked on enough times. He was tall, skinny, wore peepers, and worst of all—knew a lot more than his classmates. He studied hard, read books, memorized facts. Who in the so-called Wild West ever did that?? Maybe it was his "book larnin'," or maybe it was his funny looks (funny to his classmates and the town); nevertheless, Kat's dad, the marshal, wasn't crazy about him. The lawman had grown up in a west where children were working the farm at age ten, and learned how to fire guns at eleven. Leo was not the usual two-fisted roughneck a two-fisted lawman desired in his daughter's choice of dates. Fortunately, because he was bright, Leo didn't stammer and he wasn't shy about what he knew. But when it came to telling Kat he *really* liked her, well, that was always a problem...

Leo looked up and saw her and couldn't help but sigh. Then he straightened up as best he could and tried to act like his heart didn't skip a beat whenever she appeared.

Kat spotted him right away and met him outside the fence. Her smile lifted his heart.

She asked, "Why are you waiting out here?"

"I don't know," he replied with a shrug. "Guess I had some time to kill..."

Kat nodded, understanding. She knew he didn't want to run into any bullies who would start making fun of him at exactly the moment she appeared; so after his own classes, he usually kept his distance from the school.

They walked down the road.

"I'm glad you waited, Leo. Something awful funny is going on."

Leo looked over at her, his eyes cherishing what he saw; her shiny dark-blonde hair with the pins in it, her pert nose, the dimples, her sleek long neck, the full mouth and near perfect teeth—he started to feel urgings he had never felt before. He strained to keep his mind on the subject.

"You mean the disappearances?"

Kat stopped and looked at him. "That's right! How'd you know?"

"It's all over town. Folks on the trails getting snatched. Or some such nonsense."

"Why do you say it's nonsense?"

"Because people don't just vanish. A human engine must be responsible."

"A human...*what*??"

Leo started walking again and she did also.

He sighed. Kat was not much of a book reader.

"Some *person* is responsible for the disappearances," he continued. "Or maybe more than one. You should hear the folks in town. Especially the older ones. They act like there are still witches around taking people's souls. I mean, we're headed for the twentieth century, for God's sakes! I've read of inventions they use back east which will revolutionize industry and make things easier for everyone!"

Leo knew that when a young man was trying to court a young lady, they probably *didn't* want to hear about the wonders of the Industrial Revolution. But he couldn't help himself. He was fascinated by what was happening in the world and hoping that someday Kat would be too.

Meanwhile, Kat nodded and watched him as he walked. She remembered he was the son of a tailor from some village in Eastern Europe. Enjoyment to him was probably a dog-eared copy of Mark Twain, a history book, and a good math problem. She wondered what else he did in his spare time.

Now it was her turn to sigh.

Getting back to the subject, she blurted out, "I followed this strange woman the other day."

Leo stopped and stared at her.

"That's not a nice thing to do, Kat."

She looked down briefly to hide her embarrassment. She didn't know why she had to admit that to him. But she did, so she owned up to it.

"I think this woman had something to do with the disappearances."

"Based on what?"

"Based on my friend Josie's word. She says she came in town and she keeps to herself and—"

"Josie Arnold??"

Kat nodded. They both started walked again.

"That woman's really something," he said, with some skepticism. "I mean, with her phony spirits and conjures."

"I know. But *she* believes in it."

"And so do the poor folks who pay her, unfortunately. Anyway, what you were doing was...following some stranger. Stalking this woman like you're a hunter and she's some animal in the woods."

Kat put her hand on him and stopped him. Leo's eyes went to his forearm. He certainly didn't mind her touching him, but when he looked up at her eyes, they were hard.

"Listen, Leo Groman, I'm no doddering old woman making up stories! I *know* she has a gun in her purse! I even saw her pull a knife on Alvin Willis!"

His eyes widened.

"Pull a knife?"

Kat nodded.

"*And* a gun?"

"She had one!"

Leo then held his hands apart a couple feet.

Smirking, he asked, "And was the knife this big?"

He was fond of Kat, but the wiseacre in him couldn't help it.

"And was the gun a flintlock?"

Kat's eyes narrowed and she shouted at him, "What's the use talkin' to an egghead?!"

Leo's heart sank. That's what the schoolyard bullies were calling him.

Kat instantly saw his hurt expression and realized she had let her temper win out again.

She softly touched his arm and said gently, "I'm sorry, Leo. I was stupid to say it. Guess I have my pa's temper."

Leo gave her a weak smile.

Then he lied. "It didn't hurt me, Kat. It's okay."

Kat stared at him, still feeling sorry for what she said.

Then she put her arm through his and continued walking down the road.

Leo was shocked at the gesture, but he gladly let her walk him down the road.

"Kat, folks are going to see us!"

She said firmly, "Let 'em!"

His heart rose and he couldn't help smiling.

The tree branches above them swayed as a northern wind pushed through the town...

THEY ALL HELD hands around the kitchen table. Martha Aschville wanted to shove back a wisp of her iron-gray hair that had fallen into her right eye, but knew she couldn't break the circle. She was on Josie's right.

Her eldest daughter, Nan, was in the circle as well. The teenager tried to stay interested in what this strange woman was making her ma do, but she found her eyes wandering to the ceiling where she noticed the crossbeams above them for the very first time.

Nan's uncle, Thaddius, the deceased's younger brother, was ushered into the séance against his will, but Martha insisted, saying that Josie needed another pair of hands to complete the circle. The flinty old man believed in Josie and her powers even less than Nan did. He was between Martha and Nan (he did *not* want to hold hands with Josie!).

"Spirits of the dead!" Josie intoned with fervor, her eyes tightly closed, her nostrils flaring.

Thaddius muttered, "Good grief."

Martha roughly squeezed his hand and hushed him.

Thaddius gritted his teeth and kept silent. But this wasn't his idea of spending a quiet evening.

"Zebulon Aschville!" Josie called in a trembling, almost sing-song voice.

Martha scanned the ceiling, anxiously watching.

Josie's eyes were wide open as she stiffened.

"I feel his presence!"

Thaddius said nothing, but he was thinking, *I bet you do, you young faker!*

Not as jaded as the old man, Nan's eyes darted back and forth wondering where all this was going to end up. Had her mother not enlisted her in this nonsense, she would've visited her friend, Kat. And maybe brought along her boyfriend, Richard, and Kat could bring along that four-eyed friend of hers, Leo something-or-other.

Josie intoned, "The spirit of Zebulon Aschville is strong! He wants to communicate with you, Martha Aschville!"

Martha couldn't help asking, "But...but how?"

"He will come!"

"Yes," asked Martha worriedly, "but how??"

Josie, still staring straight ahead, replied, "The Spirit World has a door! That door must be opened before he can speak to you!"

Thaddius muttered, "Must have a strong lock..."

Martha squeezed his hand so hard, it hurt. He gritted his teeth again, but kept silent.

"Wait!" Josie shouted. "I feel the door opening!"

Martha asked timidly, "Is...Zeb comin' through it?"

Nan asked, "Is Pa gonna show up? I got some studyin' to do."

Martha snapped at her, "Hush!"

"Everyone be quiet!" Josie shouted. "He's appearing!"

Still holding hands, everyone at the table except Josie looked around the room.

As if answering them, Josie quietly said, "He will come through me!"

Thaddius blurted out, "Through *you*??"

"Through me!!"

It was no more than half a minute before Josie spoke again. But this time, her voice was low and grating, with a southern drawl dripping of corn pone and hominy grits.

"Mar-tha! Mar-tha! How's y'all? You keepin' my memory alive?"

Nan couldn't help saying, "But Pa's from Chicago!"

Thaddius followed that up with, "That don't sound like his voice!"

"Hush!" said Martha for the third time. "'Course he don't sound like himself. He's come through the thick mists of the netherworld, and now he's goin' through Josie!" Then she addressed her "husband." "Tell us, Zeb, how are you doin' up there? Your daughter and I miss you somethin' awful!"

"I know! And I loves ya both! Ya hear? Now, you and Nan must prepare!"

Martha looked at her oddly. "Prepare? Prepare for what, my love?"

"Prepare to follow me!"

Martha audibly gasped.

Nan swallowed in fear.

Thaddius stared at Josie, not liking this at all.

Frightened, Martha asked, "You...you mean, Nan and I...are going to the great beyond?"

Josie's face remained expressionless when she nodded.

"But when? How?"

"Soon!"

Nan's eyes widened and she looked at her uncle worriedly.

Martha's face was crumpled in despair; tears were now in her eyes.

"No! I'm not ready to die!" she said. "Maybe I'm old, and believe me, Zeb, I do miss you so, but..."

Josie asked, "But *what*?"

"But...Nan is so young! She's barely seventeen!"

"The Spirit World knows when folks live and when they die!"

"But *how* can we stop this? How can we be spared the Spirit World's judgment?!"

Josie barely paused before she made a fervent pronouncement.

"You are to trust my spiritual conduit on earth! Josie Arnold!"

Thaddius frowned at that, but held his tongue.

Martha asked, "You want us to trust you—I mean Josie??"

Josie/Zeb nodded solemnly.

Then Nan hesitantly asked, "Um, this is what you want, Pa?"

"Yes!"

Thaddius then asked, "And just *how* is Martha supposed to 'trust' Josie?"

"By compensating this talented young woman for her trouble."

"What??"

Martha said, "I was going to give Josie a ten-dollar gold piece!"

Nan said, "Ma!"

Thaddius added, "That's kinda steep, Martha."

"All right," said Martha urgently. "If it buys our safety, I'll make it twenty dollars!"

Thaddius broke out of the hand grips of Nan and Martha and said, "This has gone far enough!"

Josie suddenly swooned.

Sounding exhausted, she said, "He...has left this mortal plain."

Thaddius rose from the table and said, "Yeah, but not before *he* tried to hold up Martha for twenty dollars! Lord, that's two weeks' pay where I come from!"

Nan looked back and forth between Uncle Thaddius and her mom, wondering if she'd have to part with the two dollars and sixty-eight cents she saved up in a small wooden box in her room.

Josie blinked her eyes innocently at them and asked, "What happened?"

Nan asked, "You mean you don't know?"

"No, child," she answered. "When I'm called to the other world, I'm just a vessel for the dead to speak through."

Thaddius growled, "That *vessel's* been sproutin' leaks, if ya ask me."

Martha spoke to Josie, her voice trembling.

"Zeb said Nan and I were going to join him!"

Josie rose and quickly embraced her. "Oh, my darling! I'm so sorry!"

Thaddius looked at the two women in disgust.

Still in her arms, Martha added, "But he also said, that if I pay you, which I was going to do anyway..."

"Yes, dear," Josie said soothingly. "The five dollars for my services."

"But Zeb said that in order for Nan and I to continue living, we should pay you twenty dollars."

Josie held her at arm's length and looked into her eyes.

"Now, honey, you know that ordinarily I wouldn't want anything from you, but my regular fee." Nan and Thaddius looked at each other thinking the same thing: Five dollars was a high enough price for the show this young woman was putting on.

Josie then added, "But if your dear husband wants you to reward me for my services..."

"Yes! Yes!" Martha cried, tears coming down her cheeks. Then she moved to a shelf where she kept an old box with coins. Thaddius quickly stood in front of her.

"Hold on, Martha!"

"Thad, I must!"

"And I say, 'You must not!'"

Josie's eyes narrowed and she said through her teeth, "How dare you! Your own flesh and blood commanded her—"

Thaddius cut her off. "If that was my own flesh and blood, then Abe Lincoln died 'o indigestion!"

"Thad!"

"No, Martha! Ol' Zeb wanted me to watch over you in case of any shenanigans and I'm seein' a bellyful of it now!"

Josie glared at the old man.

She said, "Don't blaspheme the dead!"

Thad pointedly replied, "You first!"

Off to the side watching this, Nan smiled. *That a boy, Uncle Thad!*

He turned to Martha and said, "Now pay 'er off and get 'er out of here."

"You haven't heard the last of this!" Josie shouted. "The spirits are strong!"

"Yeah, and they're not cheap either! Now, good night, young...lady!"

Then he turned and went into the living room. Confused on whether to stay or not, Nan followed him.

Defeated, Martha went over to a rolltop desk and

opened it. Josie watched her, her eyes shining when she saw the cash box. She approached her.

When Martha turned around, she jumped when she saw Josie right behind her.

"Oh! Josie, I'm sorry about that. Zeb's death hurt Thad as well. After all, he was his brother."

"I understand, dear."

She quietly squeezed a ten-dollar gold piece into the young woman's hand and whispered, "I'll get more!"

Pulling her eyes from the cash box, Josie smiled at her. Then she said, "How would you like to come to my home? Then we can continue the séance without... interference."

Martha squeezed the younger woman's hand and smiled.

"That would be wonderful!"

Nervously, Josie looked back toward the living room.

"Oh, don't worry about Thad."

"Perhaps you shouldn't tell him about your visit to us. Or your daughter either..."

"Us??"

"Oh, I live with my family."

Martha nodded and said, "I see."

"Well," said Josie, squeezing her hands in return, "God bless you, dear!"

"Thank you! And may God bless you too!"

"I'm sure He does!"

They embraced again. Then she walked Josie to the door and she left.

As Martha watched her go down the walk, she thought, *What a special woman...*

THE SUN WAS BEGINNING its descent when Deputy Grimes rode a tall horse, the kind that would support his massive bulk. The day was bright and clear when he passed through the open fence not too far from where Franz and Viktoria Schuler were caught and butchered. Once he was in the barn, he dismounted, as usual, with difficulty. Then he put his big horse in one of the stables. Waddling out of the barn, he headed toward the Krainer house. Mose stood outside the open cabin doorway and silently watched him.

Passing him, Grimes nodded and attempted a smile, but something about the big mute always disturbed him. After the nod, Mose didn't respond, but his watchful eyes followed the deputy as he headed to the house.

Grimes climbed onto the porch, and before he could knock on the door. Liz opened it. She smiled widely at him.

"Deputy Grimes! What a surprise!" she said, too cheerfully. She took him by the arm. "Come in! Come in! Get a load off your...feet."

Grimes returned the smile and took off his Stetson.

"Why, thank you, Mrs. Krainer! You know, not too many folks are as welcoming of the law in their homes as you are!"

"Aw," she scoffed while leading him through the doorway and into the kitchen. "These folks have no respect for the law like Pa and I do! Have a seat!" She could not get the wide grin off her face, nor the exaggerated cheer from her voice.

Grimes sat his massive bulk on one of their stronger chairs.

"So," Liz asked, injecting *some* concern in her manner. "What brings you to our humble home?"

"Well, Mrs. Krainer," he asked, "you've heard of these disappearances."

"Oh! Yes, of course," she answered, while busying herself with something on the stove.

"Well, we were wondering...that is, *I* was wondering, if you had seen any strange folks around here lately."

"Strange folks?" Liz asked, as she tried to straighten the old stove door, which looked like it was off its hinge and would swing open any second. She had forgotten to tell Mose to fix it.

"Yeah!" Grimes answered, trying to spy the cabinets overhead. He was hoping there was a pie inside one of them, and also hoping he'd be offered a slice—a big one.

Following his gaze, Liz chirped, "Oh! First, before I forget! I know you've had a long journey here and you must need some sustenance. So...would you like some of our special blueberry pie?"

Grimes smiled and tried not to sound overjoyed when he said, "That would be great, Mrs. Krainer!"

"All right then! But first...why don't you take off your gun? After all, no need to use it here, is there?"

Humoring her, he said in agreement, "Why, of course not!" And he dutifully unbuckled the holster from around his huge waist and handed it to her. Liz took the holster with the loaded Colt sticking out of it prominently and stood on her toes to store it on a high shelf, far out of anyone's reach. Then she went over to a cabinet and started to take down the pie.

But as she did so, she asked, "Now you were talking about these...disappearances?"

Grimes sat back, trying not to think of the pie, and said, "Well, yes! We wondered–that is, *I* wondered–the marshal's so busy with his bratty daughter lately–I was wonderin' if any...oh, boarder or traveler came by that looked like he's a criminal. Maybe some highwayman who murders folks, you know, maybe stashes their bodies in some hole somewheres and–"

Liz turned around to face him, looking quite shocked. "My word, Deputy! That sounds horrible! Such ugly things happening to good folks! Why, I think I'll have nightmares all my days!" She suddenly grasped her chest.

Now sorry that he spoke out of turn, Grimes rose from his chair and was prepared to catch Liz if she should suddenly get that heart episode she implied she was going to have and keel over.

He stammered apologetically, "I'm so sorry, Mrs. Krainer! I...I shouldn't have told you all these things in such detail!"

"It's all right, Deputy," Liz said, pretending to calm down. "I...I think I'll survive."

"Good!" he said, already regretting his need to make himself look important. He added, "Just forget what I said. It's obvious that you and your family know nothing of–"

The hollow clang of metal sounded beside them and the oven door swung open wide.

Deputy Grimes looked up and had a crystal clear

view of the Schulers' body parts, mainly Viktoria Schuler's right arm and both her husband's ankles sitting in the oven waiting to be cooked. The deputy's eyes widened when he saw them. He released Liz and backed away, frightened. So frightened that he completely forgot the holstered gun hung up on a shelf at the other end of the kitchen.

Liz quickly shut the oven lid loudly, but it was too late and she knew it.

Grimes slowly backed away as he stared at her.

Liz tried to talk her way out of it, but deep down she knew it was pointless. She smiled weakly and said, "We were having lamb for dinner. It's amazing how pieces of lamb resemble human body parts!" She then followed the explanation with an unconvincing laugh.

"The hell!" cried Grimes, and he turned and darted out the front door.

Liz quickly ran to the door and held it open. She shouted, "Mose!" The giant appeared in the cabin doorway, claw hammer in his big fist.

Liz pointed at the waddling lawman as he fled.

Mose lurched forward after him.

Grimes tried to run, but his fat legs refused to increase speed. He knew he couldn't reach the barn and get to his horse, so he ran toward the fence that fronted the property and hoped to flee out the open gate. As he ran, he thought he heard the vague sound of a buckboard pulling up in front of the property, though it sounded like it stopped before it arrived at the fence. Maybe he could jump on the buckboard of whoever was driving it and get away from these maniacs–get back to tell Sam about them.

He huffed and puffed as he stomped toward the opening, sweat covering his shirt, his lungs on fire as he moved. Finally, he was outside the open gate and was ready to run hastily in the direction of where he heard the buckboard stop when the thin arm sprang out of nowhere and slammed the claw hammer into his skull. His big body froze in its spot, the searing pain jolting through his head. But he lived long enough to move his eyes to the left. His face registered shock as he recognized the person who killed him. Then the hammer was roughly yanked out of his skull as the big deputy dropped heavily to the ground.

Just then, Mose caught up to them and looked down. Then he looked up at his stepsister.

"Here!" she ordered, handing it to him.

Gus also got off the buckboard and looked down. He had purchased some new cooking utensils in town and he had picked up Clarissa on the way back. Liz came up to them then.

Clarissa faced her mother and said viciously, "What the hell were you thinking by coming after this fat law dog? Haven't you got any brains? Jeez, I'm always bailing you two out of some trouble!"

Infuriated, Liz said, "Watch it, young lady! I'm already sorry me and Pa didn't send you back to where you came from!"

Gus interjected, "She's got a point, Liz. Of all the jaspers we could get, why did you come after *him*?" He pointed down at the corpse and added, "He's a moron. But Gelder isn't! How're we gonna cover *this* up??"

Liz's anger quickly left her. "I'm sorry, Gus. It's just that...he looked so filling!"

Mose's eyes went from Liz, then to Gus, and finally to Clarissa. Then, without a word, he bent over and lifted up the big deputy and draped him over his wide shoulders. Staggering somewhat as he headed with his catch back to the cabin, his parents and his stepsister continued to argue...

FOUR

A WHITE-HAIRED TEXAS PREACHER NAMED ARTHUR Kingston had married them somewhere outside Galveston in January 1867. The Man of God tried not to notice her sizable baby bump when he had them proclaim their vows of faithfulness and eternal love. Then he charged them two dollars. His doddering wife was the witness. In lieu of any rice, they threw birdseed at the happy couple, of course, not telling them what it was, though their caged parrot did squawk a little *too* loudly at the sight.

The couple had very little, but they would make a go of it, come what may.

They killed their first victim as a married couple somewhere along the north Texas line railroad tracks. A poor jasper from Topeka had fallen off the train and was wandering the territory when they happened upon him in their buckboard. They quickly gave him a ride, telling them they had just gotten married (which was true by two and a half weeks) and that they were going to drop him by the marshal's office in the nearest town (which was false).

Instead, Gus stopped the buckboard and got off, complaining about a bent rear wheel. And despite their passenger saying he didn't feel there was anything wrong, he still got off the buckboard at Gus's insistence. So did Liz. So when the man's back was turned and he bent over one of the rear wheels, Liz swung the claw hammer and crushed his skull. The man dropped onto the ground and then the two hauled him into the back into the buckboard and covered him with an old blanket.

They called it a delayed wedding feast.

Three months later, after being laid up in a small hospital in San Antonio, Liz gave birth to a rather large dark-haired baby boy weighing twelve and half pounds. In honor of the man who had brought them together, they named him Mose. Still ailing, Liz was put up in the small cabin of a midwife who helped her with the delivery. Then, one day, hungry beyond belief (the regular food they gave her didn't seem to be enough), after the midwife's husband went into town, Liz found a kitchen knife and stabbed the midwife when her back was turned. Then, after using the blade to help carve up the corpse into smaller edible pieces, Liz breast-fed Mose. Staying in another room, Gus was shocked at his wife's lack of decorum, but still quickly hauled the woman's body out of the house and tossed her into the pigpen, where the hogs finished the job.

Not waiting for her husband to return, and despite Liz's weakened condition, they packed up and fled the area, never to return.

As a child, Mose never spoke much, but his fate was

sealed one late afternoon at a schoolhouse outside Denison. His parents were already planning to move from the area. The rumors of people disappearing as soon as they had moved there were gaining speed, and the family was already barred from entering certain establishments.

One day, Mose, an oversized child who was shy and rarely spoke unless prompted, was cornered by three of his male classmates on an Indian trail Mose sometimes took on the way home.

Ernie, the eldest boy, pulled out a folding knife and whipped it open. Then, as the other two held Mose down on a carpet of twigs, Ernie forced his mouth open and cut out his tongue. During the attack, Mose never uttered a scream or any other expression of pain.

It was fortuitous that Gus happened along carrying his Springfield repeating rifle. Aware of the rumors accusing him and Liz, he had been hoping to wean both of them off human flesh. Therefore, he journeyed out into the woods looking to shoot some rabbits and skin them before putting them over a fire at their small cabin.

But when he came upon the scene, the enraged former soldier in him—as well as angry father—took over and he raised his rifle. The three boys, eyes widening and a couple of them relieving themselves, started to beg for mercy when Gus fired the first shot at Tommy Paris. The boy's corpse flew across the clearing like a sack of laundry. Then Cliffie Smalls turned to run only to get a Springfield cartridge in the middle of his back.

Ernie sprang for the scene, moving fast along the forest's uneven ground. Mose rose slowly and his dad had tears in his eyes when he saw the blood flowing from his mouth, but Mose could only raise his hands to Gus. Nodding, his father quickly realized what his son wanted him to do. Stiffening himself through his tears, Gus pulled the claw hammer out of his waistband and handed it to his son.

The boy took off like a gazelle, springing easily over rocks and high grass like a true predator. Panting, Ernie looked back in mid-run and was suddenly slammed in the face when he crashed into the tree directly in his path. He fell over a nearby log and lay there in the grass, insects already making a bead for him as he lay there.

By the time his vision cleared, he saw Mose on top of him with his dad's claw hammer in his upraised hand.

The beginning of a scream formed in his throat, but Mose cut it off by burying the claw part of the hammer into the young man's head. Gus arrived then and pulled his boy off the dead hulk that used to be his classmate.

Then, dropping the hammer, Mose burst into tears and tried to put his arms around his father's legs, but due to the boy's already large size, his arms ended up around his waist.

As his son cried, Gus bent over and quietly picked up the bloody claw hammer. Then he and his boy turned away from the sight and went back to their home.

After trying to stem the flow of blood as best they could, Gus and Liz took their boy and disappeared from the area that night. The bodies of the three young boys would not be discovered until the Krainers had crossed the Texas-Arkansas border and headed north.

And Mose never went back to school...

IT SEEMED like a simple house standing in the middle of a surrounding forest of lush cottonwoods. Wooden walls sturdy, roof slanted enough to reflect the light from a full moon; even a chimney that was not in current use but seemed a natural addition to the property, as normal as every other home along the Arkansas-Oklahoma border. There was even a small cabin a few yards away, he assumed, for guests.

Dirk Johnson had ridden past Greenwood, skirting the town's perimeter and avoiding the local law as much as he could. He was sauntering his way down the road toward Fort Smith when he spotted the Krainer place. He sat his horse and looked closely at it, taking a mental picture of where everything was—he *had* to—this family could pretend to feed and comfort him, then send their eldest son out with a fast horse to the local marshal. What he saw seemed normal enough; house in the center, barn and corral on the left, and that lonely little cabin on the right. It looked okay. And he was tired and hungry as hell.

But then he scanned the barn and was able to look inside through the open doors. He couldn't have made a mistake; along with the horseflesh behind closed stall gates, he saw *two* buckboards. That was strange. One would've been enough for a prairie family; why two? They also seemed to own a lot of horseflesh for such a small property.

Nervously, he glanced down at his full saddlebag. The greenbacks from the Hot Springs Bank were bursting it at its seams and he had to stuff the corner of a bill back under its folds. Good thing he had had enough provisions when made his getaway up into the Ouachita Mountain range or he would've starved up in those hills. Freezing in his bedroll was one thing, but freezing on an empty stomach was beyond his many talents. Then his mind went back to when he gunned down that mousy little teller who helped him with the robbery. He almost hated the man getting on his knees on the cold ground and begging mercy—*I mean, begging mercy, come on!* He shrugged then. He shot the little teller several times until he finally shut up—his blathering, after all, *was* getting on his nerves. Anyway, a one-way split was always more desirable.

He looked up at the sky and saw the dark clouds forming. It had been a mostly rain-free sleep up in the Ouachitas, but he had no desire to get soaked in his bedroll sleeping in these damp bottomlands; nor of spending soggy greenbacks despite the tough, horse-hide leather saddlebag which held it. His other saddlebag had held his provisions, and they were now starting to run out. He had the money to pay for some shelter and grub, if need be—though he preferred that they just be "neighborly" and *not* charge him for it.

Johnson was of medium height and he wore his battered Stetson well enough and carried himself well enough to not call attention to himself. The four-day growth of brown beard topped the image he wanted; he was just a drifter who meant no harm and wanted no attention called onto himself—unlike the other young men his age, boastful showboats who *had* to make a big deal about themselves and their talent with a gun.

He felt the first drop off the tip of his long, sharp nose, and at the first clap of thunder, he knew what he had to do. Seeing no one around, Dirk just rode his horse over to the barn and put him in one of their stalls. Looking around, he still couldn't believe all the horses these people had, more than the average farm family anyway.

The rain was now starting to pelt the worn fence in a steady drizzle. It would get worse by the time he appeared on the doorstep. Running through the rain the short distance to the house, Johnson landed on the doorstep a little winded. He then knocked on the old front door, which was already showing long splinters in the wood. Idly, he glanced back and looked at what passed for a front yard; dead grass, some muddy spots here and there, with a pathetic attempt to grow vegetables—long devoured by smaller creatures, and another attempt was never made.

Also, now that he was at the house itself, he couldn't escape a pungent smell which seemed to be coming from the cabin. Fanning his nose, he wondered what could be making it.

Dirk heard the heavy footfalls, a hand on the other side turning the doorknob and then saw the door swinging open. He found himself looking up into the black eyes of Mose Krainer. The hulking young man looked down on him as if he were a gnat.

Dirk wiped the shock off his face and said, "Uh, I been travelin' through here and I could use a room for the night. It's starting to rain." When Mose just kept looking down at him without responding, Johnson added, "I'll pay for the night."

That's when Liz's voice cheerfully sang out, "Let the young man in, Mose! Can't ya see? It's raining outside. And we always try to be hospitable to our guests..."

THAT NIGHT, just as Dirk Johnson was entering the Krainer house, Kat was standing with her arms folded, staring through the rain-soaked windowpane in the two-story frame house she lived in with her dad. Kat had cleaned the dishes, but Sam Gelder was still seated at the table absorbed by the articles in his newspaper—which he couldn't help talking about.

"President Cleveland's going to intervene in that Pullman strike," he said. "Good for him!"

Kat wasn't listening; she was watching the wind pound sheets of rain against the window. She was glad she was inside a warm home and not traveling anywhere, but even then her mind was on other things. That strange woman who stopped Alvin Willis in his tracks with a knife. Who was she? And with a loaded gun in her bag, she sure wasn't like the more "genteel" ladies of the town, even if she did dress like one of them. And she sounded like she's from the north too, maybe one of their big cities.

Gelder went on, "I hope Cleveland can crack down on some o' these labor troublemakers. They're gettin' out of hand." He then folded the paper and set it on the table. "Now there's a president for you! Gets elected again four years after finishing his first term. Huh! That'll never happen in this country again!"

Not hearing him, Kat kept looking through the rain-swept window pane, the rumble of thunder and the sound of pelting raindrops reverberating within the confines of the warm house. But then her mind wandered from the mysterious woman whom she had been following to her friend Leo. Absently, she sighed thinking about him. Tall, blue eyes, wasn't bad-looking if he shed those peepers. She thought of how hurt he was when she called him an egghead. Then she realized something else: If she thought of him as a boy who was always thinking *too much*, what did that say about *her*? She had always thought of herself as smart, but opposite Leo, she now wondered: Was she truly using the natural intelligence that God gave her—or was she just following the crowd?

Hearing no response to his words, Gelder turned around and watched her. He tried not to think of how closely she started to resemble Marian. So without thinking, his tone became hard.

"Are you *all right*?"

Snapping out of her thoughts, Kat turned around slightly.

"I'm all right, Pa." But then she turned back to the window, a reaction which started to make him angry.

Sarcastically, he said, "I hope I'm not keeping you from something important."

His tone hit her hard and she tried to hold in her own temper, a trait inherited from her mom.

"No, Pa, I've just been thinking."

"You're a young lady," he replied. "You shouldn't be *thinking*—except about your studies."

Kat faced him and said, "Well, maybe I've been thinking about other things."

"*What* other things?"

Trying to avoid telling him she was thinking about Leo, Kat shrugged and replied, "You know, about what's been happening around town."

"Oh? And what would that be?"

"Certain things like...those disappearances."

"I told you, that shouldn't be your concern. That's *my* lookout."

She sighed, having heard this old tune before.

"And furthermore," he added, "I've been hearing some other things about *you*."

Kat looked at him sharply, already knowing what he was going to say, but still she asked, "What other 'things'?"

"Yesterday, Grimes saw you walking with Leo Groman. He says you two were arm in arm." Though he didn't mention it to Kat (nor was he about to), Grimes hadn't appeared back at the jail all day. Sam had gone to his house and found that he wasn't there. He wondered if he had gotten into some trouble—or he had found out something about the disappearances and had it in his head to take all the credit for solving the mystery. Gelder was well aware that Grimes would love to have the marshal's job.

Resentfully, Kat said, "Deputy Grimes should be finding those missing people, not worryin' about young folks walking arm in arm."

Gelder rose from his seat then and went up to her. Already disturbed by Grimes's own disappearance and angered over his daughter's "attachment" to Leo Groman, he was ready to raise his hand to her again.

Trying to suppress his fury, he said, "You know what he and his old man are? Some of that rabble who came here from Eastern Europe!"

"So now it comes out," Kat said, not flinching. "Before, I thought it was because he's smarter than most of the kids at school and he wears cheaters and he's not a two-fisted buckaroo from the age of ten!"

"That's not so!"

"It sure as hell is! Either you're not being honest with yourself or you're not being honest with me!"

The hand was about to come up.

Then Kat suddenly turned her left cheek to him.

"Here, Pa! Hit this one! The other one's still red from last week!"

Gelder stopped and stared at her, a look of pain and shock on his face. Shock from the realization that his hitting her was becoming routine—as well as the fact that her mother had reacted more or less the same way when she herself had been hit in the face too often.

Gelder lowered his hand. Then suddenly he didn't want to be in the house. He wheeled around and went to the coat hanger. Grabbing his Stetson and rain slicker off the hooks, he awkwardly put them on and reached for the door.

Concerned, Kat asked him. "Where are you going? It's pouring outsi—"

Not answering her, he left the house, slamming the door.

She ran up to the door and was going to open it, but stopped. Then she leaned her head against it and cried.

Gelder's horse could be heard galloping out of the barn and onto the muddy trail.

Kat stopped crying then and looked up when she heard the sounds. She was afraid he would do something crazy, maybe even get drunk in town, and once that happened, he could get into some barroom brawl or worse. Not being totally alert, he could become the target of some hardcase who decided to take a potshot at him.

Quickly, Kat went upstairs to her bedroom. She shed her house dress and put on one of her ma's old hand-me-downs; in this case, her used white blouse, a pair of Levi's and a worn pair of brown leather boots. Without telling her father, she had snuck into their room one day when he was gone and tried them on—she was pleased that they now fit her tall frame. Then she found her old black rain slicker and put it on, topping the ensemble with her ma's old tan Stetson. After she was finished, she paused and wondered if she needed anything else. She was becoming more worried sick about her pa as she stood there. Then she made a decision. She went into his room. She saw the many photographs of her ma, and a couple more that were framed, like their wedding picture and a shot of them at a social in town, both on his night table.

She reached into the top drawer of the wooden corner desk and withdrew a loaded Colt .45. Just to make sure, she cracked open the cylinder just like she had seen her dad do many times and checked the loads. Then she expertly snapped it back and shoved it into the waistband of her mom's trousers. Turning, she ran down the stairs and headed out to the barn, sheets of rain pounding down on her Stetson and her slicker. She saddled and mounted her mare and headed out of the property.

As she walked her horse up the muddy trail, she tried to make out the tracks of his horse in the driving rain, but it was hard. However, she realized that if it was anywhere her dad would go—as well as the likely place he would get in trouble—it would be in town. Her decision made, she picked up speed and trotted the mare in that direction...

Dirk Johnson sat at the long wooden table with Gus at one end and Liz at the other. It seemed that the Krainers were short on meat and most other foods. He poked his fork without enthusiasm at the meal of fried potatoes and a small portion of grits. He was about to reach for his mug of supposedly hot coffee when Liz rose and said, "Would you like a little extra in it?"

Johnson's eyes practically lit up and he said, "Would I?"

She nodded with a smile on her face and said, "I thought so."

He agreed. "It's mighty cold out there now with the storm and all."

"I have no doubt. Well, relax, young man. You're in a warm place now." She went to a cabinet and pulled down a bottle of Old Hickory and unscrewed the cap. Then she poured a hefty amount into his coffee mug as he held it for her gratefully.

"Thank you kindly!"

"No trouble, young man." She held on to the bottle then, knowing he would want more. "Plenty more if you want it."

"I probably will. Thank you!" He sipped it experimentally. Then he swallowed whole mouthfuls of it. Its warmth filled his belly and hit the spot, more than making up for the paucity of the meal. As if she was reading his mind, she leaned over and refilled his mug.

"Oh, thank you again," he said gratefully, and drank some more. Then the effect of the booze hit him hard, right to his head—even when mixed with coffee. He shook himself and wondered about that. He usually took hard drinks better than that. But he shrugged off the effect and tried to keep focused.

But while he was doing that, he missed Liz and Gus nodding at each other.

Trying to keep his mind working, he idly asked them, "That young man who answered the door. Who is he?"

Liz didn't expect that, and the fact that Johnson was still alert, even partially, didn't please her. She also wasn't crazy about his question.

Awkwardly, she answered, "Oh...Mose is our son."

"Oh really?" he said, trying to shake off the drowsiness and sound conversational. "I think I can see the resemblance."

Gus swallowed uncomfortably and Liz openly frowned.

"He's a big man," said Dirk, getting woozy. "I guess he helps you a lot on the property."

"That he does," answered Gus, without committing himself any further.

Liz poured more into his mug, then figuring he must've had enough, she set it out of his reach on the table. Trying to distract him from talking about Mose, she said, "So...you're not from around here."

"No, ma'am," Dirk answered. His vision was starting to blur. "I'm from around Fort Worth," which was true. He put his hand to his forehead. He felt like he was floating in space, without any earthly worries to keep him awake. Liquor wouldn't affect him this badly. Then he suddenly realized what was wrong.

With anger inflaming him, he found the energy to rise stiffly from his chair.

Liz and Gus looked at each other with alarm, not expecting this. They looked toward the front door when Mose entered from the barn, dripping wet. He nodded to them and touched Dirk's saddlebags which were draped over his shoulder.

Turning around and seeing this, Dirk had the energy to shout, "Thieves!" Then, out of reflex, he drew his Colt and started to raise it as Mose backed away.

Quickly, both Gus and Liz came at him from either side and grabbed his gun arm just as the cocked hammer was released. The shot was thunderous in the confines of the small kitchen, and the bullet smashed the bottle of Old Hickory, splattering it to pieces.

Dropping the saddlebags, Mose quickly pulled the claw hammer out of his belt holder and raised it toward Johnson. But before he could use it, the outlaw collapsed in the arms of his parents and they both let him drop to the floor.

Liz looked resentfully at the splinters of the smashed bottle and Old Hickory seeping onto the tablecloth.

"Damn it!" she shouted. "That was my last bottle of chloroform!"

"You'll get more in town," Gus counseled. "Tell 'em you need more 'cause Mose is still having trouble sleeping, that's all."

Angrily, Liz kicked Johnson in the ribs, but he was beyond feeling it. Then she grabbed up the coffee mug from the table and flung it across the room. It splattered against the wall.

"Stinkin' outlaw! Next time I use a double dose and we make sure these jaspers take off their hardware *before* they sit at the table. Agreed?"

Both Gus and Mose nodded obediently.

Then Gus said to his son, "Better start slicing him up. And get to feedin' our new horse out in the barn."

"Don't start choppin' him up yet," Liz said. "His body is saturated with dope, and I'm not eatin' that!" To Mose, she ordered, "Put 'em down under the trapdoor in the cabin first until the effects disappear. Maybe a few hours. Then you can gut 'em."

Mose nodded. Then he lifted the outlaw up off the floor with no problem and carried him out into the driving rain.

Gus picked up Dirk's fallen Stetson and said, "Wonder if it fits me."

Liz said good-naturedly, "Long way off from those plumed cocked hats you used to wear in merry old *Deutschland*, huh?"

Gus agreed. "A *long* way, Liz."

"Sorry you're not back there?"

Gus smiled at her. "I'm glad I found you in that general store and I've enjoyed the ride ever since."

Liz laughed. Then she hooked her arm into his and they went through the small walkway to the back room where they had their worn mattress.

Mose would handle everything while they were busy...

FIVE

Gelder's stallion stopped in front of Natalie's Palace on Hall Street, the main thoroughfare in the center of the town. He dismounted, tied his horse to the hitching rail, and went inside. Despite the bad weather, the place was still open and a good-sized clientele was crowded around the bar. The smell of cigarette smoke rose in the air and beer and whiskey seemed to be on everyone's breath. Everyone's but his. Ordinarily, Gelder had had a drink now and then, sometimes with Grimes. Certainly, not like he used to in the old days before he was married and became a father. His law duties and his raising Katherine had kept him away from going on a tear, but tonight he felt different. He felt that Kat wasn't listening to him anymore, and though he didn't exactly feel like celebrating, he also felt like bending his elbow just for the hell of it, or at least, that's what he told himself.

He ordered a bottle of rye, took it in his fist when it came and retired to a corner table, far away from the smell of the patrons. He sat there and drank, thought about his newly defiant daughter, then drank some more. That's when a tall, straight-shouldered, honey-blonde woman in her twenties named Natalya Petrovich, a.k.a. Natalie Patterson, exited from the rear office and spotted him at the table she was about to pass.

"Marshal!" she said as she gazed down at him in surprise.

Gelder looked up with still-sober eyes and similarly answered, "Natalya!" Only her friends were allowed to call her by her real name.

"Don't see you around here that much, at least not as a customer anyway." Despite her Russian accent, Natalya was schooled in English from the time she was sixteen. Her folks wanted to escape the deprivations of Ivan the Terrible and settle for the corruption of the Grant administration, so they sailed for America.

Gelder poured a stiff one into his glass as Natalya silently watched. While he wasn't looking, she quietly shook her head. The marshal was a good man, not like the flotsam who came into her "palace." She knew something must have happened at home to make him like this. He downed the glass in a gulp and started to pour another.

She asked him, "May I sit down?"

"Would you join me?"

"Afraid I can't. I'm on 'duty.'"

"Then you can't sit down."

Natalya then pulled out the opposite chair and sat down anyway.

"This is my place. I don't need your permission."

He eyed her sardonically, the rye whiskey starting to bring out his sense of humor—or what he thought was a sense of humor.

"You know," he said, "if I were a Cossack, I could have you beaten up for that."

Natalya gave a wan smile. "If I were back in the old country, a Cossack would've banged me, finished up two minutes later, and then had me arrested for prostitution. You planning to wave your billy club at me?"

Not answering her, Gelder poured himself another one.

After looking at him a moment, Natalya raised her hand. "Josef! Another bottle of rye here!"

A big man in a worn apron and checked vest appeared from behind the bar with a bottle and a glass, quickly went to their table, and set them down before her. Then he went back to the bar as Natalya poured rye into her own glass.

Sam asked, "You drinkin with me after all?"

"Why not? It's my place."

He shrugged as she also drank her glass down in one gulp.

"Not vodka," she said, "but pleasant enough."

"Never saw *you* drink before."

"Never had anyone to drink with before who didn't come here every day."

Feeling warm, Gelder suddenly removed his slicker and draped it behind his chair.

Natalya watched him then, taking note of the sudden, almost irritated movement, the sullen eyes.

She said quietly, "What *really* brings you here, Sam?"

He looked at her with suspicion. She had never called him by his first name before.

Leaning back in his chair, he was impressed with her striking good looks; her blonde hair pinned up over her ears, her green eyes, the full lips with just a touch of lipstick, and her broad shoulders which were fully exposed under her sparse and frilly "saloon queen" getup. Pointedly, he asked, "What part of Russia are you from, Natalya?"

The question surprised her. But she answered anyway. "St. Petersburg, why?"

"Just wondering."

"Wondering what?"

"Are the gals in St. Petersburg better than the gals in Texas? Or should I say the Arkansas border country?"

She shrugged, made a face, and said. "You can find out."

Sam took another drink.

Natalya reached out and touched his hand. "You don't need that."

"I don't?"

She shook her head.

His eyelids were getting heavy and he worked to keep them open.

"What did you come here for, Sam?"

"Why, to see you, of course." He couldn't keep the wry tone out of his voice and Natalya picked it up immediately.

She asked again, "Why are you here, Sam?"

He saw that she wasn't refilling her glass and said, "You're not touching your drink anymore?"

"Why, Sam?"

Gelder looked at the floor, not knowing what to say to her.

Then he asked, "You know the Gromans?"

Natalya looked at him oddly and said, "Yes, why?"

"What're they like?"

She shrugged her beautiful shoulders and said, "They're good people. Why?"

"Hmm. Just curious." He downed his glass.

She added, "They're not from *my* neck of the woods, if that's what you're thinking. They're from Poland. Meaning we were all in the same boat as far as the Czar was concerned." Then she looked down at her glass for a moment and said, "But maybe they had it worse..."

"Yeah? How so?"

She faced him again and replied, "They're Yids."

"Figured."

"Not that that's supposed to matter here, is it? I mean, we're in America. We're all equal now, right?"

Gelder shrugged. "I guess..." Then he poured himself another.

"The Poles burned down his tailor shop."

Sam looked at her with glazed eyes. "Whose shop?"

"Herschel Groman's." Natalya paused then and said with emphasis. "He's Leo Groman's father. The mother died on the voyage here." She looked off for a moment and added wryly, "Things like that happen in steerage..."

Upon hearing Leo's name, he took another drink.

Watching him, Natalya said, "That boy is a real catalyst, isn't he?"

"A real *what*?"

"Catalyst. I did learn *some* new words after I got off the boat."

"That's nice. And what does it mean?"

"A trigger, a spark. Something that sets off something else. That Jewish boy sets you off and you don't realize it."

"You're full of it."

"So I've been told."

He poured another shot. "Probably many times."

"Now you're being nasty."

Watching the liquor splash into his glass, he said, "Am I?"

"I'm getting close to the truth as to why you're here."

Sam looked at her and said, "I told you. I just wanted to see you."

"Bullshit. If that's the case, what're we dilly-dallying for? Let's go upstairs."He drank again and then banged his glass loudly on the table. "All right then!" he said decisively. "What're we waiting for?"

They both got up and Natalya called out, "Josef! Unless the place is on fire, I'll be busy!"

Sam said confidently, "And I can promise you, honey, I'll take more time than a Cossack!"

With the trapdoor pulled aside, Mose dropped the limp body of Dirk Johnson down the hole. Fortunately, most of him first bounced off the remains of an old couch before he rolled off and hit the dirty floor with a thud. A cloud of dust rose when his body made impact and wisps of dirt and grime shook off the three wooden posts which held up the floorboards and piles of earth overhead. Dried blood had soaked into the soiled floor and the air held a stench so thick it took but six and a half minutes before Dirk breathed it in fully and snapped awake.

He felt the pain in his limbs as he rolled over onto the ground, his outstretched right hand feeling one of the fallen cushions which tumbled to the floor alongside him after his fall. Darkness surrounded him. Blindly, he reached out for something to get hold of and finally grasped on to the arm of the sofa as he attempted to rise. But he slipped on something and fell back onto his rump, the pain suddenly awakening him to his surroundings. Nervously, he looked around and knew he was in their cellar—a rather huge cellar.

In fact, the place had actually been an underground shelter carved into the earth decades ago by the property's previous owners during the wars with the Kiowas and Comanches. Old furniture and supplies were still there; even rarely used lanterns. When the Krainers got hold of the property after the previous owners moved to Wyoming, Mose was ordered by his parents to dig a cellar beneath the lone cabin. That way, instead of a burial place where they just shoved in the mutilated corpses, they now had the perfect place to dump all the bodies—especially leftovers. But while Mose was digging a hole in the middle of the cabin floor, he had broken through the top of the Indian shelter and his parents were delighted—the "cellar" was already there. After digging the hole, Mose covered it with a large wooden trapdoor.

Johnson looked up and noted that he dropped probably twenty feet or so. Had he not fallen onto the old couch, he'd likely be dead instead of racked with pain, especially in his back. Just then, his nostrils got another whiff of that smell and he winced.

Dirk glanced upward and saw a vague light seeping through the edges of the trapdoor above. Reaching into the pocket of his jacket where he kept the makins', he got out a match. He flicked it alight with his thumbnail and held it high. He saw some old furniture: chairs, a couple straw mattresses, even a wooden table, spread over the length of the "room." Then he found a lantern on a built-in shelf next to one of the wooden posts. Moving with some pain, he strode over to the shelf and took down the lantern and, after blowing off the dust, lit the lamp. Then, before it would burn his fingers, he blew out the match. Holding the lantern as high as he could, he looked around. The room illuminated as much as possible under the circumstances, though harsh shadows and wide spaces of darkness remained.

Johnson remembered the days of Indian fighting as a kid and guessed that this place might be a shelter with a passageway to the main house. Holding up the light, he looked all the way to his right and found a short hallway just a couple feet long that could've led to the main house. He walked over and soon found a door, old and covered with cobwebs. But the knob had fallen off, and when he put his shoulder to it, it didn't budge. In fact, it was like moving stone; he realized then that the family above might have filled in the passage with rock and soil to prevent escape should they throw a live captive down the trapdoor—like, for instance, *him*! Though why anyone in their right minds would do this, he had no idea.

He turned around then and saw something white that was across the "room," leaning at the base of one of the wooden posts which seemed to reflect a dull light even in the gloom. He walked slowly across the dirty floor and, holding up the lantern, squinted his eyes to see what it was.

Then he saw it clearly. It was a thighbone leaning loosely against a larger pile of human bones.

"Jesus!" he said, stepping back across the floor.

He then looked down at his right hand as it leaned on a table. Blood was on his palm and fingers. He gasped. Then he anxiously wiped it on his Levi's.

"What the hell kinda madhouse is this?" he asked himself out loud.

He had other matches on him, but wisely figured to save them until absolutely necessary. He didn't know how long he was going to be down there, and why the hell they would go to the trouble of knocking him out. The money, of course! He had seen the big one with his saddlebags. But then, why would they even bother with him anymore? Why are they still keeping him alive? They could've killed him, taken the money, and dumped his body in a ravine that flowed into some larger body of water and goodbye forever to ol' Dirk Johnson. No one would be the wiser and less folks would even care.

But then, it hit him quick enough. He looked again at the pile of bones in the corner and quickly looked away. He felt sick. Absently, he ran his hand back through his hair and realized his Stetson had fallen off his head when he lost consciousness upstairs. He looked up then, spying the meager splash of light from above. How long had he been knocked out? He cocked an ear and tried to listen, for what he wasn't sure. But he noted the sudden vibrations in the thick walls around him, the slight shifting of earth due to the powerful storm still raging above. This was verified when he heard, faintly at first, then louder as the seconds ticked by, the sound of rushing water. Suddenly alarmed, he lifted the lantern high and shone it on where he thought the sound was coming from. It was then that he saw a cascade of water pouring onto the floor from a huge gap in the wall at the far end of the shelter.

He couldn't help saying, "Oh boy..."

If the water at the end of the room continued to build, and he couldn't get out of there, he wouldn't have to worry about ending up as a three-course meal for the Krainer family...

Leo Groman watched the storm rage as it pelted the windows of his family's small house on the outskirts of Greenwood. He'd seen thunderstorms in the area before, but not like this. He had heard trees torn out of the ground far from his home, causing him to imagine one of those tall, wooden monsters toppling on *his* house. His dad was the local tailor, not a member of the town council. Even if they survived something that terrible, their home would be destroyed for good; his father didn't have the funds to rebuild and they would be homeless. Forget the town! To these people they were "Jew foreigners," not of this country and not of this people. They merely tolerated his father, not embraced him as a citizen. He sewed up tears and took in pants, he didn't till the soil or enforce the law. The Gromans weren't even part of their place of worship.

Herschel shouted from the living room. "Leopold! Come back to your studies!"

Leo answered, "In a minute, Papa!"

"All right. But I can keep the prayer book open so long. Then I start to fall asleep and it kind of closes itself..."

Leo smiled and said, "Soon, Papa."

"All right."

It wasn't that Leo had an aversion to learning Hebrew, an important language, it was just that he saw few opportunities to use the language in the Arkansas border country, with Oklahoma right next door and a very large land mass called Texas right behind them. But Herschel was always one of the faithful, not only to his religion, but to the woman who was his wife from the old country. Herschel had promised her on her deathbed to teach their little son the ways of their faith, including its ancient language. It was a vow Herschel meant to keep, whether it was going to used in this new land or not. Maybe, just maybe, his son's children or even his grandchildren might find more opportunities to use it in the future.

It was then that Leo was jolted from his thoughts by a rumbling sound outside. At first, he thought it was more thunder, but then he bent forward and practically pressed his nose against the cold windowpane. He saw it clearly, even through the pouring deluge, a horse and rider coming fast up the road. He squinted his eyes trying to make out the figure as it got closer. He saw it then, a red mare with tan patches, ears pricked up, muscles working, and reins tightly held by a tall yet thin figure in the saddle. He knew by the shape and size that it was either a boy, or more likely, a young woman. Then he remembered the horse and suddenly realized it belonged to Kat. His eyes widened as he now saw her dark-blonde hair tied up above her ears and stuffed under a wide Stetson. He saw the drenched slicker she wore and caught a glimpse of the determination on her wet face. She thundered past the Groman property as if the Furies were in pursuit, clumps of wet earth flying upward from the ground as horse and rider thundered past.

He stood back from the window, worried at what he saw. Then the worry turned to fear. Where was she going in such terrible weather? And why? It's as if his heart was speeding down the road along with her; he couldn't help himself.

"Papa!"

Herschel entered the living room, a lit pipe in one hand and the Good Book in the other.

"I must go into town."

Herschel asked, "Tonight? But why?"

"*She* just rode past the house and was headed into town. I think she's in some kind of trouble."

Herschel knew who the "she" was that his son was talking about. He had confessed to his dad many times how he felt about her.

"This...young *shiksa*. Are you sure she's worth it?"

Leo answered sincerely, "Oh yes, Papa!"

Herschel sighed. Then he looked at him steadily and said, "Then do what you have to do to protect her. But be careful."

"I will, Papa..."

It was February of 1872 at what used to be the Comanche camp within a stone's throw of Sulphur

Springs, not too far from the Texas-Arkansas border. The Krainers were moving through the area on a buckboard piled up with their belongings, Gus at the reins driving two old nags who had seen much better days—like the shelling of Fort Sumpter. Liz was seated on the right with a tall-for-his-age Mose between them. At five and a half, the boy was already tall, his shoulders broad and his head big, with knotted black brows crowding his face as if he were some bird of prey.

Both his parents had thicker frames now, having fed on the flesh of the people whom they had once called their neighbors. And again, as they would for many years since the end of the war, once authorities were alerted to the disappearances, the Krainers moved on, always alert, always searching for greener pastures, always looking for a new way to feed off the fat of the land.

Mose looked up at his ma, hitting her in her left arm without restraint.

"Ow!" Liz looked down on him, though not by much, since his head was practically level with hers.

"All right, Mose! Just calm down. We'll get food soon! Don't you worry." She turned forward to the trail. "*Someone's* got to show up soon..."

As if in answer to her prayers, as the horses went up a rise, the camp came into view.

Liz leaned forward. She pulled out a pair of binoculars, she had swiped off the corpse of a cavalry lieutenant two months ago. The family had found him delicious.

"Comanch!" she said.

Gus pulled on the reins and stopped the horses.

"How many?"

"Hard to say. Looks quiet."

"The Comanche quiet? That'll be a frosty Friday."

"No, really," she said, still watching the camp. "No movement..."

"Maybe they're asleep."

"Not likely. They would've heard this wagon and rode out to meet us by now." She put down the binoculars and said to him, "We're practically on top of 'em and we've still got our hair."

Liz then pulled out a Winchester rifle and jacked a shell into the chamber.

"Maybe we better turn around," said Gus.

"I say, maybe go ahead, but *slowly*. Any red nigger appears, that'll just be too bad—for him!"

"Huh." Gus smiled. "Can't say I've ever had Indian meat before."

"But we *did*, Gus. Don't you remember in '70? That Kiowa at Forked Plains?"

"The scout?"

She nodded. "Mm hm. Riding point for the cavalry, and when he got deep in the grove o' cottonwoods, Mose dropped out of the trees like a bat outta hell and crushed his skull with the hammer."

Gus nodded and said, "Oh yeah! Now I remember! He was kinda tough, ya ask me."

Liz looked ahead and said, "Well, let's see how this bunch acts."

"You're the boss," said Gus, shaking the reins.

In a few minutes they arrived at the camp. All of them got out of the buckboard, and Liz had the rifle's barrel up and ready for trouble. Gus had drawn a Colt from his holster and pointed it at nothing in particular. Mose wandered off looking around and childishly picking up moth-eaten blankets and other tribal belongings and then throwing them down when they failed to amuse him.

Liz scanned the area. The place had been the site of an attack. Dead Comanches, both warriors and women, were scattered around the well-trod ground.

Soon, she spotted a still-burning cookfire in the distance.

"Whoever did this, it must've been recent."

"Cavalry? Another tribe?"

Liz shook her head. "Don't know. Coulda been either. The Comanches make enemies o' both red man and white-eyes. Don't know which ones did the deed, but lookin' at all these corpses, I could see who won..."

Then they heard little crunching noises close by.

Liz ran over to Mose and roughly yanked him to his feet. The boy already had blood on his mouth. He had been nibbling on the arm of a dead warrior.

She shouted at him, "I told you before! Wait till we look 'em over before you start chompin' on 'em! You don't know where they've been! 'Specially Indians!"

Mose wiped his mouth on his sleeve and looked ashamed.

She then hugged him. "You're our beautiful baby boy!" She kissed him on the cheek and then said, "We just want you to be *careful*, that's all!"

It was a small sound at first, but then it grew as the seconds wore on.

Quickly releasing Mose, Liz pulled up the Winchester and aimed it at a spot several yards away, the barrel pointing toward a Comanche lodge. Similarly, Gus whirled around and aimed the Colt at the same place.

They waited but a few seconds before the sound became a wail, then a cry.

The two looked at each other, and then they both slowly advanced to the sound. Mose watched them curiously, then slowly followed at their heels.

They got to the entrance of the lodge and looked at each other again, both realizing what the sound was.

Gus put his hand on the tepee flap and said, "Get ready, Liz."

She replied, "I'm ready!"

They had silently agreed that the noise could've been a ruse to lure them closer to the lodge so that they could be attacked; Comanche, especially, were known for such tactics. But when Gus threw back the flap and held it open, nobody leaped out with his tomahawk screaming in their faces. Instead, they found a dead Comanche woman hugging an infant. Upon hearing the Krainers' approach, the infant finally found her voice; a pleading, screeching, voice begging for love and attention.

Mose ran forward then, reaching out for the baby girl.

Dropping the rifle, Liz caught the boy and yanked him back with all her strength.

"No!" she shouted in his face. "No! You'll be fed, Mose! I promise you! But not this way!"

Mose pounded his fists at her face, and then reached up with his big hands, pulling her hair down around her ears. Liz screamed and then hauled off and slapped Mose hard in the face. The boy fell back to the ground and then crumpled in tears beside the body of another dead Comanche woman.

Shoving her hair out of her eyes, Liz said, "We better feed the boy fast! He's gettin' famished!"

Gus said, "Well, we've got plenty of nourishment all around us. But what about their friends?"

Continuing to shove her hair behind her ears, she said, "Yeah. The larger band will find out what happened and they could be headed this way."

"And what about that cryin' little red-hot over there? Take her with us as an appetizer for Mose or..."

"No," Liz said, looking down at the baby, who gradually stopped crying and looked up at the Krainers with adorable green eyes. "We'll take her with us."

"Her crying could alert the tribe if they're close by."

"She's crying because she needs to be fed. And I got more than enough breast for that." Then she looked again at the infant.

"You see that, Gus?"

"Yeah," he said with concern. "Green eyes." Then he went off, scanning the area.

Liz asked no one in particular, "Wonder which parent was white?"

Gus called, "Over here." He was holding open the flap to the tepee for her.

After retrieving her rifle, Liz walked over to the lodge and peered inside. She saw three white women in various stages of Indian clothing, all lying on the ground with their throats cut. A dead warrior with a blood-soaked knife lay not far away.

"Hostages," she said. "Probably kidnapped from their homes."

"So when the cavalry or maybe an enemy tribe showed up..." Gus made a slicing gesture across his throat.

Liz nodded and said sadly, "Poor things..."

"Now we know where that little half-breed is from."

Gus holstered his gun and went to the buckboard. After a few seconds, he dug out a hatchet and came over to her.

"In the meantime," he said, "Mose has got to be fed."

Liz nodded. Then she walked back to where the infant was. Bending over, she gently pulled the baby girl out of the dead Indian woman's embrace and picked her up. She smiled at the baby, who smiled in return and started gurgling as soon as she was in Liz's arms. Then Liz pulled down one side of her old ranch shirt and exposed her breast. She smiled down at her and said, "You're gonna live with us, little one! And we're gonna give you a feast you'll never forget!"

As if in response, the baby girl ravenously locked her lips on her exposed breast. Liz laughed as she gazed down at the infant and bounced her in her arms.

Stopping by with the hatchet, Gus asked, "So she's going to stay with us, huh?"

Liz looked up at him and nodded solemnly.

"You fell for her really quick, didn't you?"

"Only like a ton o' bricks."

Gus looked at the baby, forming a smile. Then he got serious and said to Liz, "She's another mouth to feed. You know that, don't ya?"

"I know it."

Gus looked again at the baby, weakening.

"What're we gonna name her?"

Liz watched the baby as she suckled her breast.

"I once had a baby sister named Clarissa. She killed herself after the Yanks had their way with her..."

Gus nodded. "Clarissa it is then."

Then he turned away.

As she fed the child, there were chopping sounds from inside the lodge with the dead women and warrior. Gus had not mutilated the dead women; instead, he had used the hatchet on the warrior who murdered them. After he was finished, he threw the parts Mose's way. Still sitting on the ground, the boy grabbed up the pieces and ate hungrily...

SIX

She had been at practically every saloon on Hall Street and no one had seen her pa. The only one she had not gotten to yet was Natalie's at the end of the street.

Kat was certainly a strange sight to the drunken men in each saloon, dripping wet, the water rolling off her Stetson, her boots, and her slicker dripping on the wooden floors, her breathing fast after her long, fast ride into town. Everything about her aroused more than a few of the patrons who saw her.

But she got the same answer: No one had seen the marshal; it was as if he just disappeared off the face of the earth. However, she *did* get offers of company from their clientele; men who seriously believed that their thick, scraggly beards, smelly bodies, filthy come-ons, and all-around slovenliness would be enough to attract a young lady of Kat's beauty and stature. In a way, she was almost glad her father wasn't around when she showed up at these places because he would've killed these men on the spot.

Then, as Kat walked down the street, hugging herself from the cold and the splatter of rain still pouring down, she heard a movement near her, just as she passed the mouth of an alley. The arm shot out like a huge paw and grabbed Kat around the waist, yanking her back into the darkness. She started to scream, but the other hand, hairy on the knuckles and smelling of spilled whiskey, covered her mouth before the scream fully formed.

They crashed against a wall, and Kat struggled to break out of the man's arms. She whimpered behind the hand, trying to scream. Then she bit down on it hard. Yelling in pain, the man quickly spun her around and slammed her head against the brick wall. She cried out in pain as her Stetson fell off and her dark-blonde hair tumbled down. Grabbing a fistful of it, he yanked her head back and again slammed her head against the wall, causing her to cry out again. Awkwardly, she drew the gun from her waistband and cocked the hammer, but a meaty hand swatted the barrel away just as it fired. The shot was loud in the alley, but was barely heard by anyone else as rain loudly pelted the street. Her attacker grabbed the Colt and yanked it out of her hand, tossing it deep into the alley.

Angry, Kat quickly lifted her booted right foot and sent the toe right into Tom Carrow's crotch.

In pain, he cried out, "Damn you, bitch!" He smashed her across the face, knocking her off her feet. Landing near a garbage can, she felt her face and absently reached behind her with the other hand. Whipping off the garbage can lid, she slammed it at Carrow's head when he bent over to reach for her. Uselessly warding her off with his hands, the big man then lifted his foot and kicked the lid aside. It flew down the alleyway, bounced loudly against the brick wall, and rolled into the other cans.

"HA!" Carrow yelled triumphantly. He reached down and got her right wrist in an iron grip and was ready to roughly yank her to her feet.

But the barrel of a .38 Colt struck the big man square on the back of his skull. He groaned in pain and his legs buckled under him, dropping his body to the soaked alley ground.

Shoving her wet hair out of her eyes, Kat looked up and saw Josie standing there with the gun.

"Josie!"

"Take it easy, Kat! He won't bother you again!"

"How did you—why are you here?"

"I was doing a séance for the McGruders a block away. I was on my way down the street in my buckboard when I heard the shot. Then I saw this *creature* attacking you!" Josie then offered her hand and Kat grabbed it, allowing herself to be lifted to her feet.

"I can't believe this!" the younger woman said tearfully. "All I was trying to do was find my father! I must've been in every saloon on this street!"

"Obviously, this trash followed you, hoping to get you in an alley alone." Then, with rage etched on her face, she looked down at the unconscious man and brutally kicked him in the stomach.

Kat's eyes widened as she looked at her.

Josie caught her look. Quickly, she dropped her angry expression and smiled at her, reassuringly touching her hand.

"Don't worry, dear! It's just that these...pigs anger

me no end!" She gave the figure on the ground a dirty look.

Breathing fast, Kat said urgently, "But I have to find my father! I have to find—" It was all too much for her. Getting dizzy, she limply collapsed in Josie's arms in a dead faint.

While still barely conscious, she heard her friend say, "It's all right, darling. I'll bring you back to my house. You'll be safe there..."

Leo had ridden into town on his dad's bay horse wearing a Stetson and a rain slicker, all while keeping his eyes on the soaked trail for the hoofprints of Kat's mare. It wasn't easy, with the rain pelting him from all directions as he shaded his eyeglasses from the onslaught as best he could so as not to get the lenses wet. At least the brim of this wide western hat helped. In the old country, he wore caps; they didn't have Stetsons.

He knew she was headed into town on the simple assumption of *where else* could she be going at that time of night? Just why she was doing so was the mystery. But the thought of Kat on her mare thundering past his house during a raging storm worried him no end. This was not a night to go gallivanting outdoors. She was in trouble. However, the big question for him was, what was *he* going to do about it when he did meet it? He decided to table that question for later; in order to help her (if indeed she needed help), he had to go after her first, think about the solutions to her problem *later*.

Leo rode into the rain-soaked town and ended up on Hall Street. Cautiously, he looked at the closed doors of the saloons. No one was on the street. Lights were on behind the many bat-wing doors, but no one was staggering drunkenly in front of them. Was he going to ask every sleazy person who went into these places if they saw a young woman of Kat's description? He'd be laughed out of every one of them. But he was prepared to do so if necessary.

Then Leo froze as he spotted the lone mare tied to the horse rail in front of a closed saddlery; it was a few doors up from Natalie's Saloon and across the way from the three-story Jackson Hotel. She was red and her coat was dotted with tan patches; there was no mistaking it. This was Kat's mare.

He quietly rode over to the horse and looked her over. The coat was wet, but when he put his hand on the horse's right flank, he felt the warmth in the coat, the trace of lather that came from a horse who'd been galloping fast. He looked up then, scanning the street. Still no one around except a woman on the other side of the street maybe twenty yards away. She was walking fast, but then stopped when she saw him. She was tall, had her reddish hair piled up under a Stetson and wore a ranch jacket and Levis. She was also wearing glasses like he did. They looked at each other from that distance for what seemed like a long time, but was actually moments. Then he broke out of the staredown and turned his attention to the ground. He dismounted then and wrapped the reins around a nearby post. Then he crouched down.

Leo immediately saw deep buckboard tracks in the muddy street near the mouth of the alley. They were very close to where Kat had left her mare. Then he saw something that *really* frightened him. Her Stetson and a small-barrel Colt were on the ground. Then he spotted boot tracks near the mouth of the alley. One pair were those of a big man, a pretty heavy one at that. The impressions in the mud were deeper. Besides them were the prints of other boot heels, this pair being lighter. He had seen Kat in her boots during inclement weather and he knew he was looking at the boot imprints of a tall young woman. He noticed that the two pairs of boot prints were haphazard, as if there had been a struggle. Then he saw a *third* pair of boot prints originating from the street where the buckboard must've been parked. Another woman's boots, deeper than Kat's, but not by much. He guessed they were made by an older woman, though still a tall and thin one. This woman's prints originated from the street, then they moved into the alley.

And then he spotted something which chilled him: bloodstains. Not a lot, but little droplets of blood near the wall, right in the midst of the scuffed and disarrayed boot prints of the big man and a young woman who may have been Kat. Still in a crouch, he followed the bloodstains onto the boardwalk, then they ended at the street near the buckboard tracks.

Coming to a decision, he climbed back into the saddle and, turning to the mare, expertly shook the smaller horse's s reins off the tie-rail and led her down the street. Totally forgetting about the woman who had stared at him, he rode up the street to a stable. He paid the hostler to shelter the mare out of the rain and then turned back to the street. After he rode out of the stable, Leo looked for the woman, but saw that she was gone. Probably back indoors like normal folks.

He rode back to the mouth of the alley and observed the still-deep tracks in the road, though they were starting to fill with little pools of water even as he looked at them. He had to move fast or there would be no trail. Turning the horse around, he followed the tracks as far as he could, not knowing where they would lead. But he knew that Kat would never leave her mare out on the rainy street for an extended amount of time. She figured to leave the mare on the street for a short period of time while she did something else, but while she was returning to the horse, something interrupted her. Kat certainly didn't go to a saloon to "have a few"—she was only seventeen, for God's sake—and those buckboard tracks were a little *too* close to that horse for comfort. That and the sure signs of a struggle made him scared for what might be happening to her.

He hunkered down under his slicker and rode out of town, following rapidly disappearing wheel tracks in a torrential downpour so he could rescue the girl of his dreams.

But if he actually *did* meet trouble, who was going to rescue *him*??

EXACTLY TWENTY-TWO MINUTES before Leo rode into town, in room 312 on the top floor of the Jackson Hotel (named after "Stonewall"), Susan York was getting ready for bed. Tiredly, she rubbed her eyes, the redness on the bridge of her nose prominent from her eyeglasses. It was a long day, or maybe that was how it felt. First it was breakfast in the hotel's dining room, where practically everyone she ran into asked her what she was doing in town. She steadfastly refused to say, *not* making friends with those people who couldn't mind their own business. But she had a rule about that in every town she had traveled to so far: To tell them what she was doing there was tipping off the murderers of her brother, and that she was certainly *not* going to do.

Sue watched the raindrops running down the panes and sighed, shaking her head.

Then after breakfast, she was going to the marshal's office and decided to cut through that alley. Then, before she knew it, out pops an oversized orangutan who smelled of half the distilleries in her native Baltimore. Then he decided that she was the woman of his dreams (God help us what *they* looked like!) and put his gorilla paws on her. Against her better judgment because she wanted her presence in town kept quiet—she had to pull her knife on him. Then, to top it all off, by accident, the pistol in her purse had fired when Simba knocked it out of her hands.

Why didn't she just take out a newspaper ad announcing who she was and why she was in their Godforsaken little town??

Sue shook her head again. Then she had a visit with the marshal to find out if anyone had information about who killed her brother. She had trailed the killers for months and over many miles. She knew it was a family that was responsible for his death. William York had been the kindest soul anyone could have known, a much-loved doctor and noble human being. But then, Bill York thought he could do more for humanity by being a doctor out west where eastern progress had not yet taken hold. Maybe he could even make a gold strike and have money to build a hospital so he could do even *more* for humanity—or at least that's what he told her and his many patients. Maybe it had been wanderlust, or maybe it was just plain greed, or more likely his generous spirit to do good for those in need, but he listened to Horace Greeley and went west (though he was no "young man"; he was pushing forty).

Then he suddenly disappeared somewhere around Mount Pleasant in Northeast Texas. It was almost a year ago when she received the last letter from him, postmarked from that area.

Leaving her teaching job, she withdrew all the money she had in the State Bank of Baltimore and set out to find him. She had no other family, no husband, and no children. Though actually quite pretty, the appearance of her wearing glasses, along with her sharp intellect, turned off a lot of men. In fact, those who knew her already considered her a spinster at her present age of thirty-five. She certainly didn't miss her provincial town, nor the gossips and their snide remarks as she was determined to find out what had happened to Bill York, come what may.

Traveling to Mount Pleasant, she asked around. She spoke to the marshal; she spoke to the townspeople; she spoke to the doctors, lawyers and judges who were respected figures of the town. Then she spoke to the cowboys who rode the trails; of course, some of them tried to paw her (apparently the cheaters didn't stop them), but most of them actually were respectful and sounded eager to help. All of them, every one, pointed toward a family that lived in some house at the edge of town with a cabin next to it; apparently a location where these riders had stayed and been fed. Someone of Bill's description had gone their way and, from eyewitness accounts from other riders, he *had* stayed with this family. According to what they told her, the family appeared normal, if slovenly. A middle-aged man, his wife, a big young man who was their son who never uttered a word, and a striking young woman who was the little sister. Indeed, the men never forgot her; she was tall, attractive, with dark hair, green eyes, high cheekbones, and a full mouth made for kissing (she tried to keep these cowboys back on the subject). But several of them noticed something else about her; they couldn't exactly put their finger on it, but there was something in those bright green eyes that scared them. The woman smiled a lot, dressed well (unlike the family), seemed extremely charming, and normally radiated cheer when they were around her. But when one of them spilled something on the table or refused to believe in her power to contact the Spirit World, she would give them a cold stare that made them swallow in fear—and these men didn't scare easily.

Sue thought about what happened to her brother and shivered. The family was gone from Mount Pleasant by the time Sue got her court order to have lawmen search their property. So when she and several deputies arrived to question them and found the family gone, Sue insisted that they not only search the house and nearby cabin, but that they uproot the place as well. The marshal tried to dissuade her, but she kept at them. In fact, her brother wasn't the *only* person who had disappeared from the area lately. Therefore, the marshal and his men *had* to take her seriously. Primitive earth-moving equipment pushed the house off its foundations and the lawmen soon found what they was looking for. Beneath what had once been their cabin, they had unearthed a mass grave filled with mutilated body parts and the remains of human bones.

Then she found one, a tall skeleton wearing the tattered remnants of a broadcloth coat worn by her brother; it was even wearing a garnet ring on his left ring finger which, apparently, someone in the family had tried to rip it off the corpse's finger, but eventually gave up. Only Dr. York's leather physician's satchel was missing.

On her knees at the burial site, Sue covered her face and cried. As her body shook with sobs, the marshal came up behind her and sympathetically put his hand on her shoulder. Then he and a deputy gently lifted her to her feet as she continued crying.

He said, "You were right, Miss York. I'm sorry for your loss..."

It didn't end up doing anything as far as apprehending her brother's murderers, but at least it was better than what she got from the pig-headed lawmen she had spoken to earlier. First, there was the fat one named Grimes. He wouldn't say anything until his boss, the marshal, showed up. And then when this rough-looking man pushing forty showed up with his badge lazily pinned on his shirt, he tried to sweet-talk her into being patient. He knew of the disappearances, but apparently they didn't spark his interest as much as some bank having been robbed in the middle of the night. They exchanged sharp words. Maybe the marshal was overworked, but she had just been manhandled by a big drunk and she was in no mood for the usual condescending attitude from thick-headed men.

Then, almost against her will, her mind went back to the marshal and she pictured him, both at his desk at the jail and strolling around town. He wasn't a bad-looking sort, and was even kind of handsome for his age. The only thing missing from his personality seemed to be a good dose of manners. Going about town, she had seen the gruff way he was treating his daughter and it angered her no end. *Now, if I were her mom...*

And then, as she stood with her arms folded, just seething at the thought of that obstinate lawman, she heard it. It was muffled, but the noise was sharp and shrill, like a scream, and then a gunshot following almost immediately. She went over to the window and threw it open. Looking out, despite the pouring rain, she saw them. She reached back to the night table and put on her glasses shading them with her right hand so they wouldn't get wet and blur what she was seeing.

There was a young woman in the alley across the way being attacked by a man. They struggled briefly before someone else showed up in a buckboard. *Another* woman, maybe a little older, wearing a little hat on her head and an eye-catching red dress, came over and struck the big man over the head with something. Then the younger woman collapsed in the other woman's arms. Her head rolled into the glare of the streetlight as raindrops pelted off her fresh young face. Sue gasped when she saw it.

Then, her eyes widening, she couldn't believe what was happening next.

Not only did the older woman put the girl in the back of the buckboard, but she also, albeit awkwardly, picked up the big man and put him in the back next to her. Then the woman threw a thick blanket over both of them, quickly got back in the buckboard's driver seat and drove up the street.

Sue threw the window open higher and leaned out. At the top of her lungs, she screamed, "Help! Help, someone!" But a clap of thunder roared over the area, shaking the earth and totally obscuring her shouts. By the time she looked up the soaking street, the buckboard had gone.

Frightened, she pulled herself back in the room, soaking wet from the rain. She ran her hand back through her wet hair and then turned around, reaching for her clothes. In her bones, she *knew* that this was the woman who belonged to the family who had murdered her brother. She pinned her hair back up and, instead of the little hat she had been wearing, put on an old Stetson that had belonged to her father. Then she pulled on Bill's old trousers and a rough calico shirt which she had brought along. She yanked on her own boots and then donned a slightly used buckskin jacket which Bill had worn when he went hunting. It was a size too big, but it helped protect her from the rain. Then she strapped on her dad's old holster. Moving fast, she pulled open her top dresser drawer, found her newer model Colt .45, and shoved it into the holster. She also shoved the switchblade knife into her pocket.

She remembered that particular horse that was still tied beneath the saloon overhang, keeping it out of the rain. She had seen it in town earlier and knew it belonged to the marshal.

Ignoring the usually sleeping desk clerk, Sue went out into the street, hoping to get to the stables nearby and rent a horse quickly. She looked up the street and knew that the buckboard and its passengers were well out of sight. Then she froze when she noticed a young man with spectacles like hers, watching her from the same alleyway where the girl was kidnapped along with her attacker. They watched each other for a few seconds, then she saw him get off his horse and bend down at the alley's mouth, studying the tracks.

Was he with the family or was he tracking them? Sue didn't have time to think about it, and couldn't take a chance if this kid was with the family anyway. Ignoring the pelting drops, she ran across the street, the rain rolling off the brim of her Stetson, and she made it through the bat-wing doors into Natalie's Saloon.

As she entered the place, Sue was praying the marshal was still there.

For she now realized she had seen the young woman who was thrown into the buckboard along with her attacker and taken out of town. She had even seen her in the marshal's office when she attempted to speak to him about what he was doing about finding her brother's killers.

The young woman was his daughter...

Natalya was standing at her bureau, still in her nightgown, smoking a cigarette. She idly looked in the mirror and saw Gelder in the reflection. He was lying on her bed, arms outstretched, face buried in her pillow, and snoring loudly—and still in his clothes. She sighed and shook her head.

He had collapsed the moment his head hit the pillow.

Then the snoring veered off sharply and Sam's eyes

shot open. He sat up quickly, hair disheveled, shirt and vest in disarray, his Stetson on a coat hook. He blinked his sleepy eyes and saw her brushing her hair in the mirror.

He paused as he watched her. She turned around then and looked down at him, taking a drag on her cigarette and not saying anything.

Uncertainly, Gelder asked, "What happened??"

Blowing out some smoke, Natalya just said, "You were...*magnificent*!"

Gelder put on an awkward grin.

He didn't want to say he knew he still had it in him, but he felt like it.

Then they heard the commotion outside and the door opened. Sue pushed past Josef and entered the room. She looked at both Sam and Natalya with disgust.

The saloon queen shouted, "Who the hell are you?"

Josef said apologetically, "I'm sorry, boss, but this... lady was stubborn!"

After glaring at the barman, Sue turned back to Gelder and said, "Marshal! Something's happened!"

Suddenly recognizing her, Sam said, "Wait a minute! You're Susan York! You've been to the office every day since you hit town bothering me and Horace."

Ignoring him, Natalya came forward and started to raise her hand toward Sue. Through her teeth, she said, "Bitch, I know what's going to happen to *you*!"

Quickly, Sue drew her gun and pointed it at her.

"Back off, trash!"

Natalya paused, eyeing the gun. But she was ready

to knock it out of her hands when the opportunity arose.

Angrily, Sue said, "So this is what the law in this town does when people are in trouble!"

Gelder sighed and said, with feigned patience, "Miss York, put down the gun. I know you're upset that we haven't found your brother's killers, but—"

Sue shouted at him, "Goddamn you! Your daughter's been kidnapped! I saw it happen outside while you're in here sampling *her*!"

Gelder turned pale as he stared at her. Natalya froze where she stood and the blood drained from her face. Then, when Josef was trying to reach for Sue's gun from behind, Natalya shouted, "No, Josef!" And then quietly, "Leave her alone..." The barman stopped in his tracks and stepped back.

Sam leaped off the bed and, ignoring the gun, grabbed Sue by her shoulders.

"What the hell are you saying!?"

Shoving the gun back into her holster, Sue looked up at him. "A few minutes ago! A young woman grabbed her and this big man and put them into her buckboard!"

Gelder shouted at her, "You're not making any sense! Kat's home! I left her at home before I came here."

"And I'm telling you I saw her being put into a buckboard along with some big man who had attacked her—"

"Attacked her?!"

Sue nodded and said, "And this young woman took her and this big man who attacked her and put them in the buckboard. Both of them looked like they were out cold. Oh, come on! We're wasting time!"

"I don't believe you! You're making this up to lure me out of town for some reason."

"Your daughter wears a tan Stetson, a black rain slicker, and rides a red mare with tan patches?"

Gelder backed away, staring at her. Then he quickly took his Stetson and holster off the coat-tree and put them on. As he was tightening the belt, he said, "If you're making this up..."

"As God is my witness!"

"Which way did they go?"

"I can show you."

He looked at her hard and said, "You're not coming with me."

Sue returned his angry look and hissed at him, "If these are the people that murdered my brother, no power on earth will stop me!"

Natalya watched them both, convinced that Sue was telling the truth.

"Listen to her, Sam!"

Sue glanced at her then, quietly grateful for her support.

"All right," he said. "And if you want to go with me..."

She replied, "I'd go *without* you if I had to..."

SEVEN

THEY STOPPED BRIEFLY AT THE STABLES DOWN THE block and Sue rented a gelding. Riding slightly ahead of him, she guided him out of town and the two kept watching for wheel ruts in the road.

Their tracking was made easier when the rain started to slow down, and then, after fifteen minutes or so of diminishing drizzle, it stopped altogether. After the clouds parted, a bright full moon hovered over them as they rode.

Shedding his slicker and stuffing it beneath the pommel, Gelder said, "Glad the rain stopped. And a full moon's comin' up."

"It'll make tracking easier, a little anyway."

"Now, Miss York."

She looked up at him.

"You said that this...young woman also kidnapped some big man."

"That's right. I saw her awkwardly pull him onto the rear of her buckboard and close the end-gate. Then she drove it out of town on the same trail we're on now."

"Now...kidnapping a young woman, someone like my daughter, is one thing. But why would this person also kidnap a big man? Doesn't make any sense."

"It's not strange at all, Marshal," she said while watching the trail. "The family I've been tracking eats human flesh."

Sam stopped his horse and stared at her. Sue stopped as well. The teacher had said it so casually, he didn't think he heard right.

"Come again?"

"They eat human flesh."

"Are you right in the head?"

"Listen, you stubborn fool! You've received reports on what they do to the people they capture. Lawmen have discovered graves with body parts in them. There have been other disappearances from one state to another, depending on where they settle down. And the territory's been alerted to their atrocities—"

He nodded and said, "I *know* that! But I always thought they were exaggerating! I've heard of outlaws who were supposed to be eight feet tall and spat fire, and when they show up in town, they're little runts who need a seeing-eye dog."

"Marshal, this family is not out of some penny dreadful written by Ned Buntline! They're savages! And now your daughter might be with them."

"I hope you're wrong, Miss York."

"I hope I am too, but I don't think so."

They started down the trail again. As they rode, she told him all about her being a teacher back in Baltimore and giving it all up to find her missing big brother, of how she and Texas lawmen found his skeleton in that grave in Mount Pleasant, how she decided to track down his killers, a family of butchers who travel from one location to another. The more she told him, the more he believed her, especially after she gave a razor-sharp physical description of Mount Pleasant's marshal, Hank Wilson, whom he knew personally.

Nodding after she was finished, Sam said, "Yep, that's old Hank, all right. Right down to the scar on his neck put there by the Kiowa."

Sarcastically, Sue asked, "Any other descriptions you'd like me to give, like what Mount Pleasant looks like? Or the town cannon in the park dedicated to Jeb Stuart?"

"You have quite a sharp tongue, Miss York!"

Watching the trail, she said bitterly, "I'm not out here for *fun*, Marshal Gelder..."

He watched her then as they rode. She wasn't bad-looking, he thought. Now if only she had some *manners*!

Trying another tact, Gelder said, "Well, anyway, you've been through a lot."

"So have the relatives of many of their victims."

"Yeah, but you're going out and *doing* something about it!"

"Well, thank you, but I—" Then Sue remembered something. "Oh, another thing. A young man was following the buckboard."

He stared at her, dreading the answer. "*What* young man?"

"I've seen him around town, sometimes with your daughter. Like me, he wears glasses."

Sam stopped his horse. Though facing her, he could've been talking to himself. "No! *He's* out here too??"

"Who is he? Your daughter's boyfriend?"

Sam turned to look at her, resentment in his eyes.

Sue caught the look and said, "Apparently, you don't like this young man."

"She can do better!"

"Better? This kid went out on a night like this, probably miles from his home, to follow your daughter's kidnappers and probably try to rescue her. I can't think of a better young man to go out with *my* daughter!"

Gelder faced the trail again and said irritably, "Well, she's not *your* daughter, Miss York."

Sue burned her gaze into his. "Oh really? Well, I've seen the way you treat that girl in town. Yelling at her and threatening to raise your hand to her. If that's an example of how you also treat her at home, then you're some special kind of asshole!"

Gelder looked at her and said, "I'm also some special kind of single parent!"

Sue stopped then and stared at him.

"Then her mother is..."

"Yeah. She caught the fever almost a year ago. Been raisin' our daughter on my own ever since..."

Sue quickly dropped her anger, and her expression became sympathetic. She, of all people, was not about to dismiss the loss of a loved one.

"I'm...I'm sorry."

He faced the trail again. "Not looking for any sympathy, Miss York."

"I know. But seeing your daughter in town, I'm sure that her mom must have been a lovely woman."

Sam still rode, but his eyes were losing their anger.

Sue gently added, "I guess your daughter takes after her."

Quietly, Sam just said, "That she does."

"What's her name?"

"Katherine."

"A pretty name."

"I call her Kat for short."

Sue looked down briefly. But when she looked up again, she tried to sound hopeful. "I think we'll find her."

They rode for a while without saying anything, just watching the trail in the cold moonlight. Then, still thinking about his daughter and trying to keep his voice from breaking, Sam admitted, "She's all I've got, Miss York. I'd be nothing without her..."

Sue looked at him and swallowed. Then she reached over to him and squeezed his hand as it held the reins.

Sam looked down at her hand. No woman had ever touched him since Marian died—or at least, not in *that* way. Then he thought back to his time in Natalya's room; belatedly, he realized that nothing had happened between them.

Still looking at Sue, Sam gave her a weak smile, which she returned.

Then the two went back to studying the trail...

ABOUT A QUARTER MILE from the family homestead, Josie stopped the buckboard. She couldn't hold it in any longer.

She got out and walked to the back of the buckboard. Then she threw the blanket aside to check on them.

"Okay, folks! Be patient! I got some 'business' to do."

Gradually, Kat's eyes fluttered and then she was fully awake. The first thing she saw was Josie smiling down at her. The second thing she saw was that she couldn't move her hands because they were tied tightly behind her back.

"What?? Josie, what's this?"

Josie hauled off and backhanded her across the face.

With tears in her eyes, Kat stared at her "friend" in fear.

Josie hissed at her, "*That's* what's happening, you little bitch!"

"But...you're my friend!"

Josie picked up a handful of her hair and yanked it back. Kat gritted her teeth in pain.

"My *family* are my friends. And pretty soon, they're going to have *you* for dinner!" Then, with her other hand, she punched Carrow's ribs brutally and added, "You and this big piece of sirloin!"

Now fully awake, Carrow groaned and shouted, "You're crazy!"

His hands were also tied behind his back as he laid next to Kat.

Josie replied lightly, "I'm sorry, dear, did you say something?"

Then she let go of Kat and plowed her fist deep into Carrow's stomach as he groaned in pain.

Continuing the light tone, she said, "Don't worry, big guy, no one to hear you out here." Then she shouted, "Now shut the hell up as I go back yonder and water the plants!"

With tears in her eyes, her voice pleading, Kat cried, "Josie! Why are you doing this?"

"Josie" leaned over her, eyes narrowed and looking meaner than many had ever seen her.

"First of all, 'dear,' I was never your *friend*. You were just the marshal's daughter, someone I could get close to and find out if he getting close to *us*..."

"*Us*??"

She nodded wickedly and said, "I'm Clarissa Krainer! That name mean anything to you?"

Kat didn't answer, but her eyes grew wide. Her enemy saw the fear behind them.

"That's right," the older woman replied. "*You* told me that lawmen all over the territory were concerned over disappearances. Even your father was told about it, but he didn't take the reports seriously. Well, he will now! Starting with him finding the remains of his precious little darling!" Then she punched Kat in the face. The beaten young woman cried out as blood formed on her mouth and a huge red bruise colored her face.

Clarissa then went off some distance into the woods.

Carrow said to Kat, "I don't know about you, but I'm gettin' away from that crazy sow!"

With desperation in her voice, Kat asked, "What're you gonna do?"

"I'm gettin' outta here!"

"She's out there! You'll never make it."

"I'll take that chance."

"Please help me! Get to town, tell my pa!"

"Hah! You're on your own, sweet cakes!"

"No, wait! Please!"

Ignoring her, and with his hands tightly tied behind his back, Carrow lurched forward and jumped off the end-gate. Stumbling at first, he got to his feet and ran off into the woods.

It was but ten seconds after he made his escape that Clarissa gave an angry scream and gave chase.

Kat was leaning against the end-gate and had a bird's-eye view of Carrow's flight. Without the freedom of his hands and arms to balance him, and in unfamiliar territory, the big man stumbled several times. On the last stumble, he fell flat on his face, covering it with dirt and crawling insects starting to get into his thick beard. He rose again halfway off the ground, spitting them out, and tried to rise fully. But Clarissa suddenly appeared and jumped on his back. Wrapping her arm around his neck, she tightened the stranglehold as he tried to rise. In her other hand, she held a wicked bone-handled knife with an eighth-inch blade.

Grinning, she looked down at her prey and sliced his throat from ear to ear.

Kat screamed. Then with tears in her eyes, she struggled to break out of her ropes. Still smiling, Clarissa got off the corpse and strode up to her. Then she wiped the bloody blade on the young woman's trousers. Kat whimpered when the knife touched her.

"That'll give you an idea of what'll happen to you if you try to leave us before we've had our dinner. Oh, and you can scream all you want, we're not far from the place, and no one else is out here to hear you. Now, if you have no complaints, I'm going to try again to do my business..." She punctuated her statement by shoving Kat's head back against the floor of the buckboard; the girl cried out as her head hit the hard surface.

Then her former friend turned around and walked back further and further so she would have some privacy.

Kat's face was streaked with tears and she tried to get off the rear of the buckboard, but she was afraid she would get the same treatment as the big man.

Suddenly, she heard someone next to her whisper, "Shhsh!"

Her eyes became alert and she turned to the sound of the voice.

Leo leaned over her and pulled out his penknife.

"Leo! Thank God!"

"Shh, Kat! She's probably not that far away."

Obediently, she kept quiet as she leaned to the right and allowed him to slice her ropes. After he was done, he physically carried her off the back of the buckboard.

Gratefully, while he was still holding her, she put her arms around his neck and leaned her head longingly against his shoulder.

Leo stared at her then, breathing hard and wanting desperately to respond to her, but there wasn't time. He carried her farther away from the buckboard and deeper into the woods, opposite the direction Clarissa had gone.

Leo asked her gently, "Can you walk?"

She nodded and said, "Uh-huh."

He set her down on her feet as she gazed at him.

Deep down, Kat didn't care if she was in his arms forever, but this was not the time. An armed lunatic was nearby.

This was verified when they heard Clarissa give a loud roar when she found that Kat was gone. But to the two young people, it sounded like a wild animal.

"Oh God!" Kat said in fear.

"Sounds like something caught in a steel trap!"

"Let's keep moving!"

They dove through the woods as Leo's eyes scanned the area.

"I left Mitzvah tied to a tree. I know he's around here somewhere..."

Unfortunately, in the quiet of the forest, their voices carried, despite their distance from Clarissa. Suddenly, there was an explosion and the large branch of a tree right about them fell to the ground.

Kat started when she heard the shotgun and flew into Leo's arms to avoid the falling branch.

Clarissa shouted, "Come along quietly, Kat! Don't want to have to blow your head off! Ma don't like bullets or shotgun pellets in her food!"

Leo said, "Bullets in her *food!* What the hell is she talking about?"

Frightened, Kat replied, "I know what she means! We've got to get back to town and tell my father about her and her whole family!"

"Come on! I thought I heard my horse a few yards back..."

They scurried through the dense underbrush like oversized squirrels, and though Kat was on the tall side for a teen, the even taller Leo was the one who had to dodge branches overhead. The full moon helped them see better, but scrambling through a still-dark forest in the early morning drowning in fear and panic was not an ideal situation, as tree branches and shrubbery seem to reach out to them with every step they took.

Suddenly, in the middle of their run, they heard Clarissa crowing at them from a distance.

"Hey, Kat! I don't know who your friend is who cut your ropes and all, but I've got his horse!"

Leo said, "Damn!"

"Don't worry! He'll come back to the house with me, and he can be part of our stable! But you two are now on foot and you're near our spread, so you're as good as caught as if you were wolves in a bear-trap. Hey! Do you hear me?"

Then she fired another blast at a tree branch ten feet above them.

As they were showered with bark and leaves, Kat started to cry out, but when Leo put a finger to his lips, she quickly stifled it. As quietly as they could, they moved on. Again, they scurried through the foliage, trying not to make too much noise as they did so, avoiding snapping twigs and rustling fallen leaves they had trod underfoot.

Then, without their fully realizing it due to the covering shade of the cottonwoods, the sun rose, lighting the area with its glow and, unfortunately, making it easier for their pursuer to find them.

It took a few minutes of running before they found an open clearing, now bathed in sunlight.

Kat clearly saw the edge of a fence, and an excitement went through her.

"Leo!" she cried. "We found a house! Come on!"

Still partially hidden behind some shrubbery, he warned, "Kat, wait!"

But it was too late. She left the underbrush and made herself seen. The click of the rifle was not far behind.

Gus and Liz closed in on her from both sides.

"Looks like breakfast is gonna come early!" said Liz, smiling.

Gus said, "Come out, mister! Or your girlfriend's gonna die right now!"

Leo emerged from his hiding place and stood before them, his hands raised.

Liz then squinted her eyes at him.

"Aren't you the Jewish boy I've seen in town?"

Leo answered wryly, "I'm the one..."

She replied, "Huh! I never did have kosher food before. Should be an experience."

Kat embraced him then and turned to face the Krainers.

"Let him go! *I'm* the one you want! I'm the marshal's daughter!"

Leo quickly said to the two Krainers, "Don't listen to her! Keep me and let *her* go! I'm nothing to the marshal! But if you kill his daughter, he'll track you to the ends of the earth."

The old couple just stood there and stared at them.

Hearing their plea and seeing the young couple in each other's arms, Gus said, "Kinda gets ya, doesn't it, Liz?"

Liz replied plainly, "No, not much."

She gestured with the rifle barrel. But before they moved an inch, Clarissa rushed out of the woods with her shotgun. Whirling the barrel in a wide arc, she slammed it into Leo's head. He crumpled to the ground as Kat turned on her angrily. Balling her right fist, she punched Clarissa hard in the jaw.

Momentarily stunned, Clarissa fell back a step and felt her mouth. She then looked at her fingers and found blood on them. Stepping toward Kat, she raised the barrel of the shotgun and seethed, "You little—"

"Hold it!" shouted Liz, as she barred Clarissa from getting to Kat with her rifle. "Let Mose finish the job."

Wiping more blood off her mouth with the back of her hand, Clarissa glared down at Kat as she cradled Leo's head in her arms.

Quietly, the youngest Krainer said, "Eating her will be a pleasure..."

THE WATER WAS NOW JUST above waist level, despite the fact that the storm had essentially stopped and there was no further cascade of water coming into the shelter. But it would still take days for the water to go down fully. Most of the old furniture in the shelter was now underwater, but sometimes someone's bones or a lighter object might float by.

Dirk stood there, water all around him, slightly above his belt. He was glad that he had the foresight to put the lantern on the upper shelf of what was once a bookcase; he then fixed it there by jamming his jacket against it and the inside wall of the bookcase to hold it still; he would have light as long as the wick burned and was kept far above the water.

Curiously, he looked up and saw that the crude ceiling was held up by three thin wooden posts, all now slightly bent under the weight of the cabin's floor some twenty feet above. How long would it be before flowing water, age, and rotting wood that had seen better days, cause these posts to shatter and cave in the ceiling?

All they needed, he surmised, was just a little push.

Then he decided on something. Finding the first wooden post close by, Johnson put his shoulder to it. Clumps of sod came down and bounced off his head and shoulders. He looked up again.

He didn't know if his plan would work, but if it did, it would give him a way out, and maybe, just maybe, a chance to get back at his captors and retrieve his money...

Clarissa was in the barn leading Leo's horse into a stable. She knew that her ma and pa had brought the two young people to the cabin for Mose to hack up. She smiled when she thought of what was in store for them. And she was going to be there to watch it happen...

Then she jumped when she heard a noise behind her.

She whirled around and saw Mose standing there, mouth open and staring.

"Jesus, you nearly scared the hell out of me, you damn gorilla!"

He just stared at her.

"Well, what is it you want?"

Mose lifted his huge arms and gestured at Leo's horse.

Clarissa shook her head at him. "No, you're not getting him. He's mine!"

Mose made guttural noises, which, if he could speak, would've been angry complaints.

"You already *had* a horse! Is it my fault the poor thing collapsed under you? God, you ruin everything we ever gave you!"

Angrily, Mose plunged his hand down and broke a wooden railing with a loud crash.

She stepped closer to him and said defiantly, "You don't scare me, monster boy! You're just the butcher around here, nothing more! Mom and Dad *always* loved *me*! You can't talk! You have no brains! I'm ashamed to even call you my brother! You know that Mom and Dad are keeping you around only to chop up the meat and hide the evidence! You're a creature out of someone's nightmares, and should be extinct like every other dinosaur!"

With a macabre expression on his face, Mose lifted his hand and almost touched her.

Without thinking, she fearfully stepped back.

But, recovering quickly, her arrogance returned.

"Go ahead, you circus freak, kill me and see what Ma and Pa will do to you! Especially Ma! You saw what she did to that whiskey drummer last week! She hollowed him out like a Halloween pumpkin!"

Then they heard Liz call.

Clarissa shouted toward the barn entrance, "We're comin', Ma!"

Then she turned back and looked up at him. Tall as she was, he towered over her, but she stood her ground.

She smiled up at him.

"Yes, Mose," she said quietly. "You *are* an inferior being. But maybe someday, after you're long dead in the ground—buried in a piano case, of course—maybe I'll be able to summon *you* during one of my séances..."

She then turned and confidently walked out of the barn.

Mose watched her, breathing fast.

Then he turned and punched one of the horses in the head with all his might.

The horse collapsed in the stall, dead of a broken skull...

The sun had risen fully and they were riding faster toward the sounds of the shotgun blasts they had heard a few minutes ago.

Sue asked, "What do you think it is?"

"I don't know, but I intend to find out!"

Soon enough, they saw the Krainer property in the distance and slowed their horses to a walk.

"Better be careful, Sam. If those two kids are with them, and they hear us coming..."

Gelder said quietly, "I know. We've got to have a plan." Then, unusually for him, he turned to her and asked, "What do you think we should do?"

To his surprise, Sue already had the answer.

"Let me go in! You remain outside the place and block their escape."

He looked at her and said, "And what do you think *you're* gonna do?"

"Get them to focus their attention on *me* instead of the kids!'

"I'm not havin' it, Sue! If they're the ones responsible for the disappearances, one pretty girl is not gonna mean a damn thing to them!"

Sue took her eyes off the house and looked at him. She asked, "You think I'm pretty?"

He shrugged and tried to sound casual.

"Yeah, you're good-lookin' enough. Maybe...maybe if you dropped the peepers. You have pretty eyes."

Sue turned red then. Smiling, she looked down briefly, then said, "Thank you, Sam. But...you know, I'm hardly a *girl*."

"I figured that!"

"I'm coming up on thirty-six!"

A thought came to him then that he would turn thirty-eight in August.

Not mentioning his own birthday, he said, "You've kept yourself pretty well. In fact, it's a surprise to me why you haven't been hitched by now."

Again, she tried to hide her embarrassment. She couldn't recall when a man had spoken to her so openly. *Especially* a man from back east!

"Well," Sue began lamely, "a lot of men don't like a woman who's..."

Sam finished it for her. "Got a lot to say and doesn't blindly obey orders?"

She stared at him then, not answering.

"I once had a woman like that," he added, holding back tears. "But I was too damn stupid to appreciate it..."

Her heart went out to him then. But she knew there was nothing more to say. They both had a job to do, and neither of them knew what they would find once they got *inside* the Krainers' spread...

A FEW MINUTES LATER, they both dismounted and tied their horses to a couple cottonwoods out of view of the house.

Sue took off her jacket and stuffed it under the horse's pommel. Then she drew the Colt out of her holster and checked the loads. Watching her, Sam shook his head and asked, "What kind of schoolmarm are you?"

"Hopefully, one who's a good shot." Then she snapped the cylinder back into place.

They looked from one end of the property to another. They saw the barn, the house, and finally the cabin on the right.

Sue quietly said, "If we storm one of them, they could be in the other building and kill the kids."

"Then we'll have to separate."

"It would seem so. I think the two most likely buildings for someone to be in would be either the house or the cabin. So why don't you sneak around the back and get into the house and I'll hit the cabin?"

"Now wait a minute!" Sam argued. "*I'm* the lawman here."

Sue looked up at him and held his gaze.

She repeated, "So why don't you sneak around back and get into the house while I hit the cabin?"

Belatedly seeing that her way was probably right, he sighed irritably and said, "Yes, ma'am..."

EIGHT

Both of them had their hands tied tightly behind their backs and were seated on a wooden bench against the cabin wall. The place stank of blood and human remains. A long work table was against the other side of the cabin drenched in dried blood. On the wall next to the cabin's only window, various tools and other supplies were hung on iron hooks, along with a heavy coiled rope. On the table, however, was a huge blood-stained cleaver, and next to it a large saw, its teeth also reddened by dried blood. By this time, Leo had regained consciousness and the two young people were glumly watching Mose as he prepared to do his work.

Gus and Liz, still carrying their rifles, stood by as their son shoved other "residue" off the table, making room for the two captives, or at least one at a time.

Kat looked at Leo and said, "I never should have gotten you into this."

"You *didn't*, Kat. I followed you!" Then he whispered to her, "'Wherever thou goest, I shall go...'"

She looked at him with some confusion, and said apologetically, "I'm sorry, I don't—"

"It's from the Book of Ruth."

Tears formed in her eyes. She said, "Oh, darlin', if only my hands were free—"

Clarissa stepped before her and suddenly grabbed a fistful of her hair. Then she slammed the teen's head against the cabin wall.

"Ow!"

Imitating her, Clarissa repeated, "'Oh, darlin, if only my hands were free!'"

Then she slapped Kat across the face.

Fighting the ropes that held him, Leo angrily said, "Always attacking your victims when they can't fight back! I've seen enough of your kind in Poland!"

Clarissa screamed in his face, "Shut up, Jew!" Then she stood upright and said more quietly, "At least you won't die in a pogrom..."

She then pointed to the big trapdoor in the center of the room.

"You see that?"

Kat and Leo looked at it with apprehension.

Clarissa grinned again.

"That's where what's left of you is going to end up!"

Their looks of fear made her smile wider.

Then she turned to a small shelf on the wall and brought down a black satchel. It had previously belonged to the late Dr. Bill York. She opened it and pulled out the blood-stained claw hammer.

She said lightly, "It can also be used to separate the skin from the meat!"

Then she kissed it.

Mose finished cleaning off the table of body parts

and then went over to the trapdoor. He bent over and was about to open it when Gus interrupted.

"Hold it, Mose!"

The giant stopped and looked up at him.

Liz asked, "What's wrong? We've delayed this long enough. I'm gettin' hungry."

Gus asked, "Don't you hear it? Don't you even feel it??"

"Feel *what*??"

"Be quiet, I said!"

Obeying him, they all kept still. Even their captives listened, hoping against hope that it would be someone trying to rescue them.

The muffled tremor sounded again, but louder this time. The floor beneath them started to shake.

"You hear it?"

"Yeah," said Liz, "I do now. Sounds like the cellar."

"The cellar?" Then Gus remembered. "Damn! That outlaw with the saddlebags full of cash! I forgot about him!"

Liz turned around and faced Mose.

"Lift it up, Mose..."

She then jacked a shell into her rifle.

Mose obediently bent over again and lifted up the big trapdoor. Its hinges creaked loudly as the giant pulled it all the way open and set it back on the floor. The hole had been widened during construction and it was now a full three feet by three feet, large enough for the purpose of dropping a full-grown adult a good twenty feet down into the former shelter.

The pounding was louder now, and the cabin seemed to shake more.

Peering down, Liz said loudly, "What the hell?"

They all looked in and finally saw him.

Thanks to the lantern that was mounted on a shelf high above the water, there was enough light for the four of them to clearly see Dirk Johnson crashing his body fully at a wooden post. He had been taking turns on each one; ramming one post, then going to another. With each slam, the old supports started to crack. And with every crash of his body against them, the shelter's ceiling was starting to sag. Gradually the cabin floor was tilting to one side.

Raising her rifle, Liz aimed at Dirk's back, whenever she could get a bead on him, but he kept moving fast from one post to another. Still, because the shelter was already illuminated by his lantern and he had been busy slamming the posts, Johnson failed to notice that Mose had fully opened the trapdoor and the four Krainers were looking down at him.

With Dirk's final strike at a post, the cabin floor shook. Then Liz lost her balance and she dropped her rifle. Gus dropped his own rifle on the cabin floor and threw his arms around his wife before she toppled through the hole. Her rifle, however, fell freely through the opening and hit the water far below. In fact, it splashed not far away from where Dirk had struck the last post.

Belatedly realizing where the extra light had been coming from, Johnson turned around just in time to see the rifle hit the water. Ignoring the four people above, he quickly waded toward the floating rifle, trying to keep his balance as he moved.

Picking up Gus's rifle, Clarissa jacked a shell into the chamber and aimed it down into the void. Smirking, she said, "Like shooting fish in a barrel..."

Dirk was able to get to the floating rifle, but before he could put his hands on it, Clarissa fired a cartridge into his back. The outlaw cried out and reached for his back. Not hesitating, Clarissa jacked another shell into the chamber and fired again. The second cartridge struck Dirk in the back of the neck and came out his upper breastplate, severing his windpipe. Limply, he dropped into the water and quietly sank beneath the surface.

"Well," said Clarissa triumphantly as she lowered the rifle. "That takes care of him. You won't have to worry about the posts in the cellar breaking anymore."

Liz said, "Mose, you better go down and fix 'em tomorrow. No tellin' what that man did." The giant nodded as he glanced down through the trapdoor.

Kat and Leo stared at them, trying to figure out what was happening, or who Clarissa had just killed.

The window crash from the house suddenly made the Krainers jump.

Liz said, "What the hell's going on now?"

"Someone in the house," said Gus, and then to Clarissa, "Give me that."

She handed the rifle to him, and he and Liz left the cabin and headed toward the house.

Clarissa then walked back to the two captives and looked down at them.

"Don't worry, children. I can still promise you, it'll be a slow, agonizing death."

The two were buoyed by the interruption of the window crashing and hoped it was someone trying to rescue them, but Clarissa's last statement chilled them. They both looked up into her eyes and saw that, no matter what happened, she meant every word of what she was going to do.

When the two older people stood outside their home, they saw nothing amiss. They looked at each other.

Talking about their old dog, Gus said, "Maybe it's Bart..."

Liz replied, "Don't you remember? Mose butchered him last week. Had 'em for dinner..."

"Oh, yeah! I must be gettin' old."

"So was he..."

They both climbed the steps onto the porch and Gus opened the front door and backed away quickly to the side, experimentally poking the rifle's barrel into the house. When nothing happened, he came forward and showed himself in the open doorway, his rifle at the ready. Liz hovered close by.

Then both of them felt a presence behind them and quickly turned around.

Sam stood a few yards away, near the fence, aiming his rifle at them.

"Stand still, both of you!" he shouted. "I made that noise to get you two out here." To Gus, he ordered, "Drop it, Krainer!"

Liz shouted, "Bullshit!"

Using that as a signal to fight, Gus raised the rifle and fired. Sam dove behind a bush near the fence as Gus and Liz started to back into the open doorway of the house.

Recovering quickly, Sam poked the rifle barrel around the bush.

Then, Gus fired again, the slug coming uncomfortably close to the marshal's left shoulder as it veered off the hard wood of the fence. Unfortunately, after the rifle slug ricocheted so close to him, Gelder's immediate reflex action was to pull the trigger of his own rifle just as the barrel moved a few inches to the left. Still on the porch facing the marshal, the unarmed Liz felt the cartridge hit her in the pit of her stomach.

She doubled over and almost fell. Anxiously, Gus wrapped his arm around his wife and dragged her back into the house. Then he slammed the door.

In the house, Liz was on the ground bleeding heavily from the stomach as Gus set his gun down and started crying. His wife was pale, and it was obvious she was fading fast.

Angrily, Gus rose and picked up his rifle. Then he went over to the front window and poked the barrel through the glass pane, shattering it. He fired again even though he couldn't actually see the marshal, who was still concealed behind the thick bush by the fence. The old man fired again and again as tears rolled down his cheeks, never once hitting his target, but effectively pinning him down. Then a lucky ricochet off the fence behind Sam hit him in the right forearm, causing him to drop his rifle and writhe painfully on the ground, his hat rolling off as he gripped the wound tightly. Using his legs to push himself back behind the huge bush, Sam awkwardly pulled off his neckerchief and, using his teeth as well, wrapped it tightly around his arm, above the wound.

Inside the house, Gus's rifle gave its final empty

click, though the sound was not loud enough to be heard by the marshal. Then the old man got up from the window and tossed the useless weapon away. Loudly, it flew into some pottery on a shelf, shattering it.

Standing over his dying wife, Gus howled with rage, the tears covering his ruddy face.

Then he walked back deeper into the house, and the next thing the marshal knew, he was hearing the sounds of glass shattering, though he didn't know why. By the time Gelder had pulled out his Colt with his left hand and rose from behind his shelter, he smelled smoke, and when he looked across the lawn, he saw flames rise to the roof of the simple dwelling. He ran toward the house and tried to get in, but the flames had engulfed the front door and had spread to the rest of the windows—exactly as Gus had planned when he threw every lantern in the house at any possible point of entry. The oil he purposely spilled from their wicks all over the house also increased the spread of the flames.

Inside, as fire rose around them, Gus embraced his dying wife as tears soaked the shoulder of her well-worn dress. He stroked her hair, massaged her face, but he was never going to get her back. As he gazed down at her, he saw her skin turn white and sweat soak her forehead. She gritted her teeth in pain as she looked up at him.

Weakly, she said, "Was a good ride, wasn't it, Gus?"

He answered, "The best I ever had, Liz..."

With her vision fading, her husband's tear-streaked face would be the last thing she would ever see...

Throwing his good arm up protectively, Sam was forced to back away almost to the fence. He looked at the house sadly as its walls started to fall with a loud crash.

With no support, the burning roof suddenly caved in and buried both Gus and Liz Krainer within a smoldering wreckage with a temperature of over 1,000 degrees...

But before Sam had even shouted his warning to Gus and Liz Krainer to surrender, Clarissa approached the two tied-up young people while brandishing the bloody claw hammer. They stared at her with some fear as she hovered over them.

Viciously, she hissed, "I don't care who's out there. If you think I'm gonna let you two live..."

Then, she sensed a hulking figure coming up behind her and quickly turned around to see Mose standing there shaking his head.

"What?" she said sarcastically. "You don't approve?"

Mose's face grimaced and he shook his head. But he couldn't speak and was poor at pantomime. No one would ever know if he was just plain sick of all the killings and mutilations, or whether he suddenly got sentimental at the sight of the two young people suffering at the hands of a sadistic woman, or maybe he was falling for Kat and didn't want her to end up as just another of Clarissa's many victims. Or maybe he knew the jig was up and it would be better for all of them if they finally backed off, at least this one time.

Still brandishing the claw hammer, Clarissa asked

him, "A little late for you to change your diet, don't you think?"

Because he couldn't respond verbally, Mose again shook his head and pointed at the two young people seated on the bench in the corner as if she didn't get it by now.

Holding the claw hammer before her threateningly, Clarissa stepped forward. Showing some fear for the first time, Mose backed away until he finally bumped into the edge of the long blood-drenched table.

"You know, Mose, if it wasn't for Ma and Pa, I would've gutted you like a trout by now. And it won't be a loss to any of us either, much less humanity itself. We can train *anybody* to do your job." Then she added, shouting at him angrily, "And he'd be better to look at too!"

Already backed against the table, Mose quickly reached back and wrapped his fingers around the handle of the cleaver.

But Clarissa was faster. Quickly seeing what he was up to, she swung the claw hammer in a wide arc, striking him in the left side of the forehead with the flat part. The solid iron slammed against his skull and caused him to fall back against the edge of the table. Weakly, his fingers released the handle of the cleaver, and both of his big hands came up to his head. Despite the blood now spouting from his skull and the searing pain, Mose tried to stay on his feet, but he only tottered a couple of steps instead. Then Clarissa stepped back as the giant fell to his knees. Then he hit the floor fully, shaking the already tilting floor.

Clarissa looked down at him then. She was trying to remember, but couldn't, all the times in much better days, when she had actually called him her brother. Staring at him now as he lay prone on the slanting cabin floor, she refused to shed any tears.

In fact, she quickly realized that she couldn't anymore.

Frightened by the murder they had just witnessed, Kat and Leo stared at Clarissa, not knowing what was going to happen next.

Their answer came shortly after Mose had hit the cabin's floor.

They all heard the sounds of gunfire outside.

Clarissa said, "Shit!" Then, gesturing with the claw hammer, she faced the two young people and shouted, "*Anything* happens to us, you two won't live through it!" Then she moved away from them and headed for the doorway to see what was going on.

But a movement from the open window caused her to turn around before she got there.

"Drop it!" ordered Sue as she stood before the window, pointing her Colt.

Glaring at her in return, Clarissa reluctantly dropped the bloody claw hammer into the open satchel on the floor—as if she was going to use it again.

"Now back away from it."

Scowling, Clarissa reluctantly took a few steps back.

Gratefully, the two young people looked up at Sue. Then Kat examined her face more closely. She couldn't believe it. The red hair, the cheaters! This was the woman she had suspected was responsible for the disappearances, but now it looked like she was rescuing them!

Finally, she asked Sue, "Who are you?"

"Susan York. I came here with your dad."

"Daddy's here!" she said happily.

"He's outside trying to take the others." Sue took out her switchblade knife and flicked it open. "Now let's get you kids out of those ropes."

The two young people helpfully got off the bench and turned around, presenting their bonds to her. Sue glanced at the bleeding Mose lying on the floor, but figured that keeping her eye on Clarissa was more important; what had happened to him will come out soon anyway. Quickly, she cut Leo's ropes. Then she gave him the knife, and he sliced apart Kat's ropes and threw them to the floor. The teen gratefully rubbed her wrists.

Then Sue noticed the bruises on Kat's face. She put her free hand on the teen's chin and gently lifted it to the sunlight streaming in through the open window.

Indicating Clarissa with her gun, she asked her, "Did *she* do that to you?"

Kat just looked down shyly and nodded.

Sue turned back to Clarissa, trying to restrain her anger.

At that point, she caught the brunette trying to inch her way toward the satchel. Beating her to it, Sue kicked the satchel away from her. Then she stopped and took a second look at the bag. She gasped as she stared at it.

Clarissa saw her reaction and suddenly realized why.

Grinning, she said, "*That's* why that satchel means so much to you." She then looked at Sue appraisingly and said, "The same eyes, the same chin! You're Dr. York's little sister!"

Sue didn't answer. She just stared back at her with

narrowed eyes, the gun following the brunette as she confidently circled the room.

Clarissa continued, "*That's* why you're here! To avenge big brother!" She laughed then and clasped her hands. "This is rich! You're here to get us because we made him into the most delicious soufflé we ever had!"

Kat and Leo glanced at Sue worriedly, but the redhead said nothing as she just stared at the crowing woman before them.

In fact, everyone there was ignoring the sounds of gunfire and shattered lanterns outside. It was as if the world had stopped and everything of significance was happening only in that cabin.

Clarissa stepped forward boldly. Still gloating, she said, "Let me tell you something, little sister! Your brother wanted me like it was nobody's business! And he was easy to get too! He was in my bed when it happened! In fact, I was on top of him, riding him like a stallion up in my room in Mount Pleasant. And when he came—*just* at that moment when he came, I reached under the mattress and pulled out that claw hammer! And those prongs were bigger than *he* was and I buried it in his skull so deep that I was able to lick pieces of his brain off it!" Her smile was wide and arrogant.

Kat and Leo stared at her, their mouths open as they heard language and sexual descriptions—not to mention a confession of a gory murder—they would *not* have heard at any time in their mostly quiet and sheltered young lives.

Sue, however, continued to stare at Clarissa, breathing fast, her gun still pointed at her, her thumb almost ready to pull back the hammer and fire.

Then, controlling herself, she turned to the two young people.

"Leo," she casually asked, "can you handle a gun?"

Leo started to reply, "Well, no, I've never used—"

"Good!" she said, shoving her gun into his unprepared hands.

Then she bent forward and dove headlong into Clarissa's stomach, the impact throwing the two women backward. However, when Sue launched her attack, she didn't consider that Clarissa had moved right in front of the open trapdoor. The two women fell heavily through the opening and plunged the twenty-two feet downward, finally hitting the water with a loud splash.

When the two women, both gasping and in shock from the fall, surfaced, they both tried to orient themselves to their new surroundings. Sue's hat and glasses had fallen off and were floating in the dirty water, and her soaked red hair was now plastered to her eyes. Similarly, Clarissa shoved her own hair back from her face and glared at Sue. It took but a moment before the two women came together and punched, clawed, and kicked each other before they fell into the water again, rolling around and around in the waist-deep muck as they tried to kill each other.

Kat and Leo peered over the edge of the hole and watched as the two women fought frantically. At times the combatants switched roles, as one, and then the other, tried to drown the other one.

Kat said urgently, "Good Lord! We've got to stop them!"

"How?"

"Well...*you've* got the gun!"

"And who do I shoot first? The woman who wanted to butcher us or the woman who rescued us?"

Confused, Kat could only say, "Uhh..."

Meanwhile, Clarissa ruthlessly pressed her hard fingers into Sue's eyes and open mouth, shoving her head under the surface as she did so. Up to this point, they had fought each other to a draw, with neither woman delivering a knockout blow. But with her oxygen now being cut off and her vision blocked, Sue suddenly found the strength to reach up and sock Clarissa hard in the left eye. The brunette cried out and fell back, almost going under. Her mouth and eyes cleared, Sue plunged forward, landing on top of her opponent, a wave rising up with the impact. Then they rolled around in the water again and again, their boots frantically rising above the surface as they fought. In a few seconds, their journey stopped at one of the wooden posts.

Again landing on top of her, Sue used her long fingers to close tightly around Clarissa's throat.

Not knowing her own strength, even she was surprised at how quickly Clarissa was already choking and turning blue. Not stopping there, the teacher then shoved her enemy's head under water and held it there. Bubbles rose to the surface in a haphazard fashion as Clarissa frantically waved her hands above the water trying to stop her. She tried to put her fingers on Sue's face again, but the teacher held on, increasing the pressure. Ignoring her red hair hanging down in her eyes and water dripping off her face, she tightened her stranglehold. A few seconds later, Sue could see Clarissa start to lose consciousness as her head limply fell back under the surface.

Then, as quickly as she had started it, Sue took her hands off her enemy's throat and stood up in the water. She swept her wet hair back from her face and was breathing hard as she looked down at Clarissa's limp form. Then she shook her head and said, "No, bitch, I'm not like you. I'll let a hangman's rope finish the job..."

Watching the two women fight, neither Kat or Leo noticed that the bleeding Mose had slowly crawled to the trapdoor hole.

Weakly, Mose also looked through the hole and saw the fight. He even smiled when he witnessed Sue strangling his arrogant stepsister. But then he saw her suddenly stop and stand up in the water. She was going to let her live!

Then, as she and Leo were smiling at Sue's victory, Kat looked up and saw Mose push himself forward. But before she could shout a warning to Leo, the giant had plunged through the open trapdoor and fell into the water with the impact of a twentieth-century bomb. The huge wave caused by his body threw Sue off her feet and she fell back into the water. Again, frantically pushing her head above the surface, Sue shoved her wet hair out of her eyes and tried to focus. Slowly, she got to her feet. But before she could do anything else, Mose was striding through the water as if it were no trouble at all, reached out with his meaty hand, and shoved her hard in the face. Again, she fell back into the water and splashed around before she found the strength to get to her feet.

Getting to his stepsister, Mose picked her up and looked down at her face, now covered with bruises and scratches which Sue had given her, as well as an ugly black eye. Still dizzy from the strangling, Clarissa's eyes slowly opened and she looked up at him.

But something in her stepbrother's face made her eyes widen in terror.

"Mose! No! No!"

Ignoring the pain searing from his bleeding skull, Mose moved with a fury he had not felt before. Dragging Clarissa by the hair, the giant pulled her through the rising waves to one of the bent wooden posts that Johnson had already broken.

"NO!" she screamed one more time.

Then the giant slammed his stepsister's body against the broken post. The noise echoed in the cavernous shelter, and the two young people above them watched in horror. Mose kept slamming her body against the post again and again as Clarissa screamed.

With every slam of her body against the post, the floor sagged more and more. At one point, Leo had to grab the screaming Kat around the waist and stop her from falling in through the opening. Pulling her back from the edge, Leo set her down several feet back from the hole.

But the floor shook again after Clarissa's body struck the post.

Kat shouted, "Sue's still down there! If the floor collapses, it'll bury her too!"

Leo quickly returned to the open trapdoor and shouted down to Mose, "Stop!"

When the giant continued to slam Clarissa's body into the post, Leo pulled Sue's gun out of his waistband, carefully aimed it, and fired.

The bullet struck Mose in the lower back, though it avoided his spinal column. He paused briefly, but shook off the pain, continuing to slam the screaming Clarissa's body against the post which was starting to fully crack under the impact.

"I said, stop!" Now getting used to the gun, Leo cocked the hammer and fired two more bullets, this time toward Mose's back. However, the bullets instead blew apart the back of Mose's head. The giant's last slam against the post merely bumped Clarissa's head against it. Finally, without a head on his shoulders, the big paws opened up and he let go of her. Limply, his stepsister slid down into the water as what was left of her stepbrother fell forward and sank under the surface like a dead whale.

Blood and her stepbrother's gray matter were all over Clarissa's head and neck, and she almost gagged when water flowed into her open mouth and nostrils. But it forced her to regain consciousness. Coughing, she wiped her eyes and dizzily looked around, trying to orient herself.

Several yards back from where Mose threw her, Sue rose up from the water and coughed, trying to get air back into her lungs.

Seeing her, Kat shouted, "We've got to help Sue!"

Leo said, "Wait!"

He had seen it before when they were brought into the place. Now the young man put the gun aside and went to the rear wall of the cabin, which was now slanting forward menacingly. He quickly took the coiled rope off the hook and ran back to the hole. Then he shouted down, "Miss York!"

Sue quickly snapped back to consciousness when she heard her name shouted. She looked up.

"Here!" Leo shouted as he and Kat uncoiled the rope and dropped the other end through the hole.

"I know what to do!" she shouted back. "Thanks, kids!"

She quickly tied her end firmly around her waist and knotted it securely.

Then she yanked on the rope as a signal and gripped both hands tightly to it.

"Come on, Kat!" said Leo. Straining, they both gripped the thick rope and pulled hard until their hands were red and bleeding.

Slowly, Sue was rising off the surface of the water and would soon be suspended high above it. At the point when she had almost reached the slanted ceiling with the open trapdoor, Clarissa, still bruised and bleeding, watched in frustration as her enemy was making her escape.

Then, something reflected off the surface of the water that caught her eye. She quickly spotted it practically in front of her. Liz's rifle, which she had accidentally dropped through the open trapdoor, floated invitingly within feet of her. Hungrily, Clarissa quickly waded through the water and seized it in her anxious hands. Barely concerned about her dead stepbrother in the water just a few feet from her, Clarissa had one thing on her mind.

Angrily, she jacked a shell into the rifle's chamber and raised it, the barrel's sight right on Sue as the two young people were pulling her up. Without hesitation and with her enemy in her sights, Clarissa pulled the trigger. A loud explosion followed along with her terrified scream. This was because she had forgotten that the Winchester was an older model that had now been underwater. In fact, it had flowed freely into the barrel and the stock was saturated with it.

After the explosion, Leo and Kat stopped then and almost let go of the rope. Still holding on, Sue looked back down and saw Clarissa floating in the surface of the water, her whole face and the upper part of her chest and throat covered in blood. Dangling in midair, Sue stared in shock at the bloody mess that was once a young woman. Then Clarissa's body slowly sank under the surface, the water quickly filling in the spot she had occupied. The teacher swallowed then, fully aware of what she had just avoided.

Then she looked up expectantly. The two young people continued pulling on the rope until Sue was able to put her hands on the floor and, with their help, climb out of the hole and get on her feet. She quickly stepped out of the rope and threw it aside.

Then, seeing her rescuer alive and standing before her, Kat tearfully embraced her, ignoring the fact that she was getting herself soaked as well.

Trying to hold back her own tears, Sue smiled and returned the embrace. Leaning her head on the young woman's, she gently said, "I'm glad to see you too..." Then she softly kissed the teen's forehead.

Holding on to his arm, Sam stood in the open doorway and saw them. In spite of what he just gone through, as well as the pain in his arm, he found himself smiling at the sight.

He almost hated to break up the moment, but before he could announce himself, Kat glanced toward the doorway and spotted him.

"Pa!" she shouted. Then she ran into his open arms —that is, until he winced.

Seeing the wound, she said, "You're hurt."

Gelder said dismissively, "Ahh, we'll get it patched up in town." Then he hugged her tightly with his good arm. "I'm just glad I have you back, Kitten."

Kat choked when she heard the name he hadn't called her since she was a child.

Then, while she was still in his embrace, Sam looked up and gazed at Sue. The redhead was running her hand back through her wet hair and self-consciously straightening her shirt, which was already torn at the shoulder, in a vain attempt to look presentable.

Unaware of the flooded shelter beneath them, Sam asked her, "Now what on earth happened to you?"

Before Sue could answer, Kat said excitedly, "Oh, you should've seen her, Pa!" She waved her fists around in a poor simulation of a fistfight and added, "She was beatin' up the woman who was about to kill us! I never seen such a wildcat!"

Sue looked down, trying to hide her embarrassment.

Shaking his head, Sam said, "I repeat, what kind of a schoolmarm are you?"

Sue replied sheepishly, "Right now, a very wet one!"

"Hmm..." Then he turned his gaze to Leo, though without the anger that had been inside him for so long.

Almost jovially, he said, "And you, young man!"

Before Leo could say anything, Kat again answered, "He saved my life, Pa! And he also killed the big one who'd been doing all the butcherin'! You should've seen him! He handled a hogleg like he was born with it! He even blew that killer's head off!"

Sam stared at Leo then, not saying anything, but

clearly surprised. The young man just gave a shy smile and shrugged.

Then, smiling warmly at Leo for the first time, the marshal strode up to Leo and held out his hand. The young man gratefully shook it.

Sue lightly said, "Now that all the reunions are done, I say we get out of this morgue." Quickly agreeing to that, they all went out the door, but then Sue came back and grabbed her brother's satchel. She reached inside and pulled out the second claw hammer. Then she held it over the open trapdoor hole and dropped it in. It hit the water with a splash and sank beneath the surface. She still held onto the satchel as she left the cabin.

Looking across the way, they saw what was left of the charred, but still smoldering, Krainer house.

Gelder said sadly, "I found Deputy Grimes's hat and gun in there..."

Sue looked at him soberly.

He added, "We'll come back here and take all the horses in that barn back to town. Then we'll look through the wreckage after it cools down. I'm sure we'll find a whole lot of other signs pointing to the folks who disappeared..."

The timing couldn't be better. As they all stood a good distance away from the epicenter, the cabin they had just left collapsed with a roar; the already tilted walls and slanted ceiling plunging into the watery pit, effectively burying the corpses of Mose, his stepsister Clarissa, and Dirk Johnson.

Gelder watched the now-open pit that held the Krainers' cabin, then turned the other way to look at the pile of burned wood and ashes that was once the Krainers' home.

He said solemnly, "'From Hell they came and to Hell they have returned...'"

Sue asked him, "Is that from the Bible?"

"No, I made it up."

Then Sam looked off toward the fence and saw Kat and Leo, already in each other's arms, in a passionate kiss.

Watching them, Sue said, "You'd better get used to him, Sam. It looks like he's here to stay."

Looking at them, Gelder just said, "Hmm." Though deep down, he was happy for his daughter.

Then he turned to Sue. "And what about you? Where are you gonna go?"

After putting down the satchel, she shrugged and said, "I don't know. I've spent much of the last year tracking the family that murdered my brother—especially that crazy daughter of theirs—and now...I'm kind of lost. I can't go back to where I came from. I quit my job and doubt I'd get it back."

"Well," Gelder casually said, "we could always use a housekeeper."

Her back went up then. "*What*?!"

Backing down, Sam quickly said, "Uh, let me rephrase that!"

"You'd better!"

"I mean...Kat could always use a tutor. Someone to help her, ya know, learn about life *outside* of school."

"I've got to admit, I've already grown fond of her."

"And she sure respects you."

"That she does. But where do I live? The hotel where I stayed?"

"Well, there are other options."

She asked him suspiciously, "Such as??"

"The folks in this town are not as bad as you might think. And I'm sure they'll give you a new respect when they find out how you saved the kids and solved this case."

Sue looked at him steadily and said, "You didn't do so badly yourself, Marshal."

Gelder looked away for a moment, trying to articulate what he wanted to say, but it wasn't easy.

Finally, he faced her and said, "What I'm saying is... this town needs a woman like you."

Folding her arms, Sue slyly asked, "The *town*??"

"All right, Kat needs you."

Smirking, she asked, "Just *Kat*?"

Sam then looked at her seriously and said, "No. She's not the only one."

"I figured that."

Uh...we have a spare room..."

"You know where this can lead?"

"I know."

"I'm not a shrinking violet."

"Thank God for that."

"Well then," Sue began, putting her arm in Sam's good one. "Lead on, Macduff."

Gelder looked at her oddly and said, "Macduff?"

Smiling at him, she said, "Oh, Sam. You have a lot to learn..."

Soon, all of them found their horses in various locations and they rode without incident back to town.

Far away from the now-smoldering remnants of the Krainer home and the sunken residue of what was once Krainer's cabin...

QUANTRILL'S GOLD

ONE

His horse was about played out when he rode up to the ancient stage station a few yards off the road between Independence and Lone Jack. The rain came down in sheets and splattered his Stetson and worn slicker as he sat his horse and stared at the building. The glow of lantern light shone through the front windows in the night's blackness.

Unhurriedly, he dismounted and walked his horse over to the corral gate, opened it enough for them to enter, then closed it. Pushing open the barn door, he peered into the darkness and went inside. He sensed the movement of the other horses in their stalls and, after striking one of his few dry matches against a wall, lit the lantern hung on a nail near the entrance. After leading his mount to an empty stall, he removed the saddle and soaked blanket and then threw a nose-bag around the horse's head. Raising the lantern high, he looked deeper within the building. A stagecoach had been pulled inside and four tired, soaking wet horses were in a row of stalls to the right. Opposite them, on the other side of the massive coach, was a row of stalls where the new mounts were awaiting their chance to pull the coach whenever it left. Judging by the condition of the horses on the right, he guessed that the stage must have been brought in less than an hour before.

Slowly, Hoge Farrell left the barn and then stood outside the door watching the stage station. He still wasn't sure if the marshal's posse had quit the chase, but he hadn't seen a lick of them for hours and figured he had put enough miles between himself and his pursuers to give himself a respite. He stiffened his shoulders against the night's chill and marched across the grounds over to the front door of the stage station. He entered the room without fanfare, but his entrance caused the inhabitants to stare at him as he stood there holding the door open.

Just a few people were there: a middle-aged fellow in damp range clothes and a rather short man wearing a derby and gray suit, both of whom sat at the long table in the center of the room; and a young woman who sat apart from the others at a corner table. The two men stared sullenly at him as if his entrance had disturbed their private thoughts. Only the young woman, her auburn hair pinned up under a simple brown hat and her figure snug in a tight-fitting jacket and long skirt, regarded him without hostility.

Thunder was heard and lightning flashed behind him, making his silhouette look suddenly grotesque to those in the room. It felt to him like he was a part of one of those corny stage melodramas his parents had dragged him to see as a kid, in order to instill some kind of culture in him; but all he did was laugh at the overacting of the traveling stage troupe and the pretensions of the play's script.

A voice growled from the direction of the bar. "Mister, you want to shut the door? We all don't enjoy the rain blowin' on us like you do."

Farrell saw the man, big, broad-shouldered, a thick brown mustache across a wide face and a filthy apron around his sizable belly. He tensed at the sarcasm, but decided he was in enough hot water already and shut the door.

He nodded to the others and saw no answering nod in return, so he went over to the bar. He took off his hat and shook the water off the brim; then ran his hand back through his brown hair and looked at the bar man.

"Whiskey," he said.

The man paused for a second, watching him briefly, then returned with a bottle and poured a drink. A slammed door drew his attention to the back of the room where he saw another big man, this one wearing a Stetson and soaking wet Levis emerge from a hallway leading to a back door; the man was in the process of buttoning up his fly. Seeing everyone looking at him, he self-consciously cleared his throat and then sat down at the other end of the long bar.

Farrell downed the whiskey and immediately felt its warmth.

Before he could ask for another, the bar man said, "Four bits."

Farrell said, "That's a lot for a drink. I could get the same thing for two bits back in town."

The bar man said levelly, "Then go back to town. It's four bits here. This is a swing station, not a local saloon. Hell, you're not even a passenger."

"Then I might as well make it eight bits," Farrell said, holding out the glass.

The bar man scowled and refilled Farrell's glass.

Farrell downed the whiskey and set down the empty glass, letting the tension from the encounter with the bar man go out of him. He slid a coin on the bar. The bar man slapped a meaty hand on it and took it away, giving Farrell the fish-eye as he did so.

As he wondered about his next move, Farrell noticed the middle-aged man in the range clothes staring at him. He didn't want to start any trouble there, but he was also tired and irritable from a long ride and the stare was eating at him.

"You know," he said to the man, "it's rude to stare at folks."

The man's expression didn't change, but he sounded surly when he replied, "So what?"

The bar man saw the tension in Farrell and, not wanting his furniture broken up in a fight, said loudly to the man at the other end of the bar, "You stayin' the night, right, Chet?"

Chet Riley put his huge hands together on the bar and looked at them. "Yeah," he said sullenly. "I figure the Independence road is under water 'bout now. Hope this rain stops by tomorrow. Wells Fargo doesn't like bein' late, least of all 'cause of weather."

To pull his attention away from the man staring at him, Farrell asked in a friendly manner, "Hauling any strong boxes?"

Chet looked down the bar at him and answered plainly, "No, and I wouldn't if they paid me extra either."

The little man with the derby asked, "Why is that, Mr. Riley?"

Chet answered, "Because Kate Riley didn't raise her son to be a target, that's why. I heard that before the war, a road agent would just grab a strong box and maybe the occasional gold watch, but they'd leave the passengers alive. Then the war came and the guerrillas that rode around this area changed the rules. So nowadays, every outlaw has to kill the folks they rob. That's all they can think of nowadays, kill, kill, kill. Just to get themselves a big name, like the James boys. And who do you think they shoot first, the *driver*, that's who!" He punctuated his rant by downing his drink.

The little man said, "I'm sure they're not all that way."

The middle-aged man seated opposite him growled, "What the hell do you know?"

The little man nervously blinked his eyes and replied, "Why, I heard that Jesse and Frank James are victims of the railroads and the government."

The middle-aged man stared at him as if he had just spat on his boots.

He added, "When he rode with Quantrill, Jesse James was a miserable little punk and Frank was a hot-tempered bully. They'd kill you as soon as blink."

Farrell asked curiously, "How do you know?"

The man eyed Farrell suspiciously and said, "You ask a lot of questions."

"I noticed some men are afraid to give answers."

The man tensed at the remark and leaned forward, his hand disappearing under the table. Farrell kept his eyes on the man, confident in the knowledge that he wouldn't pull a gun on him with so many witnesses around.

Then, the woman at the corner table suddenly spoke up. "Mr. Garth, I'm sure he was just making conversation. It sounded like a reasonable question. How do you know that the James brothers are..." She paused, trying to remember the words.

Chet Riley said, "Two-bit punks." Then he added, "Ma'am."

Garth's eyes regarded the woman briefly. Then, returning his gaze to Farrell, he said, "I knew a friend who rode with them during the war..." Then he leaned back and didn't say anything else, as if that was all he cared to say about the subject.

However, Chet Riley wasn't through with the topic.

He said, "I heard that the James boys would drop folks in their tracks for the hell of it. They thought killin' was fun. Bet they still do. Those guerrillas did some wicked things in Lawrence and Centralia and Baxter Springs. I'm sure there's still folks in those towns who remember how wild all those boys were."

Farrell noticed that Garth shifted uncomfortably in his chair.

The little man leaned forward and said, "Well, as far as the James brothers were concerned, their lives were ruined by the railroads. Their little stepbrother blown to bits while he was sleeping in his bed, their mother losing an arm."

Chet growled sarcastically, "I know a former Reb or two who got a leg or an arm blowed off by Grant or Sherman. They don't go around goin' 'Boo-hoo, boo-hoo, woe is me. I think I'll become a bank robber and killer and act like I'm a big hero.'" He looked at the little man and said, "I know your kind, Wentworth. You'd glorify Attila the Hun and say he had a right to conquer folks."

The little man blinked through his spectacles and said, "Now just a minute, Mr. Riley—"

Again, Farrell noticed that Garth seemed uncomfortable; he was looking down at his lap, but there was a definite scowl on his face when the guerrillas were being criticized.

At that moment, a tall, slatternly woman in a well-worn gray blouse and long skirt shuffled out of the rear kitchen, wiping her hands on a rag. Her blonde hair was mussed and her fiery green eyes gazed at the group seated around the room. The men in the room noted that the top two buttons of her blouse were open and that her breasts fairly jutted out from their confines; idly, and in their own way, they were each hoping that the third button would be open as well. As usual, the bar man was uncomfortable when she entered looking the way she did, but her lack of decorum apparently didn't bother her. The other woman in the room took note of her bold stare at Farrell, and without her realizing it, resentment began to build within her.

Pulling her gaze from Farrell, the woman then scanned the room. She said, "Full house, I see." She wasn't smiling when she said it. Farrell noted her accent and guessed that she was from the Deep South.

The bar man replied, "Better get the cots ready, Alma. The road's flooded."

Alma looked at her husband and said, "Charge 'em extra, Fred."

Wentworth said, "What!"

Garth cursed and the young woman started to

protest, but Alma cut them off. Facing them squarely, she said, "Five dollars apiece from each of you! Or else I'm bringing out my daddy's old carbine and I'm ready to use it too! You can sleep out in the damn storm for all I care! I'm not runnin' no hotel!"

Her angry glare accentuated her fiery green eyes. Despite her gruff manner, Farrell couldn't help being physically attracted to her.

At the end of the bar, Chet looked down at his empty glass, embarrassed. It was obvious he had seen this behavior from her before. Fred looked reluctant to challenge her.

She asked pointedly, "Now what's it gonna be, gents?" Then, noticing the auburn-haired woman for the first time, she added venomously, "And 'lady'?" The woman at the table glared at her in return.

Wentworth said timidly, "I have no desire to be outside on a night like this." Then he looked at Fred and added, "But, sir, I intend to lodge a protest to the Wells Fargo station in Independence."

Alma's down-home twang dripped sarcasm. "You do that, four-eyes. But when you're under *my* roof, you toe the line! Now I want five dollars in good ol' Yankee money on the top of this here bar in the next thirty seconds or y'all can take a walk outside."

Even Garth was at a loss for words. Scowling, he dug into his pockets. Wentworth did so also, and the auburn-haired woman opened her purse and searched inside.

They all went over to the bar and put their money down before Alma, everyone giving her nasty looks as they did so. Quickly, she scooped up the money and deposited it into the pocket of her greasy apron. Then she looked at Farrell and said, "Where's your contribution, mister? I don't recall saying you stayed here for free."

Fred quietly said, "He wasn't on the coach, Alma."

Alma's eyes lit up then; Fred saw this and grimaced almost immediately.

She said, "Like to travel at night in a storm, do ya?"

Farrell said evenly, "My brother in Olathe took ill. When I saw him last, I didn't ask him to get sick only in good weather."

Chet stifled a laugh, and the woman at the corner table couldn't help smiling.

Alma tensed, but kept her self-control. She asked pointedly, "You from Lone Jack?"

Farrell replied sullenly, "Yeah, I'm from Lone Jack. Now what is this, some kind of interrogation? I just come in here out of the storm for a warm place and a drink. My horse is played out and I need some rest myself. Is that a crime?"

Alma's beautiful eyes narrowed. "Your horse is played out," she repeated suspiciously. "Why? You runnin' away from someone?"

Farrell said tightly, "I said my brother's ill, and I'm needed in Olathe. But neither of us is going to benefit from my horse going lame in the middle of a storm so I stopped in here."

"Your horse is in our barn?"

"Well, I'm not leaving him outside to drown."

Alma said to Fred, "Eight dollars for him." When Farrell started to say something, she cut in, "That includes you sleeping in the barn too. *Eight* dollars, take it or leave it."

The woman at the table said, "Now wait a minute!

That's not fair! Why can't he sleep in the house with the rest of us?"

The expression on Alma's face was ugly. It was obvious to everyone in the room that she didn't like her will thwarted, and liked it even less when another woman, a younger one at that, was doing the thwarting. Fred saw the look and quickly said, "That's what my wife said, cowboy. Take it or leave it."

Farrell had been chased into the night to end up here; but he realized that a night in someone's stable, out of the storm and concealed from those hunting him, would help his situation despite the high price. Frowning, he started to dig out the money.

FARRELL FELT LUCKY, for what it was worth, that the pile of hay he was lying on was comfortable enough for him to sleep soundly for at least two hours or so before the creak of the barn door opening woke him up. There was no mistaking it; the sharp stab of moonlight as the door opened, the sound of hissing rain on the hard-packed earth outside, and the faint sound of muddy boots on the stable's dirt floor announced the sudden entrance of an intruder. He had his Stetson over his eyes, and after he lifted the brim up to clear his vision, he felt the sharp blade against his Adam's apple.

He froze and held his breath. Sweat appeared on his forehead as his eyes tried to make out the figure leaning over him. He saw only a man in a wide-brimmed Stetson silhouetted against the moonlight seeping in through the closed barn door.

"Don't yell," the man hissed.

Then the man lifted the blade enough for him to reply.

Farrell said harshly, "If this is a robbery, then you've got the wrong man. No money-bags sleeps in a barn with the horseflesh."

The man leaned back and looked down at him briefly. Satisfied that Farrell wasn't a man to panic, he rose and went over to the lantern that hung near the door. Striking a match on the doorjamb, he lit the lantern and then faced him with bright eyes.

Farrell saw that it was Garth.

He put his hat back on and rose, facing him curiously.

Garth said, "Hoge Farrell."

"Yeah?" he replied cautiously.

"Don't remember me, do ya?"

Farrell paused and studied the man's face.

"You remind me of someone, but he's dead. And when he was alive, he was a whole lot thinner."

Garth stepped forward and said, "Huntsville State Prison down in Texas, five years ago. That's where we met. You were part of the gang that robbed the bank in Trinity and they sentenced you to three years. A teller was killed during the holdup and so was a bystander."

Farrell said tightly, "Yeah..."

"Good thing everyone saw that you were just holding the horses or you would've been dropping off that scaffold along with your friends."

"At the time, I had bad taste in friends."

"No doubt. Come on, Farrell, Huntsville! You still don't remember me?"

Farrell stared at him. Then his eyes showed recognition and he snapped his fingers.

"Charles Taggert!"

The other man grinned wickedly and said, "Just plain Garth now. I'm not into advertising my identity at the moment."

"But Taggert died in a bank holdup in Waco. Sheriff said the gang overdid it with the dynamite and not only blew up the safe, but themselves as well."

The grin widened. "Now who can accurately identify *anyone* who's got his face blown off, you tell me."

Farrell shook his head and leaned back against a stall. He said quietly, "I'm beginning to get the picture."

Garth said, "It was my gang, all right. But riding with 'em was getting too hot for me. I had to get the law off my back and the addition of an extra stick or two of dynamite to the pile helped provide me my new life. I skedaddled out the back door just in time; blew the place to splinters. So everyone thinks Charlie Taggert died in some God-forsaken bank in Waco? Let 'em!"

Farrell stared at the man and said, "As the English would say, that kind of behavior is *hardly cricket*."

"Oh, don't *you* start judging me too!"

"Yeah," Farrell said wryly, "and Jesse and Frank were two-bit killers. It figures why you're such an expert on 'em. I remember now, you rode with 'em."

"Yeah, but I shun notoriety. I'm not a newspaper hog like they are. I'm after making a bigger stake with a lot less noise. That's where *you* come in."

"I was wondering where this was going to lead. But I'm through with robbing banks."

Garth approached him. Looking at him levelly, he said, "You ain't got a sick brother in Olathe or anywhere else. Your horse is all in when you came riding in here in the middle of a storm. You must've tried to break into the bank back in Lone Jack."

Farrell stood there and his mind went back over the last few hours. Garth was wrong; he *hadn't* tried to break into the bank. In fact, he had just stopped in town and was peacefully having a drink at the Parakeet when someone who happened to be from Trinity, Texas recognized him and alerted the marshal. Coincidentally, it seemed that a young woman had been assaulted and had her purse stolen around the same time he was ordering his drink. As Farrell sat there and finished his whiskey, he thought of the immediate future. He was hoping to move on and get a job at one of the outlying ranches on the Kansas/Missouri border before he turned around on his barstool and saw some ten men standing before the swinging doors and demanding that he come with them. Hell, he hadn't even done anything, but he didn't like the looks of the stern, sweaty faces that glared at him from across the room. Having been in this situation before, he gauged the problem immediately, quickly shooting out the light and running out the back door.

And now here he was, facing a man who lived by the lie and the gun and probably wouldn't believe him no matter what he said.

But he wasn't going to lie to this ex-guerrilla or anyone else.

"You believe what you want to believe," he said evenly, "but I'm not pulling any stickups for any ex-border men or anyone else."

Garth grinned again and shook his head. "No stickups, Farrell. This is another kind of robbery—but you won't need no guns or dynamite either."

He was rolling himself a cigarette. As he did so, he asked, "How'd you like to be rich, *very rich*?"

Farrell smiled gravely at him and said, "That's why you woke me up with a knife at my throat in the middle of the night?"

Garth struck a match and lit his cigarette, then blew out a cloud of smoke. The horses in the surrounding stalls smelled the tobacco and several snorted in disgust. Garth sat down on a tied-up bale of hay and stared at Farrell, sizing him up, wondering whether he was right in letting him in on his secret.

"You got a job?" he asked.

Farrell looked down and said, "Not right now, but I'm young. I'll get by."

"Doing what, working the ranches all your life?" He waved his hand dismissively and added, "You told me once you used to break horses before you fell in with that gang. What I have in mind will make sure you'll never see another bronco as long as you live."

Farrell leaned back against the wall and started to roll his own cigarette. He wanted no part of anything illegal, but he *was* curious as to what Garth was driving at.

"All right," he said, "What's on your mind?"

Garth grinned and settled himself on the bale.

"You know I rode with Quantrill?"

Farrell nodded.

"Well," Garth continued, "I was a tow-headed young whip back in '63, long-limbed and ornery and full of hell. I'd have torn your head off for looking at me wrong, that's the kind of young'un I was."

"All right," Farrell replied irritably, "I figured if you rode with that bunch, you weren't a saint. Go on."

Garth ignored the testiness and said, "Well, anyway, we stopped a stagecoach heading east on that road there just outside this door."

"The Independence-Lone Jack road?"

"Right."

"Uh-huh." Farrell exhaled smoke into the cool, damp air. Smelling more tobacco, the horses moved around their stalls, their nostrils flaring as the smoke drifted toward them.

Garth shook his head in disbelief and said, "Only the Yankees would be stupid enough to travel down a main road with Reb guerrillas everywhere you spit, with a stagecoach carrying the biggest pack of gold you'd ever see in your life!" His eyes lit up with glee and he smiled broadly.

Farrell stared at him.

"Gold?"

"Bars," Garth said. "Bars bigger than your leg!"

"You've seen this gold?"

"I've seen it. Straight from the gold fields of California, an almighty ton of it! Specially melted down into bars and shipped east. First by rail, then by stagecoach. Maybe they wanted to transfer it to another rail line; can't say for sure."

"Why would they bother to ship all that gold east, especially during a war?"

Garth nodded and said, "*That's* why! Because of the war. Seems that lanky lawyer from Illinois..."

"He's originally from Kentucky."

"All right, so he's from Kentucky!" Then Garth relaxed and continued, "Anyway, the Union government needed money. The blue-bellies were losing thousands of men at the time and England and the rest of

Europe were boycotting the Yanks because of the Trent affair and such, and anyway, the goddamn Union was running out of money to continue the war, don't you see? So they ordered this gold from California for this special purpose—to keep Grant and Sherman on their McLellan saddles waving cutlasses and the northern factories cranking out Henrys and Dragoons and pistol balls to use on good southern boys. Same reason Custer and his bunch got shot up while fighting on Sioux territory in '76, so President Grant and his crooks can have gold for the US treasury."

"So you raided the coach. How'd you know that it had gold?"

"We *didn't*! That's the thing. We just knew it was a Yankee coach and we pulled it over. We...we paroled the men guarding it--"

"You mean you killed them?"

"All right, so we killed them!" he said testily. "It's a goddamn war, not a cocktail party! What do you expect?"

"All right," Farrell said irritably, "go on."

"When we opened those strong boxes, our eyes bugged out of our heads. We couldn't believe our good fortune."

Farrell blew out some smoke and said, "You boys had to travel light. You couldn't have brought that gold with you to Lone Jack."

"Right."

"So you buried the strong boxes?"

"We buried the whole goddamn coach!" He leaned forward, getting more excited as he spoke. "We drove the thing into a gully not far from here, cut loose the horses and used a pile of gunpowder to blow the side of the hill and bring it down on the coach, which was lying on its side. We figured to come back for it later."

"You didn't tell the Reb government about the gold?"

Garth cleared his throat awkwardly and said, "Well, we kind of figured that ol' Jeff Davis and his bunch had enough problems to concern them at the time."

Farrell said wryly, "Of course."

"So why bother them with it?"

"So you figured that you and your friends would get back to the spot and dig it up after the war?"

"Only that the rest of my friends were captured shortly afterwards by Joe Hooker's men. They didn't waste any time. They hanged every man-jack of 'em."

"And you're the only survivor who knows about the gold?"

"That's right."

"You sure there wasn't some little magpie who let Hooker know just where your *friends* would be so they could be captured?"

Garth leaped to his feet and threw the cigarette to the ground. His right hand hovered near his holstered gun. Glaring at him, he said, "I'd choose my words a little more carefully if I were you, friend."

Farrell wasn't afraid of him; nevertheless, he decided to change the subject.

"But why didn't you go back for the gold after the war?"

Garth relaxed, and his hand idly went to his mustache, which he stroked.

"'Cause I was in a prison run by blue-bellies in Texas, that's why. After I got out, I tried to drift up north to Missouri, but then I got in with a bunch of other ex-Rebs robbing Yankee banks and I put the gold on the back burner. But after the...sudden death of my friends in Waco, I figured to go back and try for the gold again."

"And why do you need me?"

"I can't unbury a stagecoach full of gold by myself. Besides, I need *someone* covering my back."

"Yeah, but don't you think the Union government would've tried to find out what happened to the gold after all these years?"

"That I couldn't say. I'm sure they tried to find out what happened to it. They might *still* be looking for it, for all I know. Logically, they would think that we were able to transfer it down south to the Confederate treasury; or maybe have it shipped to England where Jeff Davis had southern sympathizers open special bank accounts so the blue-bellies couldn't get their hands on it. Gold is gold to the English or anyone else, they don't care where it comes from. But it *isn't* in Europe and it isn't sitting in someone's musty old vault in South Carolina. That's where the blue-bellies were fooled! It's been sitting in the ground just a few yards from where we first hit the stage!"

Farrell nodded. Then he asked, "And what about disposing of it? You can't just walk into a store and pay for a fine suit of clothes with gold bars."

"I've already contacted a source who'll take it off our hands for a cool ten million dollars, that is, after they transfer the equal amount to American banks to an account I'll open up once I get the gold."

"And who's the source?"

"Mexico."

"Mexico? They can't even keep their governments straight down there."

"It doesn't matter. Those Mexicans are prepared to pay us my price so they can use that gold to finance their counterrevolution. With that gold, they can double their Rurales and have enough to stuff into their own pockets besides. They'll be getting the better deal, but we'll still have enough to live free and easy for the rest of our lives. Now, you with me?"

Farrell paused, then he asked, "And if I refuse?"

Garth drew out the folding knife and flipped it open; its blade gleamed dully in the lantern light. "Then I gut you like a fish."

Farrell stared at the blade. He didn't like being bullied into making deals, even a tempting one like this.

"I could always use an extra buck..."

Garth laughed and said, "An *extra buck*!"

"But how do I know that I won't end up like your, uh, friends?"

"Are you crazy? I'm an ex-guerrilla who never took a loyalty oath. I robbed banks and killed folks. I've had wanted dodgers on me everywhere. I'm a wanted man! I'm the one who has to trust *you* not to turn me in, not the other way around! The way it works out, it's perfectly balanced. You're wary of me and I'm wary of you—and that's how we protect each other. If I killed you, I'd be exposing myself to the law, and then for sure it's the noose for me... But at the end of it will be more money than you'll know what to do with!"

Farrell looked at him and thought about it for what seemed like a long time. It hadn't been so long ago that he was released from prison. He might have been free, but he didn't like being a drifter, going from one job to another. He wanted *something* to latch on to, and it might as well be a cock-eyed treasure hunt.

He said, "Okay, Charlie—I mean Garth. I'll help you."

Suddenly, they both heard a noise at the door.

Garth became alert. Without a word, he moved quickly down the runway deeper into the barn. Crouching in the darkness behind the stagecoach, he held the knife in his sweaty palm and listened.

A gust of wind and rain blew in as Alma opened the door and entered. Then she quietly closed it and approached Farrell. She was holding her carbine in one hand, but she wasn't pointing it at him. She was still wearing the same clothes she had on earlier, only this time, the third button of her blouse was open, further revealing her breasts.

Alma looked at him levelly, her green eyes flaring excitedly. She asked, "Who you talking to, Farrell?"

He stared at her and asked, "How'd you know my name?"

"Outlaw, huh? I figured from the look of ya."

Farrell noticed that she didn't act the same way she had back at the house. Whatever rage he had seen in her earlier had vanished, and was replaced by an open flirtatiousness. Her eyes were bold, challenging. She stepped closer to Farrell and he could smell her blonde hair and the sweat of her body. He tried not to gaze down her blouse, now inches from his chest.

"Listen, Miss--"

"*Missus*, but that's my curse, isn't it?"

"What do you want?"

"What do you think?"

She suddenly grabbed him around the neck and

pulled him down. Then she kissed him passionately, her tongue searching.

He pulled her away abruptly and tried to catch a breath.

"You do this with all your guests?"

"No, just the ones who set me on fire."

She dropped the carbine to the ground and tried to pull him close again, but he pulled her arms off and stepped back.

"It's not like I wouldn't want to," he said, his face still flushed and his breath panting. "But I've got this thing about married women. Figure if they'd double-cross the old man, they'd double-cross me just the same." However, in the back of his mind, he was thinking: *Yet I'll trust Charlie Taggert; does that make sense?*

Alma was tall and her arm-reach was long; she had no problem grabbing Farrell around the neck again.

"Come on, cowboy. When was the last time you had someone like me?" She reached up and knocked off his Stetson, running her fingers through his hair and kissing him with such force it hurt his lips.

When she finished, Farrell stared into her fiery green eyes. He was breathing fast as he stared at her. He'd be a fool not to admit he was attracted, and more. Yet at the same time, he had visions of Fred catching the two of them while cradling a shotgun under his arm.

"Mmmm," she purred. "You know, darlin', I'd take you back there in the dark and do you up pretty if it weren't already occupied by your friend with the pig-sticker."

Farrell pulled her arms off and stepped back, staring at her with some fear.

"What're you talking about?"

Alma gave a charming, playful smile and said, "Why, your ex-Reb friend, Mr. Garth, or that's what he calls himself anyway."

They heard a movement from the back. Alma quickly bent down and picked up the carbine. She pointed the barrel more or less in Garth's direction as he emerged into the light.

Still holding the knife, he said, "You heard everything."

Farrell said, "But you were outside."

Alma replied, "At first, darlin', I just wanted to pay you a little visit and make sure you were all right."

"Sure. Just wanted to make sure I was tucked in."

Alma grinned at the phrase. Then she said, "Something like that. But then I started to hear voices from inside, and since I figured that my horses don't carry on conversations, all I did was plant myself in a dry spot under the overhang and put my ear to the wall. You see, we got packrats who gnaw through *anything* and there's a fist-sized hole back yonder *where I can hear every word you boys said.*" She had emphasized those last words; Farrell noted that there was no smile on her face when she said them.

Then, facing Garth, she said, "Would you mind putting that thing away? I might get nervous and pull the trigger."

Resigned, Garth sighed, folded the knife and shoved it into his pocket. "All right," he said testily, "what do you want?"

She flashed a smile again. "Why," she said charmingly, "that's no way to talk to your partner."

Garth shot a look at Farrell. Then he stamped his

foot and said, "I *knew* it! Just knew it! Bloody Bill said there would be days like this!"

Farrell asked her, "And what about your husband?"

"Well," she asked, "what about him?"

"Is it now split four ways?"

"He's got a lot on his mind lately. I wouldn't burden him with all this. He's under enough pressure."

Farrell stared at her and wryly said, "It's no wonder why..."

Garth asked, "How are you going to keep that from him?"

"I've got ways."

"I bet. So what happens now?"

Alma looked at both of them and said sweetly, "Why, we wait for big Chet to take that little man and that tart out of here and Charlie just tells 'em he'll stay here for the present time. Why not? They shouldn't care."

Garth said, "My original plan was to take the stage all the way to Lone Jack, buy some tools and then double back to the spot and commence digging. Instead, I run into a fellow badman over there and I figured we could work together. Lord knows, I could use help getting that thing out from a pile of mountainside."

Alma's eyes regarded Farrell hungrily.

"I'm damn glad of that..."

Farrell picked up his hat and put it back on, avoiding her gaze.

Garth stepped forward then, a move that made Alma lift the gun's barrel and aim it at his chest.

He said tensely, "I just want to make sure of one thing. If we bring you in on this, what're you giving us in return?"

She answered simply, "My silence. I mean, you wouldn't want the whole county to know there was gold in the bottom of that hill, now would you?"

Farrell said, "She's got us there."

Alma smiled and said, "Thanks, Brown Eyes."

Garth said irritably, "All right! It looks like you're in. I figured to camp near the site while we commenced to digging."

"Why bother? Fred and I can put you up at the stage station. We could also provide the horseflesh to drag the coach up after it's dug up. I also get a chance to keep an eye on you boys and protect my investment."

Farrell asked, "And how're you going to explain our presence to Fred?"

Alma looked at him and he quickly saw the change in her. She wasn't being flirtatious or playful now; he was looking at the face of a woman who'd cut his liver out.

"He'll bow to my wishes," she said.

THE NEXT DAY, the sun burst in through the now-open windows and the sounds of singing birds could be heard from the surrounding trees.

The guests were served eggs and bread with molasses along with mugs of steaming coffee. Yet all through the meal, no one spoke, not even the usual pleasantries travelers used during a hearty meal. Instead, they all silently studied each other, as if their thoughts might be read by the person at the next table. The tension in the room was almost visible to the eye.

After his meal, Farrell rose from his chair and left

the house, heading for the outhouse in the rear. However, before he could get to it, he stopped short when he saw the auburn-haired young woman exiting the little shack and closing the door. She adjusted her riding skirt and was heading back when she saw him and also stopped.

Farrell would've put his hand to the brim of his Stetson had he been wearing it, but he had left both that and his coat at the table in the main dining room.

He smiled pleasantly and said, "Morning, ma'am."

She replied sullenly, "Morning, Mr. Farrell."

Farrell halted her with his voice. "Wait a minute! How'd you know my name?"

She turned to face him, her blue eyes brightly reflected in the morning sun. Her voice, however, was cynical. "Don't worry, Mr. Farrell, your secret is safe with me."

"What *secret*?"

"You joined us at breakfast rather late, so you missed Mrs. Parker's speech to us."

"Alma?"

She smiled wryly and said, "I see you're on a first-name basis with her already. If you mean the big blonde who likes giving me dirty looks, then I guess that's our girl."

"And what did she say to you?"

"She said that we should shun you because you're Hoge Farrell, a notorious outlaw who's robbed banks and stagecoaches."

Farrell said sardonically, "That was awfully nice of her. Did she also say that I eat babies and crucified our Lord?"

She sighed. In a sympathetic voice, she said, "Listen, Mr. Farrell. Honestly, I understand your being angry. It was a rotten thing for her to do. But..." She seemed to be struggling to find the right words. "You're an outlaw. I'm a secretary for a real estate company. We move in different worlds. Now if you'll excuse me..." She attempted to pass, but he blocked her.

"At least what do I call you?"

She raised her eyes and looked at him levelly. Farrell noted that she was almost as tall as he was; actually, she was about Alma's height. But as he studied her face and took note of way she carried herself, he never had the impression that she was trying to dominate him or get her own way. In fact, he sensed a natural friendliness in her eyes.

Patiently, she said, "Nancy." Then, when she saw that he wanted more, she added, "Nancy Belmont. Of Kansas City."

Farrell grinned and asked, "Of Kansas City, Kansas or Kansas City, Missouri?"

Despite her reluctance to smile at him, Nancy couldn't help breaking into a grin at the situation. "Kansas," she answered, then added good-naturedly, "Now I'd like to go inside."

"Yeah," Farrell said, "I've got some business to attend to myself."

"I understand perfectly. I'll see you inside then."

"You will at that."

She passed him and he watched her as she headed inside. He started to appreciate the women of Kansas as he turned and headed for the little shack.

As he sat there in the darkness, and then afterward, as he marched toward the house, his fury grew as he thought of Alma and her big mouth. It was obvious that the stationmaster's wife said what she did so that the others would steer clear of him—particularly Nancy. He was hoping that the Kansan was smart enough to read Alma's motivation in lying about him.

Still, the revelation angered him. He felt like getting back at Alma somehow, but short of smacking her in the face, an act which would've repelled him, what could he do?

Then it hit him suddenly. A perfect way to get back at her and shake up the pot a little bit.

Farrell sat at the bar and had an extra mug of coffee. Its strong smell and even stronger taste roused him further and he looked at Fred at the other end of the bar, pouring Chet a shot of whiskey into his mug of coffee. Alma was leaning back against the kitchen door, watching the room; Farrell could tell that she couldn't wait for these people to leave so they could begin their work. There was greed in those beautiful green eyes of hers, but there was also resentment and rage, most of it directed toward Nancy at the far table, quietly sipping her cup of tea.

Wentworth sat at the same table he did the other day, with Garth just two seats away.

The little man said, "Sorry we'll be losing your company, Mr. Garth. We didn't always agree, but I found you a fascinating conversationalist."

But Garth wasn't listening to him. His face was sullen, there was a tension within him, as if he were counting down the minutes when these people, this extra baggage, could go their own way and he could begin getting to the site of the gold.

"Huh?" he asked, as if suddenly snapping awake.

"I said I'll miss your company," Wentworth repeated, ignoring his companion's rudeness.

"Oh, yeah. Sure! Thanks, Wentworth!" But there was no smile or any other sign of appreciation when he said it.

Farrell watched them with interest. Then, his eyes watching the coffee mug, he asked in a loud voice, "So, Garth, when will we head for the diggings?"

Garth turned around and stared at him. From her post at the kitchen door, Alma froze, her face a mask of rage. Everyone else stopped what they were doing and stared at him, especially Nancy, who watched Farrell intently.

Innocently, Wentworth asked, "Diggings? What do you mean by 'diggings,' Mr. Farrell?"

Garth harshly said, "He doesn't mean anything. He's just talking hot air."

"Yeah," Farrell added, "hot air worth ten million dollars."

Chet almost choked on his drink. After he coughed enough times, he stared at Farrell and said, "Are you drunk?"

"Of course he is!" said Garth, his face clouding over in anger. "Only a drunken man would say such things."

Nancy said, "I don't think so, Mr. Garth. I had spoken to Mr. Farrell outside just a few minutes ago. I detected no liquor on his breath."

Farrell couldn't help smiling. But when he turned his gaze toward Alma, he saw the hatred in her eyes now directed at Nancy. Apparently, a clandestine meeting with the lady from Kansas just a few feet from an outhouse didn't meet with her approval.

Keeping his eyes on Alma, he said casually, "I hope those horses you've got can bring the gold up out of that gully."

Alma glared at him and for one scary moment it looked like she wanted to leap across the bar and strangle him.

Fred Parker looked down the bar to Alma and asked sincerely, "What is he talking about, Alma?"

Before she could respond with a denial, Farrell said, "I guess she didn't ask you yet, did she?"

"Ask me what?"

"For me and Garth to stay here until we dig out the gold?"

Fred's eyes widened. The look on his face didn't show anger as much as betrayal.

"Is what he's saying true, Alma? I've been telling you for years that there was outlaw treasure buried in these hills and you just laughed at me. Is there *really* a cache of gold around here? And you knew about it?"

No one in the room dared breathe as they all stared at the big blonde woman standing there and pausing before she spoke.

"There...there may be something in the valley up yonder...but,"—and her eyes burned into Farrell's—"it's nothing but a *rumor*, that's all. I didn't tell you 'cause I didn't want to bother you with something that'd get you on some wild goose chase, that's all. Tain't no guarantee there's anything in that gully but a ton of rocks."

Nancy noticed that Alma chose her words carefully. This only confirmed to her that Alma *did* know about the gold. Then, turning to look at Fred, Nancy could see the hurt in his eyes, the betrayal. This man may look gruff and unforgiving, but she caught on that Alma's lie had hurt him deeply. It only made her resent the stationmaster's wife even more.

Farrell then stirred the pot further. He said, "That's not what our friend Garth says." He looked at the ex-Reb and saw the rage in his face. "Gold bars bigger than your leg. Isn't that what you said?"

"Gold bars!" said Wentworth.

"That's right, Mr. Wentworth. Courtesy of William Clarke Quantrill."

Chet said, "Quantrill! You know, there might be something to it at that. I heard stories that the ol' Reb hid away some of the loot he stole during the war. But I didn't think it was gold bars...maybe you'd better come clean about this, Garth."

"Yes," agreed Nancy, "I think you should too."

Garth could've denied everything, but he knew that the suspicion of whether the gold rumor was true would linger with the passengers and the driver all through the rest of their trip, and he knew that they would talk—and talk *a lot*—once they got to Lone Jack. Then the *whole town* would be out in those hills searching for the coach—and someone might just be lucky enough to find it before he did.

He had no choice.

"All right," he said warily. "It's true. But I'm saying right here and now, that if anyone tries to leave for town..." He drew his .45 Colt and raised it for emphasis. "I'll blow their brains out."

Chet Riley scanned the room. He said, "Put it away, Garth. We're all adults here. I could always tell Wells Fargo that the storm caused my coach to lose a wheel over a rough turn. That'd explain the delay in getting to town. Who knows? Maybe if this gold thing turns out to be true, I won't have to return to whippin' horses and having my butt torn apart from bouncing over rough trails."

Wentworth said, "I always believed that my chosen vocation of teaching children was an honorable one, but..." He cleared his throat then. "I could always use the extra funds to...live a life of leisure. Quite frankly, I'm getting tired of teaching the little..." Then, embarrassed to display any anger or resentment, his face turned bright red.

Then, as if on cue, everyone turned toward Nancy.

"Well," she began, a little embarrassed by the sudden attention, "What young lady wouldn't want to have the money to run her own business? And uh, it would also give me the security not to run into the arms of just any man so he could support me." Without thinking, her eyes went to Farrell and he smiled when they looked his way. Catching his smile, she quickly cast her eyes downward.

Wentworth said, "Just one thing puzzles me. If there is indeed gold buried not far from here, and we find it, what will we do with gold bars?"

Farrell prompted, "Mr. Garth?"

Garth glared at him, but he reluctantly answered, "The Mexican government will take them off our hands for two million dollars."

Farrell asked playfully, "*How many million*, Mr. Garth?"

Garth cleared his throat and sullenly answered, "Ten million dollars."

There was a simultaneous gasp from Nancy and

Wentworth. Fred practically dropped the whiskey bottle in his hand. Of those who weren't originally part of the scheme, only Chet understood the behind-the-scenes maneuvers of international politics which would give rise to such an illegal transaction. With a one-seventh share of ten million dollars, he could purchase his own stage line; even a string of stage lines and put Wells Fargo out of business.

"Then it's settled," said Chet. "We all agree to keep quiet about this—if we each get a share."

"Great," said Farrell cheerfully, "the more, the merrier."

Wentworth prodded, "Go ahead, Mr. Garth. Tell us more."

But Garth wasn't listening to the little man; he was glaring at Farrell, as was Alma.

Quietly, the ex-Reb growled, "I won't forget this, Farrell."

Farrell replied, "I have a feeling I won't either..."

TWO

Farrell was outside leaning back on the corral fence and exhaling smoke into the warm spring air. He had to get away from his new "partners," and think about what he had gotten himself into. As before, he had left his coat and Stetson on the table inside; he wanted the warmth of the rising sun on his face, and to enjoy the fresh Missouri air while he had the chance. With this bunch, he had a feeling he wouldn't have much opportunity to relax and reflect on his life too often. Talk of gold always put people in such an all-fired rush.

The sounds of footsteps on the grass made him turn.

It was Nancy.

She was hatless and had also left her jacket inside. Farrell noted the sun shining in her pinned-up auburn hair; her blue eyes were bright as they regarded him.

She didn't beat around the bush either. She said plainly, "I was wondering why you did that in there." Farrell knew what she meant.

He took another drag off his cigarette and stared at the hollow of aspens in back of the place, their full branches swaying in the warm morning breeze.

"You know something," he said. "I don't really know..."

"Well, you must have some idea."

Farrell paused as he watched two squirrels skittering up a tree. Were they mated? And if they were, did the female of the two henpeck her mate until he became a better squirrel? Not having made a study of squirrel mating habits, he couldn't tell.

Lamely, he answered, "I guess...I guess I just wanted to get back at her for her big mouth."

Nancy looked down at her riding boots, not saying anything for a moment. Then, facing him again, she said plainly, "That's a pretty stupid reason."

"I know it."

"Hey, not that I wouldn't want part of a gold mine. I guess I should be grateful that you let us in on it. But I'm afraid you also opened yourself up to some trouble. Mr. Garth looks like he'd put a knife in your back as soon as look at you. And I wouldn't trust Alma anymore than I would a hungry tigress."

Farrell smiled wanly and said, "You think she's a wild animal in the jungle?"

Looking at him squarely, she said, "Frankly, I think she's far worse. I don't have to be a Harvard graduate to figure out that you talked yourself into a corner. I mean, is that why you did it, to spitefully get back at her for telling us you're an outlaw?"

"No. I guess I did it because of the situation I'm in. Looking for a job, trying to go straight, seeing how hard it is. You know, when I rode in last night, a posse was chasing me because some woman had her purse stolen in town and they thought I did it—which I might add, I *didn't*. But men like that don't give you a chance to explain yourself. So I ran. This was the first place I saw to get me out of the storm and away from that posse. I'm out something like nine dollars to have a couple drinks and sleep in some filthy barn. Then Garth wakes me up in the middle of the night with this buried gold proposition. Said he'd kill me if I *didn't* join with him. Hell, I don't want any trouble with the law or anybody else. And let's face it, I could use the money. But all these folks pushing me back and forth like I don't have a mind of my own, and then Alma telling all of you I'm a 'notorious outlaw.' Hell, I just decided to rock the boat and show them I'm not their whipping boy."

Nancy stared at him for a long time. Slowly, she nodded.

"I guess I see your point, though you obviously didn't think of the consequences of your actions."

"Yeah," he admitted. "I never do..."

"So tell me," she asked, choosing her words carefully, "uh, how exactly did Alma find out about the gold?"

Farrell threw the cigarette down and said, "She overheard Garth telling me about it last night while everyone else was asleep."

"But you were in the barn last night. Why did she come out to the barn if--" She stopped short and her eyes widened. She now realized why.

Seeing the look, Farrell quickly said, "Hey, it's not what you think."

Nancy turned suddenly; she felt herself flushing

and wanted to hide it. "No," she said, "it's all right. It's none of my business."

Farrell began awkwardly, "Listen, Nancy. Alma's not my lo—"

She held up a hand and said, "You don't have to say anymore! I'm—I'm really not concerned. In fact, I think I'd better get inside. They're probably setting up what they're going to do next."

"But nothing happened—"

He was talking to no one because Nancy had already turned and marched back to the stage station before he could finish.

Again, he felt himself falsely accused of something he didn't do.

When Nancy entered, she ignored Alma's glare, but Farrell, following her by just a few steps, saw it right away. Again, Alma assumed the two of them were meeting together for some kind of tryst; but she relaxed when she saw Farrell go back to his own table and Nancy return to hers in the far corner. After they were seated, Garth stood and spoke. He was never a good speaker; even when holdups were planned with his old gangs, he was more a spectator than a leader. This time, however, he was reluctantly forced to acknowledge the necessity of having "partners" and, since they were not schooled in this sort of thing, he had to show them the way.

"First of all," he said arrogantly, "y'all going to take orders from me."

Wentworth said, "I protest, sir!"

Alma said, "You're not ordering *me* around!"

Fred added, "Nor me. I could use the money, but I'll be damned if I'll be treated like your employee."

"I'm not saying this just to hear myself speak," said Garth, though Farrell had gotten that exact impression. "I'm saying this because, first of all, *I* know where the gold is buried; and two, y'all haven't got any experience getting this stuff out and then not giving yourselves away about what you're doing. And *three and most important of all*, I'm the one who's in contact with representatives of the Mexican government to deliver the gold and get the money for it."

Wentworth asked, "How do we know you won't abscond with it when this deal takes place?"

Garth looked down at the bespectacled man and his voice dripped sarcasm. "Because, Wentworth, you could always tell the Federals about me and they'll put me behind bars for a hundred years, that's why! So you see, four-eyes, it is I who am lowering myself to trusting you all, not the other way around!"

Wentworth scowled at the "four-eyes" remark. Despite his anger, however, his curiosity got the better of him.

"Federals?" he asked.

Chet was about to answer, but Nancy beat him to it.

"The regular army, Mr. Wentworth. But only an ex-Reb would refer to them as 'federals' so many years after the war. An old habit to break, I'm sure." Then she looked into Garth's eyes and said wryly, "Mr. Garth, something tells me that you've had a whole lifetime of doing things outside the law and evading pursuit. Or am I jeopardizing my share by insulting you?"

Garth stared at her and his lips twitched as he suppressed his rage.

Farrell looked at her with admiration. He liked her

bluntness, but wondered about her timing. *Now, who wasn't thinking of the consequences?*

Chet said calmly, "Don't worry about her, Garth. You know these Kansas girls. They tend to shoot from the hip anyway. She don't mean anything personal by it. In fact, we all kind of figured you for a man who's... let's just say had an adventurous life."

Garth relaxed. And though Nancy resented Chet's remarks, she had successfully made her point about the kind of man leading them on this new "adventure."

Garth continued, "We're going to need some supplies. Now, the Parkers have very generously offered us their horseflesh for the pulling-out of the coach itself." Fred grimaced at the sarcasm and then shot Alma a dirty look, but she ignored him. "Anyway, they have but one shovel in the barn and that's been used to shovel horse manure. Not exactly the kind of tool we're going to need to dig out a buried stagecoach. So what we're going to do is this. I'll go into Lone Jack with Farrell—"

"Lone Jack's out," Farrell said.

Garth looked at him and paused. Briefly, a smile played on his lips. Understanding, he nodded and said, "All right. There are other towns nearby. Maybe Harrisonburg."

Fred Parker said, "Too far."

"Sedalia?"

"Even farther."

Nancy said, "How about Aubrey? It's right over the Kansas border and it's actually closer to here than any Missouri town."

Farrell said, "I don't see why not. Hell, it's just to purchase shovels and ropes at some general store and maybe some pairs of rough gloves to wear while we're digging. We're not staying there overnight."

But Garth looked uncomfortable. He shifted his feet and didn't reply.

Chet said, "What's the matter, Garth? It's like he said, you're just there to purchase supplies and that's that. Miss Belmont's right. Aubrey is just a few miles from here. You both should be back from there in less than an hour. We'd best get started on this digging. I can stall Wells Fargo and delay bringing back the stage just so long before they send someone out to find out what happened to it. Right now, I'm just glad it's off the road and hidden back there in the Parkers' barn, but it can't stay there forever."

"Yes," agreed Nancy. "I was visiting my mother in Kansas City, but my employer is expecting me back on the job day after tomorrow."

"Then it's settled," said Chet, decisively hitting the bar with the flat of his hand. "Just ride out there and get back and we can get to the diggin'."

"Yes," said Wentworth, "Aubrey *would* make sense. It's a nice little town too. Why, the trees alone are horticulturally—"

Alma cut him off. "Fine, fine," she said irritably. "Let's just get the show on the road. I suppose I'll have to feed the rest of ya till they come back. But if y'all want something, get ready to *pay double* our regular prices."

From across the room, Nancy stared at her with narrowed eyes.

Practically through her teeth, she said, "You won't have to feed me. I'm not hungry."

Alma smiled at her, but her eyes were clearly angry. "You're not a big spender, are ya?"

Nancy replied cuttingly, "I am when the food's worth it."

Alma's smile disappeared. Angrily, she moved down to the end of the bar with the clear intention of coming around it until Farrell stood up, effectively blocking her. He put on his coat and Stetson and said, "Let's get on our way then. I'm anxious to get to the diggings."

Concerned, Nancy watched him as he and Garth left the house, with Fred following.

As they marched out to the barn, Farrell asked, "You think you can keep your wife and Nancy apart?"

Fred answered sullenly, "I haven't been able to stop Alma from doing anything she had a mind to before. Why should now be different?"

"Besides," added Garth, "Chet Riley's in there. Though he looks like he'd pay for any bottle put before him, no matter if the price is double!"

Fred said, "That's not my idea, boys. That's Alma's."

"Hold on."

They all stopped just outside the barn door. Garth was looking at Fred up and down.

"What's wrong?"

"No," said Garth, smiling wickedly, "you're still small enough to hide behind her skirts."

Fred angrily said, "Why you!" He swung a fist at him, but Garth ducked and returned with a punch that struck Fred right in the nose. The stationmaster dropped to the ground like a sack of potatoes as Farrell grabbed Garth's arms and pulled him back. Quickly,

Garth wrenched himself out of Farrell's hold and said, "All right!"

Farrell stood back as Garth stared down at the fallen man. Fred was holding his nose painfully; blood was dripping down to his upper lip.

"If'n you tried that on me fifteen years ago," Garth raged, "I would've taken your head off! Damn apron-wearin' son of a bitch."

Then he went into the barn.

Farrell held out his hand and Fred took it; then he pulled him to his feet.

"Thanks, Farrell."

"Don't mention it."

"Guess I treated you awful last night."

"Never heard of a storm putting anyone in a good mood."

Inside the barn, Garth shouted, "Hey, Farrell, come on! Let's get this over with! Ask him which horse I take."

Fred scowled and looked inside the barn. Then he said quietly, "The brown chestnut in stall five. Give him that one."

Hearing the tone of his voice, Farrell looked at him. Then he said, "All right, if you insist."

"I do. And take the palomino in seven. He's a good pack horse."

Soon they were riding off the property and headed west on the Independence-Lone Jack road. Since Farrell was facing the trail, he didn't see Nancy anxiously watching him from the west window as he rode.

WHAT FEW CLOUDS there were in the sky had parted and the afternoon sun blazed down at them as spring temperatures rose. Farrell rode with his jacket off and his eyes gradually adjusted to the sun-bleached trail before them. He stole glances at Garth and noticed how quiet he was. Something was eating at him, and it was not the fact that he had to now share "his" gold with six other people. There was something he saw behind the grim set of his mouth and the emptiness in his gray eyes. As they approached the outskirts of the town, he also saw his companion's back stiffen, as if he were about to ride into battle.

They leisurely walked their horses down Aubrey's main street. Farrell glanced around and saw what looked like a normal town. There were folks shopping for groceries, feed, equipment for their farms and homesteads; freight wagons hauled cargo. Men in fancy duds, the Prince Albert coats, the high hats, the ties with cravats in them, standing outside the various saloons; inside were the gamblers and guzzlers, saloon gals and bouncers, as well as the bartenders wearing aprons and handlebar mustaches who served rotten whiskey and had 12-gauge shotguns within reach under their bars. Farrell had seen a dozen towns like this and more; in all of them, he learned one important thing: No matter how law-abiding he was in their town, none of these people were going to welcome strangers.

Perhaps that was why Garth seemed so edgy. Farrell knew what it was like to be on the wrong end of a chase; obviously, so did Garth. He looked again at his companion's face and saw that it was now stone. Only the man's eyes seemed alive, watching, scanning the streets and especially the alleyways they rode past, for any unusual movement that didn't belong.

As they rode deeper into town, however, Farrell also felt the tension. He looked at the people on the boardwalks and saw that several of them were staring at them as they rode in. It was not the whole town, just a few people, older folks mostly, watching them as if they were lepers on horseback.

Farrell started to say, "What the hell's wrong with these pe—"

Garth cut him off with, "General store up ahead on the right. I'll go in, get a few shovels, ropes, *and then we get the hell out of here.*"

Farrell noticed the rage behind those last few words. What was it he wasn't telling him?

After stopping in front of the store, they dismounted and tied their horses to the tie rail.

Garth said tightly, "I'll make it as fast as I can."

He started to turn, but Farrell put a heavy hand on his arm.

"Wait! What the hell's going on? These folks are staring at us like we shot their mothers or something!"

Then it hit him. His eyes widened as he stared at Garth. In that split second, he suddenly realized that the people in this town, especially the older ones, and this man now called Garth were probably far more familiar with each other than he could have dared imagined.

The ex-Reb roughly pulled Farrell's hand off his arm. Then without a word, he entered the general store.

Farrell turned back and watched the street. The people on the boardwalks still looked like they were going about their business, but their movements seemed stilted, odd; as if they were going through the motions and trying hard *not* to look in his direction as they passed. Time seemed to stretch as he stood on the boardwalk, hoping that Garth would hurry up. He wanted to roll himself a cigarette, but didn't even try because he knew that his fingers would shake. Feeling what he thought was a sudden chill in the air, he pulled his jacket off his saddle and put it on. However, it did no good; the chill was still there.

He felt strange standing there. How ironic that he had played this same scene before many years ago, staying with the horses and watching the passersby while his companions robbed the bank. Only this time, there was no robbery, no guns, no waiting for a big getaway. Instead he felt an intangible fear; a nervous kind of quiet before an explosion.

Finally, Garth left the store with three tightly coiled horsehide ropes that he carried under his right arm. He handed three big hand shovels with gleaming new spades to Farrell, who took them and tied them onto the third horse. Then the ropes were fastened on as well. Farrell could sense all these eyes on them as they were doing their work.

"Come on," said Garth quietly.

Farrell did not have to be reminded. He turned quickly to his horse, but before he could put his foot in the stirrup, a voice stopped both of them in their tracks. The voice sounded as if it belonged to an old man, a voice as scratchy and hoarse as sandpaper being rubbed against rock.

Farrell turned toward the voice and saw the man. He was a short fellow in shoddy range clothes and a slouch hat; his gray eyes were staring in their direction, but the object of his anger was not Farrell, but the man standing next to him. Farrell didn't know why, but he immediately noticed that the man's shirt was buttoned a trifle too high for such a warm day.

The man spoke again, a repetition of that harsh, awful voice.

"Taggert!" he shouted.

Garth just stared back at him. Farrell glanced at his companion and saw only the slight up-and-down movement of his Adam's apple, a nervous swallowing despite his otherwise taut exterior.

The man stood his ground from a distance of eighteen feet; his aging hands were at his sides. He wore no gun.

He shouted, "You coming back for more, Taggert!"

Farrell didn't have to look around to feel the eyes of people staring at them.

When Garth spoke, a quavering in his voice betrayed his fear.

"You got me mixed up with someone else, old man!"

With a grim expression on his face, the man shook his head. Then, in a quick movement which shocked Farrell, coming as it was from such an old man, he reached up and ripped open the top of his shirt. Two buttons popped off and hit the wooden boardwalk. Pulling the collar open, the old man revealed the bloodred streak burned around his throat.

Farrell couldn't help but gasp when he saw it.

"A souvenir you and your friends gave me!" the old man said.

Garth said harshly, "You're a crazy old man! I never seen you before!"

Farrell watched the ex-Reb closely, saw sweat

appear on his forehead and heard the fear in his voice. He had no doubt that what the old man was saying was absolutely true.

The man started to walk toward them, the look on his face getting wilder with each step he took.

"You filth!" he raged in his rasping voice.

Then his right hand reached up and touched the raw flesh around his throat.

Garth quickly drew his gun and shot the old man in the stomach before he got to them. The fellow doubled over, arms hugging his belly as blood spread across his shirt.

Farrell grabbed Garth by the shirt and yanked him around.

"You fool! What the hell are you doing!"

Garth shoved him off and raised his gun.

The seconds of shock soon wore off and the crowd in the street shouted and came closer. Out in the middle of the street, a tall man in a black suit and derby hat shouted, "Taggert!" Rage was plain on his face and he shook his fist at Garth as he ran toward him.

Garth turned the .45 toward the street and fired. The man stopped in his tracks and staggered. Then he crumpled to the ground in a cloud of dust.

The crowd now rushed at them, but Farrell saw an escape route, a clear path down the boardwalk behind them. Turning back, he ran down the walk with Garth close behind him. As they fled, Farrell heard the angry shouts getting closer as they tore down the street, shoving passersby out of their way. Garth still had his gun out, but Farrell kept his in the holster. Even in this frantic moment, he was smart enough not to appear as if he were directly tied up with Garth and had the same murderous impulses; though he realized that would be hard since everyone had seen them riding into town together.

As he ran, he saw people on the boardwalk, their eyes widened in fear, quickly diving out of their way, and he knew it was for a better reason than the fact that they would be bowled over. His answer came when he heard guns fired and a flurry of bullets pelted the walls of the buildings they were passing. As they ran, they kept their heads low, purposely ducking behind nervous horses tied to hitching rails as bullets whizzed above their heads. Then Farrell heard a gun firing much closer to him and he came to the sickening conclusion that Garth, even though he was being chased by an angry, gun-toting mob, still had the gall to turn back and fire at the crowd. He cursed the ex-Reb under his breath.

With his lungs bursting for air, he saw no end in sight as still another crowd, hearing the gunfire, started to form a few hundred feet ahead of them. He knew that if they blocked their path, they'd be finished. Then, with his lungs burning in his chest, he saw it; the mouth of an alley coming up to their right. Without pause in his flight, he turned into it, feverishly hoping that he wasn't running into a dead end.

Fortunately, the alley continued straight down the rest of the block and emptied out onto another street. Farrell glanced back and saw Garth close behind him, but with his gun back in his holster, for which he silently thanked God. Figuring that Garth was probably a veteran of these kinds of chases, Farrell knew that the ex-Reb had instinctively holstered his gun so that people on the next street, who hadn't witnessed the killings, wouldn't be alarmed when they appeared.

Suddenly, Farrell noticed that he wasn't hearing Garth's running footsteps behind him. He turned back and saw that the ex-Reb had stopped at a wooden door in a particularly dark part of the alley.

"Farrell!" he shouted.

Farrell stopped and saw Garth put his weight against the door. To his surprise, he saw it give easily. Garth beckoned and the two of them ducked inside, closing the door behind them.

Darkness enveloped them. Farrell didn't know where they were, but there was a musty odor that penetrated his nostrils. Feeling about, he touched canvases covering what felt to him like barrels. He heard a noise behind him and sensed that Garth was putting his ear to the door. They heard the mob outside passing by, yelling, blindly running through the alley, knocking over garbage cans in their rush to find the culprits.

After a couple moments, Garth thumbed a match and held it alight. Looking around, Farrell saw huge wooden boxes and barrels, most of which were covered by dust-covered canvas, against the walls. There were no windows.

Farrell asked, "Where are we?"

Garth answered, "The back stockroom of a saloon. I oughtta know. I've slept off enough benders in 'em." The match's flame almost got to his fingers and he shook it out. He quickly thumbed on another one and walked over to a lantern which was hung next to a weathered door. He put the match into the wick and the room lit up to reveal even more crates and barrels, as well as a desk and swivel chair near the back wall.

Garth said, "This is the place they tally up the supplies."

"Yeah," Farrell said grimly, "I can see that."

They saw the door they had entered from just a few feet away. Garth went over and put his ear against it. "No one out there now," he said.

Farrell sullenly said, "Maybe not out there, but we've got plenty of company outside."

"All right, what do you want me to do? Cheer about it?"

Farrell stepped closer to him and said, "I knew you weren't all-fired anxious to come here, and now I know why! Why the hell didn't you at least *say something*!"

Garth glared at him and said, "How did I know they'd remember after all these years? By now, I thought they'd forget."

"Forget! How can a person forget something like that! You and your boys hanging that poor old man! What did y'all do, put a noose 'round his neck and pull him up until it didn't seem funny anymore?"

"You shut up, drifter! I don't need no sermons from you!"

They were both yelling now, ignoring the consequences as their rage at each other grew.

"And how'd we get in this trap?" asked Farrell loudly. "Because of that gold you stashed away! Was it worth all these 'gold bars bigger than your leg'? The lives of all those men?"

"We were *soldiers*, damn it!"

"I have my doubts about that too. And that man outside--"

"He recognized me."

"But then you shot him!" Farrell shouted. "An old man you tortured! Hell, he wasn't even armed!"

"He made a move with his hand!"

"It was to his *throat*! He moved to touch the rope-burn on his throat you and the other scum put there!"

Enraged, Garth let off a string of curses that would have embarrassed mule skinners; but when he made an unflattering remark about Farrell's mother, her son punched him square in nose.

The ex-Reb fell back against the desk and put his hand to his nose. Seeing the blood, he roared and put his hand in his pocket. He had done the move so many times that the blade flicked open in less than a second. Farrell grabbed the wrist and pushed it upward, the blade jabbing the air over his shoulder. Seeing how strong Garth was, he used both his hands to try to wrest the knife out of his grip. With his free hand, however, Garth swung his arm out and put Farrell in a headlock, his fingers covering the young man's face and blinding him as they grappled.

Straining, Farrell bobbed his head downward and opened his mouth. Then he bit Garth's pinky deeply, drawing blood. The ex-Reb screamed and took his fingers off the Texan's face. With his vision now cleared, Farrell lifted his knee and slammed Garth's wrist down on it, causing the ex-guerrilla to drop the knife. Without the knife to struggle over, the two men fell back on the desk and wrapped their arms around each other's heads. Their hats fell off as they rolled over each other punching and kicking, knocking aside clip-boards and stationery. Predictably, when they got near the edge of the desk, they fell off and crashed against the corner, still tussling.

With his hand covering Farrell's face, Garth proceeded to slam his opponent's head several times against the wall, the banging noise loud in the room.

With Garth's dirty fingers covering his nose and eyes, Farrell was suffering in more ways than one. As his head was hitting the wall, Farrell was vaguely aware of a glass-covered framed picture coming off an opposite wall and smashing to the floor loudly. Blindly, with his eyes full of Garth's fingers, he reached up and took a fistful of his opponent's hair, yanking it back. The ex-Reb screamed and pulled his hand off Farrell's face. Angrily, Farrell slammed Garth's head back into the side of the hardwood desk again and again.

He did it so many times that Garth's yells soon stopped. Losing consciousness, the ex-guerrilla feebly tried to raise his hands to strike back, but it was useless. After Farrell slammed his opponent's head one last time, he groggily got to his feet. Then, after he gave himself a moment to catch his breath, he reached down and pulled Garth off the floor by his hair. With his free hand, he punched him several times in the face, his hatred for the man growing in intensity as he beat him.

Suddenly, Farrell detected a movement behind him. Dropping Garth, he whirled around and looked at the door. It was open, and standing before the doorway was a young woman in a gray blouse with a high collar and long black skirt. Her dark hair was pulled back into a bun and her mouth was covered with tasteful shades of red lipstick. To Farrell, she was a striking woman, and her beauty and poise presented a sharp contrast to the dingy storeroom she had just entered. Her piercing brown eyes regarded him knowingly, as if she had seen fights before and had long ago ceased being shocked by their violence. She was also holding a pocket revolver, the kind that ladies in dangerous professions kept hidden in their purses.

"Sorry," she said in wry apology. "Didn't mean to break up your little party."

Farrell noted the way she spoke. The accent actually sounded Texan, but it seemed layered over with the more hurried speech patterns of Northerners. Idly, he guessed that she had spent long hours trying to get rid of her original accent.

She continued, "I would've preferred you boys taking your private quarrel outside my establishment, but it's a little too late for that. Usually, I break up the boys when they're fighting in the saloon proper. This is the first time I had to interrupt a fight in the place I keep my kegs of beer."

Farrell felt himself blushing. He ran his hand back through his hair and then picked up his Stetson. Putting it on, he first became aware that his face was throbbing in pain. He felt his bruised cheeks, and then looked down at Garth still lying unconscious on the floor. He found himself smiling weakly. *At least the other guy got worse...*

"Yes," the woman said agreeably, as if reading his mind. "You cleaned his slate pretty well, I'd say."

"Uh, listen," he started awkwardly. "We'll uh, we'll leave this place, and uh...sorry to have bothered you."

She smiled. "Oh, don't run out," she said pleasantly. "I know who you are. You're the two men that crowd is looking for."

Farrell tensed up and his eyes went to the revolver in her hand.

She glanced at it and shrugged. Then she lowered it and held it at her side, her finger planted carefully on the trigger guard.

"I only brought it with me because I didn't know

what was going on in here. I just heard all this racket and I thought that the saloon down the street had hired someone to steal my stock. You know, a woman in my position has to be careful."

Farrell wasn't interested in her preoccupations. She was in her twenties; and her face, accentuated by high cheekbones and a tasteful use of makeup, would have attracted him in normal circumstances.

"And your name is..."

"Monica Lawson. And you're standing in the rear storeroom of the Silver Star."

"Hoge Farrell."

She eyed him up and down and Farrell sensed that she was enjoying the scan.

Trying to change the subject, he guardedly asked, "What do you mean we're the ones the crowd is looking for?"

With the gun still in her hand, Monica folded her arms and leaned back against the rim of a beer barrel. An understanding smile came to her easily, as if she could see into any situation without judgment or condemnation. Despite her relaxed manner, however, he also saw that she refused to put down the gun, which meant that she still didn't fully trust him.

She continued, "Two men are dead outside. From what I was able to get from those who witnessed it, your friend there shot dead an unarmed old man, killed Hiram Crawford, the undertaker, and wounded a mother of three in the butt..."

Farrell stared at her and asked, "He killed the *undertaker*?"

Monica gave her little smile again. "Funny, isn't it? Old Hiram wouldn't have broken a sweat if he unloaded a hundred bags of rocks off the back of a wagon. I heard that the only time he ever cried was when someone ran off and didn't pay for the burial of a family of four taken by the coughing sickness. But when your friend appeared, Hiram got so angry that he charged at him even when your friend had a gun. Turns out that Hiram had met him back during the war and I guess he recognized him. Hiram had two of his fingers sliced off by one of Quantrill's men." Her eyes regarded the unconscious man. "And I have a strong feeling he was the one doing the slicing..."

"And the old man? What about him?"

Monica shook her head and quietly said, "Old Jedediah Carson used to give money to abolitionist groups. Quantrill's bunch must have had him on a list or something. They attacked his farm and burned it to the ground. Then they took Carson and strung him up from his favorite cottonwood. They would've finished the job, but a Union patrol came by and opened fire on them. Most of them got away."

Though she tried to end the story with her usual wry smile, Farrell saw something else behind the controlled demeanor and careful movements.

Rage.

It was buried deep, but he had definitely seen snatches of it as she spoke.

"Uh, Miss Lawson..."

"Monica."

"Monica. Don't you...don't you blame *me* for any of those killings outside?"

She shook her head.

"I heard you two screaming at each other. You were pretty angry at him for killing those men."

Farrell glanced down at him. "He's nothing but a cutthroat. I'm still trying to figure out if I had a good enough reason for riding with him."

"You sound like you're from Texas."

"I was born outside of Houston."

Smiling, she said, "I'm from the Panhandle myself."

"Pardon me for saying it, ma'am, but you don't sound like it."

He saw her smile become bitter. "I'm up north now, Mr. Farrell. And I have a business to run. I learned very quickly to either sound like the people around me or pack up and get out..."

A groan from the direction of the floor was heard. Farrell stepped back and balled his fists. As he saw Garth rise unsteadily, he braced himself for another fight.

Garth's face was bruised and a huge ugly welt was on his left cheekbone.

When he saw Farrell, he said, "You—" He started to move toward him, but Monica raised her gun and cocked it.

"Hold it!" she commanded.

Garth stopped in his tracks, his ears attuned to hearing a gun being cocked even before the shouted command to halt. He turned to look at her.

"Who're you?" he asked harshly.

He suddenly noticed that his mouth was bleeding and wiped it with the sleeve of his shirt. Then he picked up his hat and put it back on.

"I'm Monica Lawson," she replied. "And unless I miss my guess, you're Charlie Taggert."

"Says who?"

"Oh, come on! You kill two men who recognized

you and, I might add, they shouted it publicly for everyone to hear, and you want to pretend that it was all a mistake?"

Garth said grudgingly, "No." He glanced at Farrell, then looked at her, his eyes narrow. "So you and him going to turn me over to that mob?"

Monica's eyes shone and her smile returned. Farrell noticed there was something odd about this one, as if Garth had said some kind of private joke only she understood. In a moment, he had his answer.

"I can't turn you over," she said, her eyes reflecting off the lantern light. "If I went and did that, then how can I get some of that *gold*?"

Suddenly speechless, both men stared at her.

Garth finally broke the spell by saying to Farrell, "You and your big mouth!"

Then he turned to Monica and said, "Okay. How much of a cut?"

"One third."

"One third! We already got five other partners to worry about!"

"That's *their* problem. I'd say it's pretty fair. One third for you, one third for your good-lookin' friend over there and one third for me for keeping my silence."

Suddenly a commotion was heard behind her. Several men with guns appeared in the open doorway. In the forefront was a beer-bellied, middle-aged man with a star pinned to his wide vest.

He said, "There he is!"

Monica gave the marshal her grave little smile.

"Why, Marshal Dugan," she said wryly, "come on in."

Dugan looked at her as if he had suddenly noticed

her for the first time. Farrell saw his huge face stiffen, as if Monica should not have addressed him.

A man behind the marshal cocked the trigger of his Colt and took aim at Garth, but the lawman shoved his arm down.

"What the hell—"

"He gets a trial, Abner!"

Monica said, "I'm glad you got here—that is, all of *you*." Her arm swept past the marshal and encompassed the men behind him. To Farrell, it looked like she was trying to irritate Dugan for some reason.

The marshal turned around and looked down at her as if she were some kind of insect.

He asked, "What happened?" It wasn't a friendly question.

Monica looked up at him, and again, Farrell saw the rage behind her eyes, but she changed her tune in seconds. Her eyes became wide and she put fear in them; it was now time to play the helpless victim.

"Marshal," she said, with just the right amount of breathlessness, "I heard a noise and found that these two broke in. But don't take both of 'em." She reached out and put her arm around Farrell protectively. "This is my cousin, Hoge. He rode in from Texas to visit me. He tells me he just happened upon this man on the trail and they decided to ride in together. Isn't that right, Cousin Hoge? You don't know this man, do you?"

Farrell knew she was being a bit obvious, but it was an absurd situation.

Abner said, "Your *cousin*!"

Through her teeth, Monica asked, "You calling me a liar, Mr. Perkins?" Abner reddened.

Dugan stared at both of them, and Farrell quickly

saw by the look on his face that he didn't believe it either.

Having little choice in the matter, Farrell decided to back her up. It was either that or jail. "She's right, Marshal. I was coming to visit...Cousin Monica when I ran into that man and we rode in together. I didn't know he was going to start shootin' folks."

Garth growled, "Why, you double-crossing—"

"Shut up!" the marshal ordered. "You're in enough trouble already."

Monica said quickly, "Why, look at their faces, Marshal. You could tell they were fighting. My cousin gave him hell over those killings."

Dugan looked at her and Farrell could see the distaste on the marshal's face, like he was sick of her lies. Still, he gazed at Farrell and plainly saw the bruises on his face. Then he turned back to look at Garth.

"Yep," he said, "those bruises are fresh, all right." Then he grasped Garth's jaw and held it tight in his iron fingers until it hurt the ex-Reb. "And it looks like you got the worst of it." Then he roughly let it go. Facing Farrell, he said, "You've got witnesses outside that say you weren't the one doin' the shootin'. You're lucky, friend."

Garth started to shout, "Now wait a minute—" but Abner's pistol barrel struck his head and silenced him. As the ex-guerrilla collapsed to the floor, the marshal ordered the unconscious man taken to the local jail. "And not one of you go for a rope or you'll hear from me!" he warned.

The men picked up Garth and took him out of the room. After they left, Dugan lingered, giving Monica and Farrell a long, hard look. Then, as if he suddenly realized he had no further reason to be there, he left.

Farrell noticed that Monica still had her arm around him and, clearing his throat, he gently moved out of her grasp.

"They're gone now..."

"Just wanted to get friendly with my new partner, that's all."

He stared at her. "*New Partner*! Miss Lawson—"

"Monica." She smiled up at him and he saw her gleaming white teeth framed by full red lips. Idly, he wondered what it would feel like to kiss them.

"Monica. I don't know how to say this, but I don't know beans about where the gold is. Garth did!"

Still smiling sweetly, she said, "I kind of figured that. But when that mob showed up, I *had* to turn him in. Otherwise, for protecting a murderer, we'd be joining him on the scaffold."

"Then that's the end of any gold hunt."

"Not on your life, cowboy. If your friend knows where that gold is, we can't let him rot in jail."

"*What*!"

Monica looked up at him and he could tell by her eyes that she wasn't joking.

"That's right, Hoge. We've got to break him out."

THREE

Farrell couldn't believe his ears, though there seemed to be very little he had gone through in the past twenty-four hours that he *could* believe in.

He stared at her. He didn't know if she was that greedy or just plain crazy.

"Listen, Monica, this is getting way out of hand. I rode in here with that cutthroat just to pick up supplies. Now, thanks to our coming here, two men are dead and a woman is..."

"Shot in the butt," she concluded.

"Thank you! Now, like I was saying, this is building up to something I did *not* want to get involved in. I've got a past, a bad one. I don't need any more trouble."

Farrell saw her eyes light up as they did before. "Were you an outlaw?" she asked. "Did you hurt anyone?"

"Only myself, if that answers your question."

"Hmm..." Farrell noticed that she seemed disappointed.

"Listen, 'Cousin Monica,' even if I agreed to this, how would we break him out of jail?"

"Oh hell," Monica said, with a dismissive wave of her slender hand. "It's easy!"

Farrell looked at her incredulously and exclaimed, "Huh! Get her! Belle Starr with painted fingernails."

She folded her arms and looked at him sardonically.

"Marshal Dugan may be good at his job, but Aubrey is a quiet town. Look at him. He's gotten fat and lazy. He has no deputies. There's been little crime here since Quantrill's trash left. One of us could sneak a gun to Taggert. You don't even have to enter the jail. The cell windows look out onto a back alley. Someone could distract the marshal in the front office while the other tosses a pistol through his window with a note to get ready for a quick getaway."

Farrell paused and walked over to some covered beer barrels which stood in the corner.

"Is there a chance that anyone would get hurt?"

Monica moved close and looked up at him to gauge his reaction. Studying her face in the glare of the lantern light, he couldn't help thinking that it was a pretty face, a desirable face.

She said earnestly, "The only thing that will be hurt is the marshal's pride."

"I don't want anyone killed. Is that understood?"

"Understood."

"Good."

"Shall we seal it with a kiss?"

His mind went back to the rage he sensed in her before, and he hesitated.

"I'll take your word for it," he said.

"Well, let's say I'm not the trusting type."

Monica threw her arms around his neck and kissed him so hard it hurt his lips.

Finally, he pulled away to catch his breath.

"Stick with me, cowboy, and there'll be more where that came from."

Farrell didn't answer. All he knew was that things were getting far more complicated than he could possibly have imagined.

THE CIRCUIT COURT judge would arrive the next day and Charlie Taggert a.k.a. Garth would be sentenced for the murders of Jedediah Carson and Hiram Crawford, as well as the non-lethal wounding of a Mrs. Sheila Stirling of Baxter Springs, who was in Aubrey to visit kin. It was a certainty that the verdict would be death by hanging, with many in town looking forward to the sight of one of their hated enemies from the past choking to death at the end of a rope.

It was early afternoon and customers were already starting to come into the Silver Star. Monica was in the main room serving them and watching over the place as Farrell took an early dinner in the storeroom. She decided that he should keep a low profile, and not appear in the open until after 6:00, when they would make their attempt to help Garth. The plan was for Monica to visit the marshal and keep him occupied in the front office while Farrell tossed the pistol through his bars with a note telling Garth to hide the gun and *not* to attempt an escape until dark, when there were less people on the streets to deal with and his chances of a getaway were better. Then Farrell and Monica would wait for him at the edge of town and the three of them would head for the site of the buried gold. By nightfall, Monica would get the local hostler into releasing Farrell's and Garth's horses to her when she came to collect them.

Farrell didn't like the whole thing, especially double-crossing the folks at the stage station. Uppermost in his thoughts was double-crossing Nancy. He had been playing this by ear, and as he sat at the desk in the storeroom slicing into a free steak with potatoes and washing it down with a glass of beer, he wondered if he was going to go through with the scheme. However, two things were making up his mind for him: the promise of easy riches and the charms of Monica Lawson.

As he swallowed his food, he was not aware that the woman he was thinking of double-crossing had, at that moment, just walked into the Silver Star.

Nancy pushed through the swinging doors and boldly walked right up to the crowded bar. The men in the room looked at her when she entered. She was still wearing her short brown jacket and riding skirt and her little hat was tied to her head, but her cheeks had a smattering of dust on them, as if she had ridden hard to get there. The men had never seen her before, and some of them idly wondered who among them was the lucky man she was pulling out of this den of iniquity and bringing back to hearth and home.

Without hesitation, she leaned in between two rangy men with their booted feet hooked over the brass rails and, with a confident gesture, waved the bartender over. Oscar, the bartender, a big beefy man with light-brown side-whiskers and eyebrows to match, waddled down to her end of the bar.

Scowling, he asked, "What is it, Miss?" He figured she looked too much like a schoolmarm to ask for a drink.

She ignored his gruff tone and asked, "I'm looking for a man named Hoge Farrell. I understand that the last anyone's seen of him is in this place."

Monica was standing at the other end of the bar when she saw Nancy enter. She also couldn't figure out what she wanted, but now she found herself staring at her.

Oscar knew where Farrell was, and on his boss's orders, was told to lie.

He said, "Well, he was here before visiting his cousin, but he left town an hour ago."

Nancy stared at him. Shaking her head in disbelief, she said, "His *cousin*!"

"Sure," he said without hesitation. "My boss, Miss Lawson, well, she and him are cousins. Now if you don't mind, Miss, I have work to do."

And with that, he waddled away to serve someone else, leaving Nancy totally confused. Then, as she turned away from the bar, Monica approached her. The men nearby moved away, giving them room.

"Hello," Monica said, without smiling.

"Hello."

"Are you...a friend of Hoge's?"

"Yes," Nancy replied. Then she paused and asked, "And you're his...*cousin*?"

Monica cleared her throat, already uncomfortable in the other woman's presence.

Nancy could see by her reaction that the "cousin" angle was a lie.

Recovering quickly, Monica smiled and said, "I'm Monica Lawson. What do you want to see him for?"

"Well, Miss Lawson—"

"Call me Monica."

"Well...Monica, let's put it this way. Where is he?"

"Why, he rode out of town an hour ago."

"Then why did you ask me what I wanted to see him for?"

"Perhaps I can relay a message if he returns this way."

Nancy said, "Uh-huh," and nodded, as if she expected some kind of stonewalling. "First of all, Miss—"

"Monica."

"*Miss Lawson.* First of all, he couldn't have ridden anywhere without his horse, which is being held at the stables down the street, and it still has his gear. There are also two more horses, one loaded with shovels and ropes. And second, I just visited the marshal and he tells me that Hoge's companion, a man named Garth, is being held for murdering two men in town. He also mentioned that you're Hoge's cousin and I *still* can't believe it. So, Miss Lawson, do you want to correct your story about him leaving town?"

Monica's smile disappeared and she stared at her with unfriendly eyes. She wanted to grab her by the hair and throw her out through the swinging doors, but she knew that this one would only come back.

She sighed. After glancing around to make sure they weren't being heard, she said quietly, "He's in the back room." Then she turned around and walked to the back, with Nancy following her closely.

Monica opened the door to the storeroom just as

Farrell was finishing his meal. When he saw her, he rose from his chair and said, "Nancy!"

Monica noted the familiarity and began to wonder how close they really were.

Entering the room, Nancy started to say, "Hoge! I wanted to tell you—" Then she stopped and looked at Monica; it was obvious that she wanted privacy.

Farrell said, "It's all right, Monica. She's a friend."

Monica didn't like the "friend" remark any more than she liked anything else about Nancy's visit. Wryly, she said, "Whatever you say, partner." Then she closed the door, or more plainly, slammed it, leaving them alone.

Nancy turned to face him. The marshal had told her about the killings Garth committed and that he and Farrell had been chased down the street by an angry, gun-toting mob. Now, as she looked at him, she felt like throwing her arms around him and embracing him tightly, grateful that he was still alive. She took a couple steps closer to him, but at the last minute held back, not wanting to give him any ideas.

Still, Farrell took her hands in his and held them; he was glad that she didn't resist.

"I'm glad to see you," he said, smiling.

"I'm glad to see you too, Hoge. But there's one thing I've got to get settled first."

"What's that?"

She practically shouted, "*What the hell is going on!?*"

Then she self-consciously turned back to the door to see if anyone had heard her.

Farrell released her hands and turned away, not knowing how to answer her.

Nancy said earnestly, "Marshal Dugan told me that that maniac Reb killed two people in broad daylight!"

"Uh, yeah, there was some trouble," he began lamely.

"*Some trouble*! He could've gotten you hanged! I'm glad you didn't do any shooting."

"I'm not like him, Nancy."

She stepped closer to him and put her hand on his arm. "I know you're not," she said gently. "But now I hear that you have this...*cousin* who runs this saloon. You said you were escaping the law in Lone Jack. When the decision was made to ride into Aubrey to purchase supplies, you never once mentioned that you had a cousin here."

"She helped back me up, saying that me and Garth were strangers."

"So you suddenly attained a cousin. A pretty one too, I see..."

Farrell turned to look at her, hearing what sounded like jealousy in her tone. Realizing how she sounded, Nancy quickly turned away and moved toward some covered beer barrels in the corner.

"Anyway," he asked, "what are you doing here?"

She turned around to face him.

"You were taking too long to get back. So I told the others I had had it waiting for you and I was opting out of a share of the gold. I bought a horse from the Parkers and told them I was riding to my original destination of Kansas City. That goddamn Alma charged me a small fortune for an old nag who couldn't find his way out of the barn without a walking stick. And then I had to pay even *more* for Fred to give him new shoes. So you see, I paid quite a bit of money for you. The least you can do is be straight with me."

"I am, Nancy."

"Then why is that saloon tramp calling you 'partner'?"

Farrell hesitated. He didn't know how to begin.

Nancy said cuttingly, "All right, let me fill in the blanks for you. You were grateful for her getting you out of this scrape with a lynch mob and you felt that you *had* to return the favor."

"No. She overheard us arguing about the gold."

"I see..."

Nancy folded her arms and walked over to the lantern. Farrell saw the light reflected in her blue eyes and harsh shadows fall on her lovely face as she stared at him.

"You know that the gold hunt is probably finished now. It's dead in the water and so is our friend, Garth. He won't get out of this one, Hoge. For what he's done, they'll hang him for sure."

"Not if we get him out."

Her eyes widened in fear, and when she spoke, there was desperation in her voice.

"You can't be serious!"

"Why not? If no one gets hurt, it'll go off without a hitch."

"Listen to yourself! *If no one gets hurt*! You're just burying yourself deeper! And for what? A *promise* of a big windfall in gold?"

Farrell said roughly, "I noticed that you were also going to be 'buried' in that same windfall."

Nancy frowned at him. Then she said bluntly, "That's right. I wanted a little of that golden rainbow just like everyone else. I don't deny it. But two men were alive then, and you didn't get yourself in trouble with the law."

"We'll pass an empty gun to him and he'll get out of town after dark. He'll do it quick and quiet, with no blood being shed."

"Don't you get it? Two men have died already! Hoge, this is gold stolen by the west's number one war criminal! And the man who's going to supposedly provide all these riches was one of his disciples, a lunatic and a mass murderer just like his boss. Are you so desperate for happiness that you'd forget the blood he has on his hands and make a *deal* with him?"

Farrell didn't look at her, not into those eyes; he didn't dare.

Sensing this, Nancy yanked him around to face her. "Look at me, damn it! I asked you a question!"

The door suddenly opened and Monica stood there, her hand tightening on the doorknob when she saw how closely they were standing. She was wearing a wide-brimmed sun hat and there was a light blue shawl about her shoulders. Under her arm, she held a black leather purse.

She said, "It's time, Hoge..."

Farrell nodded and stepped forward, but Nancy grabbed his arm.

"Hold it!" Then, facing Monica, she said, "He's not going anywhere! Certainly not with the likes of you!"

Monica gave her a withering look.

Farrell said, "Nancy, please!"

Still glaring at her, Monica asked, "Ready, Hoge?"

He answered, "Yeah." He wrestled his arm out of

Nancy's grip and moved forward, as much to get between them as to leave the room.

Nancy said anxiously, "Hoge, don't go with her!"

He said, "Nancy, stay here."

"If you think I'm going to stay here and let you get killed—"

Farrell pushed her away as he ducked through the open doorway. Then Monica slammed the door quickly.

"Lock her in," he said.

"You read my mind, Cousin."

Monica turned a key in the lock and then the two of them headed out the back way as Nancy pounded on the door behind them. In the alley, Monica handed him a gun with a note. Opening it, Farrell read it to check its contents. It specified that Garth was to take no action until nightfall when there would be less people on the street and then they would have horses waiting at the edge of town near the Independence-Lone Jack road. Farrell rolled up the note and put it through the trigger guard. Then the two of them walked down the street to the marshal's office, which was three blocks away.

As they walked, Farrell was tense. He was worried about locking Nancy up in that back room. But at that moment, something else was weighing heavily on his mind: Her warning about dealing with mass murderers in order to get a little happiness...

"I'll just be in there for a couple minutes," said Monica. With her chin, she indicated an alley at the side of the jail. "I'd say the window is about ten or twelve feet off the ground. I'm sure you'll find a crate or garbage can to stand on."

"Don't worry."

Then she stopped and looked at him. Her eyes were dead serious.

"I'm not worried about *me*. I'm worried about you. I'm worried if anything that bitch said made an impression."

Farrell felt an anger rise within him when she called Nancy a "bitch," but he kept outwardly calm.

"What she said didn't sway me a bit," he lied.

"Good, because if things go according to plan, I could put years of poverty behind me forever. You know, illegitimate daughters from the dirty end of San Antonio don't exactly live the high life."

"I didn't think they did."

"All he has to do is lead us to that yellow stuff and you and me could celebrate to the end of our days."

Farrell said nothing; he just looked into her eyes and saw the change in her. Whatever pleasantness was in her before was long gone.

She added hatefully, "And as far as that Reb is concerned, the hangman could have him after he does his job..."

The remark sent a chill through him. At a loss for words, he just stared at her.

Monica turned and continued down the street. He paused, watching her. Then she stopped and turned back, her expression prompting him to follow. Farrell exhaled a long breath and then followed her.

THEY LOOKED at each other one last time as Monica entered the marshal's office. Then Farrell went around the side of the building, ducking down the mouth of the alley. The marshal's office and jail were in a low brick building; the wall that fronted the alley was aged by Midwest rains and a couple garbage cans stood against it. He looked up and saw three barred windows, each of them two feet wide and a foot and a half long.

Quietly rolling a garbage can over, he planted it under one window and climbed up on the lid. He was able to see through the bars at a point up to his chin, so he'd be more than able to toss the gun in. But the cell he was looking into had no one. He quickly got off and rolled the can over to the second one. Again, the cell was empty. As he pushed the can down to the third cell at the end, he wondered about the crime situation in Aubrey; apparently, Monica was right about the marshal's job being easy since hardly anyone was in jail.

At the third cell, he peered in and found him. Garth was lying on his bunk looking at the ceiling and smoking a cigarette. Farrell noted that the ex-guerrilla looked strange without his gun and holster.

"Garth!" he hissed.

He saw the haggard, bruised face gaze up at him. Garth didn't look surprised.

"You took long enough," he growled.

Farrell stared at him. "You're not surprised I'm here. Even after our fight and everything."

Garth got to his feet and looked up at him; there was actually a wicked smile on his face. Farrell noticed the lump on the side of his head where Abner had struck him with his gun. Garth's beard seemed thicker and his hair disheveled, but the watchful eyes were very much alive.

"Gold cancels all arguments," he said. "And I know you need me to stay alive to find it."

Voices drifted in from the direction of the marshal's office.

Garth listened and said, "It's that saloon gal. The one who said she was your cousin. I should've known she'd muscle her way in."

Farrell didn't answer him. Not wanting to waste time, he shoved the gun through the bars and said, "Here."

Catching it, Garth pulled the note out of the trigger guard and read it.

Then he looked up at Farrell. "Wait till nightfall?"

"The less folks seeing you, the better."

"You're soft, Farrell," he said with contempt. "I reckon you always were. You just don't want me to kill anyone out in the street."

"Yeah," said Farrell, "I'm real soft. Soft enough to clean your map, like I did before."

Garth tensed at the jibe; then he relaxed and looked down at the gun. He opened it and spun the cylinder.

"Where are the bullets?"

"You'll get 'em when we're out of town. You can still use the gun to bluff the marshal to open the cell door."

Garth glared at him. Then, grudgingly, he snapped the cylinder back in and shoved the pistol into his waistband.

"Nightfall," he grumbled. "With no bullets."

Farrell said, "Let's say around seven. Folks busy eating dinner, less of them on the streets. We'll meet on the outskirts of town, near that big outcropping of rocks we passed when we rode in before."

Garth didn't answer; he just gave a sarcastic smile and nodded slowly.

Farrell climbed down off the garbage can and rolled it further away from the window. Then he walked over to the mouth of the alley and took up a spot where he could wait for Monica. Leaning against the brick wall, he rolled himself a cigarette; after what he had done, he certainly felt he needed it. After fishing in the pocket of his denim jacket, he pulled out a match and struck it across the sole of his boot. Then, cupping it to the end of his cigarette, he was about to light it when he heard the gunshot.

Farrell froze, suddenly confused. Then the lit match burned his fingers and he dropped it to the ground. Anxiously, he looked toward the front door of the marshal's office and saw it thrown open. Garth appeared and spotted Farrell staring at him. Without hesitation, the ex-Reb tossed the gun at him. Catching it in his hands, Farrell just stood there, too shocked to move.

Garth had just enough time to smile at him condescendingly and shake his head, as if he considered Farrell the dumbest person on the planet. Then he sped off down the street. Too dumbstruck to move, Farrell watched as Garth suddenly stopped at a horse tied to a hitching rail, yank the reins off the post and throw himself onto the saddle. Then with a shout, he jabbed his spurs into the horse's flanks and the gelding threw himself forward, racing up the street as people on the boardwalks stared after him. A man in range clothes barged out of a nearby doorway and yelled at the horse thief to stop. He drew his gun and fired two shots at Garth's retreating back, but the ex-Reb was too far away.

The shouts of passersby across the street roused Farrell from his lethargy.

Men came from all directions and were running toward the marshal's office. Instinctively, Farrell backed into the shadows of the alley behind him. As he stood there, his heart was racing and sweat broke out on his forehead. Something had gone horribly wrong. He could only assume that Garth, like the ornery kill-crazy madman he was, couldn't wait for nightfall and decided to defy Farrell and make a break for it now.

He stood there with the gun still in his hand and watched the townsfolk gathering outside the jail, trying to make himself small behind the weathered brick wall. Then he heard the voices loud and clear as a bell through the open door of the marshal's office.

"The marshal's dead!"

"He was shot by that Taggert fella!"

"Get him! Get a goddamn rope!"

Farrell's heart sank. All the things that he was afraid would go wrong, just did.

Suddenly, an arm was thrown around his neck and he was roughly pulled back deeper into the alley. He fought it vainly, but before he could strike the arm with the gun's barrel, the figure pushed him against the opposite wall of the alley. He noisily fell against two garbage cans which spilled over onto the ground.

When he looked up, he was surprised to see Nancy standing there, her bag in her hand and her small hat still set prettily on her head. Her expression, however, was anything but calm.

She said angrily, "You fool! You softheaded fool! You let a pretty face and a lot of greed get you in even bigger trouble!"

"Nancy! What the hell are you—"

A shout came from the street end of the alley. Suddenly, Abner Perkins appeared with a gun in his hand.

"Hey!" he shouted to others in the street. "They're here!"

Nancy cursed, grabbed Farrell's arm and pulled him further back.

Facing them, Perkins cocked the hammer of his gun and started to raise it.

He said, "I'll save folks the cost of a hangin'..."

Farrell's heart leaped when he heard a muffled gunshot near him. He smelled the odor of gun smoke and looked at back at Nancy. Her right hand was jammed into her small handbag and a cloud of smoke drifted up through the opening.

Then he turned back to the end of the alley. Perkins had crumpled against the brick wall, his left hand grasping the bleeding hole in his right shoulder; his gun lay at his feet.

"Come on!" she hissed at him, grabbing his arm tightly.

With her in the lead, they both ran down the alley and within seconds emerged onto the next block. By the time they appeared, however, Nancy had put away her gun and Farrell had shoved Garth's gun into his waistband beneath his jacket.

He wanted to continue running, but Nancy's tight grasp on his arm caused him to slow his pace. Then she roughly put her own arm through his.

She said quietly, "Act like we're just taking a stroll, *darling*. And please get that scared look off your face. We're just a couple of young people taking in the sights.

We don't know what the hell happened on the next street."

Farrell couldn't help but stare at her.

Nancy glanced at him, then turned her eyes back to the street.

"All right," she asked sullenly, "*what*?"

"It's like I don't even know you. It's like you're another person."

Nancy amiably smiled at passersby and said quietly, "Why? I'm still the same Nancy Belmont from Kansas City. Pretty, able-bodied and highly intelligent..."

Farrell said wryly, "And very modest."

"Very."

"And who shoots like Calamity Jane."

She finally looked at him, her blue eyes shining in the fading sunlight. There was a question in those eyes.

"I've heard of her homely looks. I hope you don't consider me in the same class."

"On the contrary," he said. "You're one of the prettiest gals I've ever seen."

Nancy faced the street again and tried to control the smile forming on her lips.

Farrell asked gravely, "So what do we do now, *darling*? This town'll be on fire when folks find out the marshal's been killed."

Nancy's alert eyes watched the townspeople as they passed them. The news hadn't traveled to their street yet, but it would soon.

"We collect the horses from that stable before the hostler hears about the marshal. He won't let us have them if he thinks we had something to do with killing him."

Farrell stopped and faced her. He looked into her eyes and said earnestly, "I've got to thank you for this, Nancy. If that jasper had his way, he would've dropped us as soon as breathe. I've seen his type in every town. When they can't satisfy their rope fever, they figure they can do the deed themselves."

He felt her squeeze his hand. "We'll discuss it later," she said softly. "Right now, let's get those horses..."

THEY HAD CAMPED in a hollow of old cottonwoods fifty yards off the main road outside of town. The three horses were tied to trees, with lush grass and shrubbery within reach.

The sun had already gone down and the shadows of tree branches cast jagged shadows on them as they sat before a fire.

Farrell smacked his neck and said, "Damn bugs!"

"Yes," Nancy said wryly, "life on the run *is* fun, isn't it?"

He stared at her. Her hat and jacket were off and her handbag was lying on the ground next to her. He noticed the firelight reflect off her blue eyes and its glow shine off her pinned-up auburn hair.

His eyes went to her bag.

"You shouldn't have shot through your bag. Now it's got a hole in it."

She shrugged and said, "Didn't have time to draw."

"We locked you in a room with no windows. How'd you get out?"

"I used a hairpin to pick the lock."

"Pick the lock?"

Nancy nodded and said, "It's been done before."

Farrell shook his head, a confused expression on his face.

"This is getting stranger and stranger."

"What is?"

His eyes finally met hers. She could see how angry he was.

"For instance," he began, "how does a secretary for a real estate company shoot like Billy the Kid. And how did she know about *picking locks*? And why did you go to the trouble of following me all the way here?"

Nancy paused and lowered her eyes for a moment. Then she raised them and held his gaze.

"My employer sent me to Aubrey to look over some parcels of land."

Farrell shook his head.

Nancy asked, "Doesn't sound right, does it?"

"Not a bit. Give me your handbag."

Nancy hesitated, then shrugged and picked up her bag. She took a pocket revolver out of it and kept it at her side, then tossed the bag over the fire to him. He caught it and rummaged through its contents.

He soon found what he was looking for. Drawing out a piece of paper with some official writing on it, he read it. Then he shoved the paper into the handbag and tossed it back to her. She caught it and returned her pistol back to its place.

With a tight smile, Farrell shook his head.

"A Pinkerton. I should've known."

"You weren't supposed to know."

"I didn't think they had lady Pinkertons."

"There are more of us out there than you think. I happen to work out of the Kansas City office."

"Kansas City, *Kansas*?"

Nancy grinned and nodded.

"Well, what would the Pinkertons want with me? I didn't think I was that important."

"No offense, Hoge, but you're not."

"Uh-huh. It was Garth you were trailing, wasn't it?"

She nodded.

"And it's to do with those Union gold bars."

Again, she nodded.

"So the government didn't forget."

"No, Hoge, they didn't. It's true, they put it on the back burner for a while. They had other fish to fry: homesteading the country, curbing the abuses of the cattle industry, building cross-country railroads and handling the Indians. But always in the back of its collective mind was the disappearance of those gold bars. Garth made sure he was the only surviving member of his guerrilla gang to know where the gold was. We had men keeping close to Garth for years, hoping he'd reveal just *where* he buried it. We put agents in jail with him, we even had a man robbing banks with him. Thanks to his reports, we were able to thwart most of the robberies before anyone got hurt. But on his last one, Garth decided to double-cross his gang in a big way. He set too many sticks of dynamite on a locked safe in El Paso and blew up the remainder of his gang. He also blew up one of our best men."

Farrell saw the change in Nancy with those last words; the grim set of her mouth, the rage behind her eyes.

"And your job was..."

"To stick close to Garth and report where he went. Then other agents in the vicinity would've taken over from me. The agency booked a trip for me on the same stage he was leaving on, figuring he was returning to where he buried the gold. We had a good idea he never had a chance to remove it from the area."

"And how am I connected to all this?"

"That wasn't our aim at all. We knew that you and Garth were in prison together, but we also knew that you had never killed anyone before. You were certainly not in Garth's class as a robber or murderer or anything else dishonest."

"Thank you."

"You're welcome. So it was obvious that Garth wanted you along just to help him bring the gold out from under that buried coach. I'm sure he had a double-cross in mind somewhere down the line after you took the gold out."

"I'm starting to think you're right."

"Yes, but you were now involved in his scheme whether I liked it or not. I even tried to discourage you, keep you far from both of us, but apparently you're not that bright."

Farrell raised his eyebrows and said, "Oh, really?"

She replied with sarcasm. "Yes, Hoge, *really*. So when you blurted out the secret of the gold stash to all those people at the swing station, not only did you get yourself unnecessarily involved in this mess, you involved four other people who ordinarily would've gone their own way. You didn't look at me then when you blabbed about the gold, but I was glaring daggers at you! I *never* wanted to throw a chair at someone so much in my life! Thanks to your big mouth, you endangered four other people. Suddenly, I *had* to agree to be part of this 'partnership' just to stay close to all of you and make sure nothing bad happened."

"I'm sorry."

"You should be!" She shook her head gravely. "I knew you were getting deeper and deeper in this mess. Why do you think I was warning you to stay out of it, just to hear myself talk?"

Farrell said irritably, "I said I was sorry."

Nancy eyed him sullenly, then looked away. After a beat, however, she suddenly continued her tirade. "And then you get involved with some greedy bitch who'd just as soon get you killed as—"

He almost shouted, "Wait a minute!"

She stared at him curiously. "What?"

Farrell reached into his waistband and pulled out the gun Garth had tossed to him. He flipped open the cylinder and spun it, staring at the chambers. Then he looked up at her.

"It's the gun Garth tossed to me after he broke jail and killed the marshal."

"What about it?"

"It's *empty*."

"*What*?"

"Yep. Empty as my head, it seems."

"I don't understand."

Farrell leaned forward and said excitedly, "I passed an *empty* gun to Garth through the window."

"All right. So the marshal obviously had to have taken Garth's gun away, but he could have had spare bullets in the loops of his holster."

"But he wasn't wearing a holster! The marshal

must've removed the whole rig before he put him in a cell."

Nancy shook her head thinking about it. Then she stared at him with a sudden realization.

"Monica Lawson killed him!"

Farrell shook his head, clearly disturbed about the whole thing. "But *why*?"

Nancy looked at him with sympathy. She said gently, "I don't know, Hoge. But one thing's for sure."

"What's that?"

"We couldn't be in any deeper than if we had stepped in quicksand..."

FOUR

Farrell was still trying to come to terms with it. For some reason, the marshal was set up to die and he had played a part in it; albeit, an innocent part, but still...

He wondered aloud, "And now they're looking for me..."

Nancy corrected him. "They're looking for *us*."

He looked at her over the fire. "I don't see how."

"This fellow you told me about who wanted to hang Garth, the man called Abner Perkins. He got a good look at me before I shot him."

"So now we're both fugitives."

Nancy shrugged her slender shoulders and said, "I guess that puts us in with Garth. That's what the people in Aubrey will think. What I'd like to know is how Monica Lawson explained herself afterwards; that is, if she did indeed kill the marshal."

"That's easy. She was carrying a black purse with her. She either put away her gun or hid it somewhere; she had that half a minute of time after she shot him to do it. Then she'd explain to those folks that heard the shot that she was just innocently visiting the marshal when Garth made a break for it. And that's why it all happened."

Nancy instantly saw where Farrell was going.

"You mean she wanted to pin the murder on Garth?"

"Why not? He's already proved himself a killer to the whole town. He'd be the most likely suspect."

"But why would she kill the marshal?"

Farrell just shrugged his shoulders. He thought of the anger he detected in Monica when Dugan arrived at the Silver Star, wondering if there wasn't a history between the two that provoked the killing.

Looking off into the night, he spied the forest around them. Idly, he asked, "So now what? I'm about ready to chuck the whole thing and ride out to I don't know where. What about you?"

Nancy smiled gravely and said, "It's not that easy for me. My mission is to continue following Mr. Garth until I'm led to that gold."

"And where would he be?"

"I don't know, but he can't be too far out of the area. My guess is that he's actually looking for us. *We* have the tools to dig up the gold on that third horse. He might still want your help in retrieving it. The discovery of a gold cache, no matter how fantastic such a discovery might sound coming as it does on the Kansas/Missouri border, is a secret men will take to their graves. Chances are that Garth won't enlist the aid of another man to help him. Enough people know about it as it is. No, Hoge. I think he's going to come looking for you again."

"Well, there's no profit for me now that I know the government is still looking for it."

Nancy shifted her position on the ground. Then she looked at him levelly and said, "Perhaps. I can't promise anything, Hoge, but for the return of the gold cache, there might be a reward."

Farrell stared at her.

"Go on," he said.

"The federal government might see it in their interests to keep all this very quiet. It comes to reason that they might pay you a reward for your assistance, as well as your silence..."

Farrell thought about this. Jobless and drifting, the money would certainly be welcome.

"So what am I to do?"

He noticed that her eyes appeared soft and dreamy in the firelight.

"I need your help, Hoge. I didn't want you involved before, but if the government understands that you've been actively helping a Pinkerton that they themselves hired, this whole trouble back in Aubrey and elsewhere might be expunged for your record."

He looked at her, baffled. "Ex...punged?"

"Removed. Taken off. If you help me, no one will ever know that you helped a mass murderer escape jail."

Farrell felt guilty enough about that. He felt guilty about the marshal's death, as well as allowing Garth to escape justice.

He said finally, "So we have to find Garth."

"No, Hoge. We have to let him find *us*. After all he's done to us, he'd get very suspicious if we were actively looking for him."

Farrell nodded. "That makes sense. So what do we do now?"

"Sleep together."

He blinked his eyes and said, "*What?*"

Nancy rose and went to her horse. Pulling down a worn bedroll, she said, "Too dark to go anywhere. I'll sleep on this side of the fire and you sleep on that side." Then she shook it out and said, "That damn Alma sold me this bedroll for a fortune. I swear to God Almighty, I'm going to report that bitch to Wells Fargo for gouging her customers."

Farrell watched her pick up her jacket, fold it neatly next to her and then lay down on the bedroll and pull it around her shoulders.

She said matter-of-factly, "Good night."

Farrell frowned and then went to his own horse for his bedroll. Annoyed and resentful, he pulled it out and then went over to his side of the fire. Then, watching her as she turned over and faced away from him, he stomped over to the trees behind him, further away from her, and laid the bedroll out there. Then he plopped down on it and yanked it over himself, his irritation growing.

He couldn't figure out why he was so angry, but there was something about a woman instructing him on how far away from her he was to sleep that infuriated him. To his male ego, it was *not* a tactful thing to do.

Soon, however, the frenetic events of the day took its toll on him and he was asleep in just a few minutes.

As the fire started to go down, the full moon rose and its brightness broke through the passing clouds overhead.

Nancy had now turned over, and as she lay there on her side, she watched him with sad eyes...

It was about four and a half hours later. The fire had long died out, leaving the odor of burned wood in the air. This too would soon vanish as the night winds blew it away and replaced it with the smell of aspens and lush grass growing freely in the warm spring earth.

Farrell was lying on his right side, sleeping heavily. He dreamed about Nancy, and a pleasant little smile formed on his face. It was the kind of the dream he wouldn't have told her about under *any* circumstances.

Then, his right shoulder hurting because of the weight he was putting on it, he rolled over and lay on his back facing the cloudless sky. The smile was still there, and the way he pictured Nancy in his dream would have been considered scandalous. His smile widened.

That's when the figure suddenly pounced on him. It was a tall, full figure too, and when his eyes came open, he saw the figure silhouetted against the moonlight. A pair of long, slim legs were planted on both sides of him, effectively pinning him to the ground. When he looked up, he saw the wide-brimmed Stetson sitting on a long, angular head, but he couldn't make out the face.

"All right, Garth," he said wryly. "We've been through this nonsense before. What's the matter? No knife against my throat?"

Instead of answering him, the figure reached up and ran fingers through his hair, then ran them along his forehead and down to his eyelids and mouth with trembling hands.

Farrell cleared his throat and said, "Hey, Garth, aren't you gettin' kinda *personal*?"

Then the voice spoke. "Darlin', I haven't seen you in so long..."

There was no mistaking the brassy, down-home drawl. *Alma*!

She pulled off her Stetson and shook her head back and forth. Her thick blonde hair fell down into her eyes and face.

Then she said hungrily, "I can't wait for us to get sparkin'." Then she leaned down to give him a kiss.

Suddenly she heard a loud metallic click behind her left ear and felt the touch of a hard iron gun barrel against the back of her skull, the trigger sight burying itself in her mussed-up hair.

"Get off of him *now*!" said Nancy, through her teeth.

Alma froze. Then she said bitterly, "Well, well, the paper-pushin' tart from Kansas." Slowly she got up and faced her, Nancy following her movements with the gun as she rose.

The hatred was plain for Farrell to see, even in the moonlight.

Suppressing her fury, Alma asked her, "What're you doing here?"

Still pointing the gun at her, Nancy said with quiet anger, "I pay rent here. What's *your* excuse?"

Sitting up, Farrell looked from one angry woman to the other; he knew that he had to keep things light. So he said, "I think you'd better answer her, Alma. You know how unpredictable these secretaries can be."

Nancy suppressed a grin and worked hard to keep her angry scowl.

Alma eyed the gun, showing fear for the first time.

"All right!" she said, betraying her anxiety. Nervously, she ran her hand back through her hair. Then she said, more or less to Farrell, "When y'all didn't come back, Chet Riley said he couldn't wait anymore. He knew that sooner or later Wells Fargo would have his hide, so he *had* to get going to Lone Jack. Wentworth was all for forgetting about the gold too. Everybody figured you and Garth double-crossed us and skedaddled off with the gold. Fred was for forgetting about the whole thing as well, especially after Garth punched out his lights. I didn't think Fred was much of a man to begin with, but I really gave him hell when he was all for quittin' the gold."

Farrell rose off the ground and faced her. He asked urgently, "And what about their promise that they would stay quiet about the gold?"

"Chet Riley was mad as hell. Fred and Wentworth didn't care about keeping it a secret anymore one way or t'other, but Riley was fit to be tied. Said as soon as he got to town, he was going to talk and talk *good and loud* about the gold. Tell everybody about it but the stable horses."

Nancy asked firmly, "Why are you here?"

Alma just glared at her.

Farrell repeated her question, though gently. "Why *are* you here, Alma?"

Alma looked at him, mollified by the friendlier tone in his voice. She said, "Because I *knew* that you wouldn't cross us! Hell, you already let us know about it when anyone with eyes could tell that Garth wanted to keep it secret! Why would you do that if you were figurin' to cross us? So I figure you ran into trouble. I took a ride into town lookin' for y'all and found out that you and Garth were part of some 'gang' that had it in for the marshal, especially after Garth was arrested for killing two men. Then I heard that 'a man and a woman...'" Her eyes took in both of them for emphasis. "...helped get a gun to Garth so he could shoot the marshal and escape jail."

Nancy and Farrell exchanged looks. They knew what all this meant: If they wanted to find that cache of gold, they had to work fast before the whole countryside went looking for it.

However, Alma read something else in the look. She stood there arrogantly with folded arms. Her eyes were mean and she smiled at them bitterly.

"Now I see it all," she said.

Farrell asked, "You see *what*?"

Alma said snidely, "Your girl over here told us she was quitting the gold, so we sold her a horse so she could ride on to Lone Jack. But instead she comes to Aubrey so she could help you bust Garth out of jail. Then all of you can go for that gold, double-crossin' the rest of us! Now I find the two of you campin' alone in the woods in the middle of the night! Bet y'all did a lot more than watch the fire burnin' the logs!"

Enraged, Nancy raised the gun closer to Alma, her finger tensing on the trigger. Alma's eyes widened in fear.

Farrell said, "Nancy!"

The Pinkerton stopped. Gradually, she relaxed, withdrawing the gun and uncocking the hammer.

Her arrogance returning, Alma glared at her.

She hissed, "I ain't going to forget this..."

Nancy snapped at her, "Please *don't*!"

Then she walked back to her bedroll and angrily shoved the gun back into her handbag, not trusting herself with it at the moment.

Farrell asked, "What did Fred say when you left?"

Trying to relax, Alma threw her attention back to him. "What could he say? He knew I was huntin' y'all. He knows in his heart that he can't stop me from doin' what I want."

Farrell said gravely, "Yeah, I kinda agree with him on that."

Alma returned his look, a bright smile sweeping her face.

"That's right, there's no stoppin' me. I see your pack horse back yonder with the new shovels and ropes. I know you're going to hook up with our friend Garth and then you're going after the gold. Well, son, from here on in, where you go, I go! In fact..." She leaned close to him. Indicating Nancy with her head, she said quietly, "Why don't we just throw this one in some ditch and then you and me can go--"

Farrell turned around suddenly and bent down to his bedroll. Alma stopped talking and glared at him in frustrated rage.

Then a noise came from behind them and they both turned to see Nancy, her handbag, jacket, hat and bedroll in her arms, moving over to a point very close to Farrell's bedroll. After she neatly spread out her bedroll and placed the items on the ground, she looked at them defiantly.

Alma said tautly, "Marking your territory?"

Nancy replied, "Just protecting Hoge from the *animals*, that's all..."

At that moment, Alma was truly sorry she was too far from her rifle.

FIVE HOURS LATER, the morning sun was shining brightly through the trees and a cool spring breeze blew down from the surrounding hills. Slowly, Nancy opened her eyes and found that she was sleeping much closer to Farrell than she had originally intended. She raised herself up on her elbows and looked over at him. Farrell was snoring loudly, his mouth half-open as he breathed. Nancy wondered if he had moved himself closer to her during the night, but she found that he had not moved from his spot on the ground; indeed, it was *she* who had moved closer to him.

Self-consciously, Nancy moved away from him and then sat up, looking around the campsite. They had left Alma sleeping in her bedroll on the other side of the extinguished fire. But when Nancy looked at that spot, she found that she wasn't there.

She glanced at Farrell, still snoring away. Quietly she rose up off the ground and scanned the campsite. She hugged herself against the morning chill, feeling the cool, crisp air on her arms and shoulders. She picked up her light jacket and little hat and put them on. Then a sudden realization struck her, waking her up faster than any mug of hot coffee. She ran over to the grove of cottonwoods back of the campsite where they had tied the three horses.

They were gone.

Alma had left them nothing. She had not only taken the horse carrying their supplies, but Nancy and Farrell's horses as well, rather cruelly leaving them out in the middle of the woods with no way to travel except on foot.

Nancy ran to the campsite, her eyes frantically searching the grounds. She soon found that her handbag containing her gun was gone as well. Her eyes again went to Farrell. He snorted loudly and moved about as if he was waking up, but she saw that his eyes were still closed. Idly, she wondered what he was dreaming about.

Sighing with exasperation, Nancy then turned back to where the horses had been tied. She looked closely at the ground and saw the parted shrubbery where the horses had been pulled through. The Pinkertons had not trained her for tracking, but she had observed a great deal as a little girl tagging along with her father while he was out hunting. Certainly, it wasn't hard to follow the tracks of four horses being pulled through a forest, especially one where the largest creatures weren't even half the size of a horse.

The campsite had been far enough off the main road to hide them, with the dense underbrush effectively concealing their campfire from passing travelers. Nancy looked back in the direction of the road and quickly realized why Alma didn't take the horses that way. Having been in town more recently than they were, Alma knew that a posse was out hunting for them. Had she appeared out in the open with three other horses, especially one with shovels and ropes, she would've had to face some embarrassing questions. Being a horse thief was still considered a hanging offense in some parts, including Kansas. The posse had obviously slowed down their search when it had gotten dark; now with the sun up, the posse would return to tracking them in force.

Nancy brightened then. Not wanting to risk being found with stolen horses, Alma had to keep them in the forest and off the main roads—at least for now. Guessing that Alma was no more than a half hour ahead of her and that pulling four horses through the woods would slow her down anyway, the Kansan thought she had a good chance of catching up to her.

Nancy soon found an Indian trail through the trees and followed it for nearly a quarter mile. It wasn't long before she found several distinctive signs made by the horses in their journey. Besides the obvious hoof prints in the soft earth, there were broken twigs and signs of bushes being pushed aside, of shrubbery trampled on and long strands of horse hair stuck to the barks of trees where they had rubbed against as they passed. She idly thought that an Indian warrior being tracked by an enemy would've wiped out all telltale signs in his wake, but she knew that Alma wasn't even half as disciplined or possessed of infinite patience to take the time to throw a pursuer off her trail. She was like an animal who just did what she felt like doing, regardless of the consequences or whom she hurt.

Nancy continued down the trail, scanning the ground, the sides of trees, anything. As she kept her gaze on the ground, her heart lifted. The tracks of both horses and human were looking fresher. As she continued, the trail gradually widened, finally opening up into a small clearing. Then she heard it; the excited snorting of horses upon smelling another human being. Pushing a low-hanging branch out of her way, she emerged from the grove of trees, and finally saw them.

Nancy looked across the fifty feet of ground between them, covered with wind-blown grass high enough to come up to her boot tops. The horses were tied very close to each other to two cottonwoods. As she came into the open, they sullenly stared at her. Carefully scanning the area, Nancy looked for Alma, but didn't see her. Then, as quietly as she could, she pushed her long legs through the high grass, her boots and riding skirt carving a path before her. As she walked, she was hoping that the hissing-like noise of the swaying weeds would not alert Alma, wherever she was. It was then that she heard the sounds of running water in the distance. She looked past the horses and guessed that there was a stream or river of some kind back of the trees. With some amusement, she wondered if Alma had gone to take a bath, but dismissed such a notion. *A bath? Alma? Extremely doubtful.*

Finally, she got to the horses. However, as soon as she appeared, they nickered loudly. She patted them all on their muzzles and whispered softly, trying to soothe them, but her presence merely excited them more. Having been roughly yanked through the woods by Alma, they immediately sensed that *this* woman would've given them far better treatment.

Nancy walked between two horses and found where all the reins were tied to the nearest tree. She was in the process of untying one horse when she heard the metallic click and felt the gun barrel pressed into the back of her skull.

Then she heard Alma's cold voice. "Get off of him—*now!*"

Nancy stopped what she was doing and slowly turned around, raising her hands.

Alma stood there looking as she did the night before, but this time she was holding Nancy's gun out at arm's length, the hammer pulled back. Her smile was wide.

"I just love it when history repeats itself," she said.

Nancy frowned and said wryly, "I'll bet."

"I was fillin' my canteen in the river back yonder when I heard the animals acting up. 'Tain't no wolves in these woods." Then she said with special emphasis, "Just *alley cats*."

Nancy gave her a withering look. Then she said, "Looks like these horses haven't had any water since yesterday. While you were getting yourself a drink, you wouldn't think to get *them* some water as well, would you?"

Alma smirked at her as if she was too softheaded for words.

"What do I care if one of them collapses? I still got three more."

Nancy's glare grew harder. Somehow such cruelty didn't sound strange from a woman who cheats on her husband and overcharges her guests for badly needed supplies.

Alma shook her head and said, "Thought you were foolin' us when you said you were going on to Lone Jack when all the time you were fixin' to run off with the gold and Brown Eyes to boot."

Nancy knew quite well who "Brown Eyes" was since she herself had noticed the color of Farrell's eyes.

Alma looked at her appraisingly and pursed her lips in thought.

Nancy asked, "Something on your mind—as if that were possible?"

Alma grimaced at the remark. Then, aiming the gun at her head, she smiled and said, "I'm just tryin' to figure out where to leave your body..."

Nancy forced a smile. It was time for an old trick, and she was hoping that Alma was stupid enough to fall for it. "I know that gun better than you," she said. "And last night, I left the safety catch on."

Alma suddenly looked concerned, and even when her well-honed survival instincts told her *not* to look at the gun, she couldn't help casting her eyes down at the trigger guard. It was for only a split second, but it was long enough. Nancy reached out quickly and shoved the gun upward.

Alma fired. The shot echoed loudly through the forest as the bullet barely missed a squirrel high in the trees doing nothing more threatening than gnawing on a pine cone.

Hearing the gunshot so close to them, the horses panicked, stomping about excitedly in their narrow area, desperately trying to pull themselves free from the tree trunks they were tied to.

Meanwhile, the two women were struggling over the gun. Situated in a narrow space between two panicked horses, they crashed back and forth against the side of one horse, then the other, but neither woman would let go. Then, angrily pushing the pistol toward Nancy's face, Alma strained to cock the hammer back. Nancy tried to stop her, but was afraid that her fingers would get caught by the hammer as it came down. Seeing Alma's finger tense on the trigger and with the barrel practically touching her cheek, Nancy quickly ducked her head.

A split second later, Alma fired. With the shot so close to her right ear, Nancy shouted. Then she heard the horse's scream just inches behind her. Swiveling her head quickly, she saw where the bullet had struck. The dying horse's four legs folded beneath him and his massive body thudded to the ground directly behind Nancy.

Ironically, the horse's death freed up some space and the two women suddenly found themselves tumbling over the horse's carcass and landing heavily in the deep grass upland from the tree. The impact of the fall had loosened Alma's grip on the gun and it flew out of her hands, landing in some bushes several feet away.

Their hats came off as they tumbled over each other on the ground, coming dangerously close to the three frightened horses. When they rolled beneath Alma's horse, the panicked animal stomped its hooves furiously, narrowly missing the two women as they fought. Then, seeing the opportunity to inflict as much damage on her enemy as possible, Alma used her long fingers to cover Nancy's face, forcing her head back against the ground. With her other hand, she tried to pull Nancy's body as close as she could to the stomping hooves.

Though blinded, Nancy sensed what she was trying to do and pushed back, using her body weight to throw Alma over.

Now free of the horses, the two women, with their arms wrapped tightly around each other, rolled over and over through the shrubbery, punching, kicking and clawing all the way.

As she fought, Nancy became vaguely aware of the

sounds of running water getting closer and closer. She already knew what was going to happen, but was powerless to stop it.

Without a pause in their journey, the two women found themselves tumbling heavily down a rocky foothill and the next thing they knew, they had both plunged into the icy river. However, it didn't stop the fight, and the two women spent several frantic minutes trying to drown each other as they also fought against the current.

Nancy had her head dunked underwater several times, and found it harder each time to fight the temptation to pass out. Her wet hair was in her face and she was gasping for breath as she fought the heavier woman. Struggling to keep her head above the icy water, Nancy knew that she was weakening and couldn't hold on much longer.

Then, after thwarting Alma's final attempt to keep her head under, Nancy broke to the surface just in time to see her opponent gradually slowing down. As she pushed her wet hair out of her eyes, Nancy gazed at her and saw that she wasn't dreaming. Alma's movements were becoming clumsy and she was gasping for breath far more than Nancy was. Knowing what she had to do, Nancy used her last ounce of waning strength to shove Alma's head under. The big blonde fought back, reaching up with clawing fingers and grabbing Nancy's face several times, but her weakness was growing. Holding her head under for what seemed like an eternity but was actually a few seconds, Nancy looked down and finally saw the oxygen bubbles rapidly floating to the surface.

As she held her opponent's head under the freezing

water, Nancy thought real hard about what she was doing. After having killed a defenseless horse and being an all-around cheating, murderous, deceitful tramp, Alma probably deserved to be drowned like a rat; but Nancy also knew that she was no murderer. Reluctantly, she lifted her enemy up into the fresh air and then swam for the bank, pulling her along by her jacket.

Breathing hard, Nancy climbed up on the bank and dragged Alma's unconscious body behind her onto a patch of thick grass. Turning the blonde's head sideways, Nancy made sure that the water she ingested would flow out onto the ground. Then, breathing hard, the Kansan got to her feet and looked down at her.

Soaking wet, Nancy's riding skirt and jacket, now torn at the shoulder, clung to her skin. Her wet hair was hanging down in her eyes and she swept it back with a bruised right hand. Then, touching her face, she felt a few scratches, but they seemed small and would probably heal quickly. She coughed loudly, trying to get out the mouthful of water she had accumulated when Alma dunked her.

Panting, she glared at the unconscious woman and said, "You damn bi—"

"Ah-ah!" said a familiar voice. "That ain't lady-like."

She looked up and saw Farrell atop the foothill watching her with an amused expression on his face.

Shaking his head, he said amiably, "What would the Pinkertons say if they saw you now?"

Between deep breaths, Nancy replied, "They'd say, 'Good work, Nancy. Now get cleaned up.'"

Then she collapsed onto the ground and lay on her back a few feet from Alma, sucking in deep breaths of the cool morning air.

Farrell came down the hill and sat down beside her.

She asked, "How much of it did you see?"

"Enough. I woke up and found everybody gone, including the horses. I figured Alma was pulling a double-cross and you were trackin' her down. It wasn't hard to follow your trail."

She looked at him curiously. "You didn't wake up when I got up before. Your snore was like a lumberjack sawing wood. What were you dreaming about anyway?"

Farrell looked out at the river and answered, "Oh, nothing worth repeating."

"You found the horses?"

"Couldn't miss 'em."

"Whose horse did she kill?"

"Yours. Or rather the one she sold you."

Nancy sat up and faced him.

"Why didn't you stop us?"

"I tried. I was trailin' you when I heard those shots. I didn't know what to think. I ran like hell to get here, but you gals move too fast for me. I'm trompin' after you and before you know it, you both roll into a river. All right, I figured you two weren't exactly friends, but I didn't expect you to drown each other."

Nancy replied irritably, "Well, it's not like we were fighting over you!" Suddenly she realized what she had just said and sat there for a moment in stunned disbelief.

Farrell stared at her.

Thinking fast, she said, "Oh my God! Those shots!" She rose quickly and said, "A posse could've heard them!"

Farrell also got to his feet. "Yeah, you're right."

Nancy said urgently, "Let's get those horses out of here!"

"And what about the dead one?"

"Well, we can't bury him!"

"And what about her?"

Nancy looked down at Alma. The big blonde's chest rose and fell rhythmically; if anyone hadn't known better, it looked like she was merely sleeping.

Through her teeth, Nancy said, "I'd like to leave her here."

Farrell replied soberly, "I have a better idea. Bring her horse over and ground-tie it next to her. Can't leave a person out here on foot, even her."

Nancy looked at him, frowning. Then she sighed and said, "You pick the strangest times to have the quality of mercy, Mr. Farrell. I was for letting the wolves have her."

"They'd probably spit her out."

"I agree."

Then the sound of a boot scraping a rock made them turn and look up at the top of the hill.

Abner Perkins stood there looking down at them, a cocked pistol in his hand. His right arm was in a sling, and his expression was deadly.

FIVE

Farrell's hand reached back for his holstered gun, but Perkins's no-nonsense voice stopped him. "Go ahead and draw, cowboy," he said. "Now you don't want to take a chance that I can't shoot your eyes out with my left hand any better than my right, would you?"

Farrell knew he'd be a fool to try to draw now. Both he and Nancy raised their hands.

Then they saw two other men appear and stand next to Perkins. One was a middle-aged man and the other a sallow-faced youth of seventeen. The older of the two was the only one holding a rifle.

Frowning, the older man said, "Joshua, I told you to stay with the horses."

"Aw, give me a chance, Mr. Sikes! I want to help."

"I said go back with the horses. We'll handle this."

Sulking, Joshua turned and went back the way he came.

Perkins and Sikes, with their guns pointed at the two, descended the short hill and stopped before them.

Sikes took Farrell's gun and stuffed it into his waistband.

Grinning, Perkins stared at Nancy and asked, "You always go swimmin' with your clothes on?"

Nancy said sarcastically, "For a tracker, you *do* notice things, don't you?"

No longer grinning, Perkins said, "Lady, you shot me while I'm trying to arrest your friend here, and you won't be joking so much after you get old and gray in prison."

Farrell said, "It looked like you were going to do something more permanent than arrest me. I say she shot you to save my life, and I don't think a jury would have any trouble believing that either."

Sikes turned the rifle his way and said, "Our marshal is dead. And you and this woman threw in with Charlie Taggert to kill him and two of our citizens. I don't know *why* it happened, but if we prove some kind of murderous conspiracy here, you two will have a long time to think of what you got yourselves into."

A movement from the ground made them all turn.

Alma, her face bruised and her clothes soaked, sat up on the ground slowly. She felt her head briefly and then ran her hand back through her wet hair.

Perkins asked, "Who's she?"

Sikes said, "I remember her." He looked at Farrell and said, "She was asking around town whether anyone had seen you and Taggert, except she called him *Garth.*"

Perkins asked, "What do you think, Henry?"

"Bring her along too. Figures she knows what's goin' on as well as these two."

When Perkins roughly yanked Alma to her feet, she

shoved his arm off and shouted, "Who you pullin' around, sodbuster?"

Perkins shoved the gun in her face and the move was so sudden, it brought her up short. An expression of fear replaced the one of defiance.

"I never shot a woman before," said Perkins harshly, "but if you're fixin' to start trouble, I'd just as soon pull the trigger on you right now."

Alma quickly raised her hands. There was a quaver in her voice when she replied, "It's all right, mister. I didn't mean nothin'. I won't be no bother."

Perkins grinned wickedly and said, "I know you won't!"

Sikes gestured with his rifle and said, "C'mon, let's get going."

The three captives climbed the hill, with Sikes and Perkins following.

Alma was glaring at Nancy, but Farrell purposely placed himself between them as they climbed.

After they all reached the top, Sikes again gestured with his rifle and they walked back to the cottonwoods where the horses had been tied. However, they weren't there anymore. It was obvious that Joshua had taken them, as ordered, to another location.

As they passed the dead horse still lying by the tree, Sikes asked, "Who did he belong to?"

Nancy said sadly, "He was mine."

Sikes then asked, "Who shot him?"

The Pinkerton didn't reply, but the dirty look she gave Alma gave Sikes his answer.

Seeing the look, he said, "Saw a couple of women's Stetsons lying on the ground back there, and by the look of the bushes and grounds, I'd say that someone had a fight. I figure it was you two gals."

"No," said Nancy sullenly, "I always look this way when I go out."

Sikes stopped and looked at her, a reluctant admiration creeping into his voice. "I'll say this for you, Miss. Your sparrin' partner folds real quick when a gun's pointed at her, but *you* don't care about pissin' us off one way or the other. Don't find that kind of sand in too many folks, women *or* men."

Suddenly uncomfortable, Nancy didn't answer; she just looked at the ground. However, Farrell was intrigued by her refusal to accept a compliment she felt she didn't merit. *My God*, he was thinking, *she's actually turning red!*

Perkins said, "Let's get on, Henry. After we lock 'em up, I'm going to Sue's for some breakfast. I didn't have nothin' but stale biscuits and cold coffee before I rode out."

No one said another word as they continued hiking through the woods. In less than ten minutes, they had reached the main road. As they emerged from the trees, they saw Joshua sitting his horse. Tied to a cottonwood a few feet behind him stood four horses, including, apparently, Sikes's and Perkins's.

As he held his rifle on them, Sikes asked the boy, "You see the others yet?"

Joshua answered, "I thought I heard old man Higgins say they was searchin' the other side of Kane Mountain."

Perkins said irritably, "I told Higgins he was takin' 'em too far off! Probably didn't hear the shots."

Sikes said, "Tie 'em up, Joshua."

Joshua dismounted and reached into his pocket. He produced three rawhide ropes, each one about eighteen inches long. As Sikes and Perkins held them at gunpoint, he proceeded to tie the captives' hands.

As she was being tied, Alma said excitedly, "You're makin' a mistake! I'm not with them!"

Sikes growled, "We'll let a judge decide that. Now shut up!"

Hearing the tone in his voice, Alma reluctantly kept quiet.

As Farrell's hands were being tied, he was measuring distance, wondering what would happen if he tossed Joshua in front of his captors' line of fire so that he and Nancy could make a break for it back into the woods. But he dismissed that idea when he realized that the boy could be shot by accident, so he did nothing.

After finishing with Farrell, Joshua went over to Nancy and started to loop the rawhide around her wrists. Shyly, he said to her, "I'll try not to make them tight, ma'am."

Nancy smiled warmly at him and said, "Thanks, Joshua."

Joshua soon finished tying her hands. Then he looked at Nancy and put his hand to the brim of his Stetson as a sign of respect. He didn't see how moved she was by the gesture because he turned away quickly and went back to his horse.

The sound of another horse coming up the road made them all turn.

Monica Lawson was walking her horse toward them. She was wearing a ranch jacket and riding skirt, a brown Stetson was atop her piled-up dark hair. She also had a Winchester lying across her knees.

Sikes said irritably, "Now, Miss Lawson, I told you back in town that I didn't want you on this posse."

Farrell and Nancy exchanged looks. They both knew that their suspicions about Monica wouldn't be believed anyway. So they just stood there and watched her, wondering what she was up to.

She wasn't going to disappoint them. Speaking fast, she said, "I *had* to come out here, Mr. Sikes! I consider *myself* responsible for the marshal getting killed! If I hadn't been talking to him when that monster broke jail..." She just let the words hang there, letting her audience fill them in.

In a quietly soothing tone, Sikes said, "Don't worry, Miss Lawson. It wasn't your fault."

Then he turned to Joshua and said, "Boy, ride over to Kane Mountain and tell the big man-hunter Clem Higgins that we have three of 'em and to get over here fast. We're going to need some help corralling them all into town on horseback."

Joshua said, "Yes, sir."

As the boy turned, he and Nancy exchanged pleasant smiles and then he mounted his chestnut stallion. He turned his horse in the direction Monica had come from and spurred it down the road, the hoofbeats sounding farther and farther away as he left the area.

Watching Joshua disappear down the road, Monica said, "You didn't have to send him, Mr. Sikes. I'm well-armed, as you can see, and between the three of us, we didn't need the others to get them back to town."

Hiding the annoyance in his voice, Sikes responded

patiently, "Thank you, Miss Lawson, but you can go back to town now. We'll handle this."

"What'll happen to them?"

"I can't say, but they'll probably have a lot of things to answer for."

Perkins laughed then, a wicked little laugh with no mercy to it.

"Aw, who're you kiddin', Henry? For having something to do with killing the marshal, they're gonna get their necks stretched!"

It was then that Alma spoke up.

"Wait a minute!" she said excitedly. "I didn't have nothin' to do with it! It was them two! They killed him!"

Perkins grinned and said, "I love seeing them turn on each other, don't you, Henry?"

Sikes said irritably, "Oh, shut up, Abner."

But Alma was just getting started. Even with her hands tied in front of her, she moved forward so suddenly that Perkins defensively raised his pistol at her. Frightened, the big blonde maneuvered toward Sikes, whom she figured was the more reasonable of the two. Silently watching her, Farrell and Nancy could see her hysteria grow as she shouted at the two posse members.

"Listen to me, and you listen well! You want to be a rich man someday?" Her next statement took in Perkins as well. "Do you *both* want to be rich? Richer than you'll ever get bein' sodbusters the rest of your days?"

Knowing what she was going to say next, Farrell shouted, "Shut up, Alma!"

Perkins pointed his gun at him and said, "*You* shut up. Let's hear the lady talk."

"I'll talk all right!" she said. "I know where there's *gold*! And it's not too far from here! And if you let me go, I'll make sure you get every bit of it!"

Sikes stared at her, not sure what to make of her claims. He said with some skepticism, "Gold? Here in the border country?"

Perkins said, "I don't know, Henry. I've heard some stories..."

Alma continued, "It's more than stories! Bill Quantrill's gold is buried back yonder somewhere off the Independence-Lone Jack road."

Nancy shouted, "She's crazy! She's been drinking!"

Perkins replied, "Well then, I'll have what she's drinkin', because I've heard the same things too. Since I was a little shaver, I've heard about Quantrill's treasure buried just over the borderline in Missouri."

Sikes looked at Alma suspiciously, his skepticism wavering. "It's just a story..."

Alma said, "I'm not lyin' and I'm not drunk! There are gold bars buried just over the border! Now if you two boys can just untie me before the posse gets here."

His excitement growing, Perkins said, "Maybe she's not lying, Henry! Maybe there *is* Rebel gold buried in those hills!" He then turned around and said, "What do you think, Miss Law—"

He didn't finish the sentence. They all heard rifle fire and saw Perkins take a full charge right in the chest. He flew off his feet and landed somewhere off the road, his Colt flying out of his hand.

As she calmly sat her horse, Monica jacked the lever down on her smoking rifle and then turned it on Sikes.

Seeing this, Farrell plowed into Nancy, throwing

both of them to the ground. Then he covered her body with his own as the shooting continued.

Having witnessed his friend's death, a shocked Henry Sikes stared at Monica and hesitated before raising his rifle, a fatal mistake. Monica fired again. The impact of the slug threw Sikes back onto the dirt road by several feet, his rifle flying out of his outstretched hands.

Again, Monica jacked down the lever of the Winchester.

Alma's eyes practically bugged out of their sockets. She saw Monica aiming the rifle at her and had just enough time to scream before one bullet struck her in the stomach and another in the chest.

Cowering on the ground, Farrell and Nancy heard the shots cutting off Alma's scream, then the sound of a tall body hitting the dirt road. They heard the rifle's lever come down again, ejecting another spent shell. Then, after an unsettling moment of silence, they heard Monica dismounting and walking a few steps, her boots making small crunching sounds in the gravelly road.

They almost jumped out of their skins when they heard the Winchester fire a third time.

Monica said crisply, "All right, you two, get up. This is all I'm going to do—for now."

Farrell hesitated. His face was close to Nancy's, and as he looked down at her, he saw that she had tears in her eyes. He then realized that they were not for herself, but because he had risked his own life to protect hers.

Monica said, louder this time, "I said *get up*! Your hands are tied, you're not crippled."

Reluctantly, Farrell pushed himself up off the

ground. Then he helped pull Nancy to her feet. Both of them gasped when they saw Alma's bloodied body lying face down in the dirt.

Seeing their reaction, Monica said, "If that bitch didn't open her big mouth about the gold, those two would still be alive. So I gave her an extra bullet because she's owed that. Don't worry, after what I did to her face, no one will ever recognize her."

Her voice thick with emotion, Nancy asked, "Why did you kill the marshal?"

Monica's eyes narrowed, and her voice, though quiet, betrayed her hatred.

"Because he'd had his way with me for the last time, that's why. All the time he was telling everyone in town what saloon trash I was, and then coming to my room late at night when no one was looking and forcing himself on me. So when your friend Charlie Taggert got himself in jail, I knew that if the marshal got killed during a breakout, they'd blame Taggert, not me."

Farrell said, "So you used me."

"Had to, *Cousin*. Now you and me are goin' places before that boy comes back with the posse. They probably heard the shots."

"Going where?"

"Why, to get the gold, that's where! I found Taggert. He agrees to a three-way split." Then she turned the rifle toward Nancy. "And that doesn't include her!"

Farrell stepped in front of the Pinkerton.

"If you kill her," he said earnestly, "you might as well kill me too."

Monica stared at him, infuriated.

"Hoge, move aside!"

"I mean it! You harm her, I won't do anything for you!"

Exasperated, Monica glanced back down the road. Facing them, she said, "Then she's coming with us."

"Why don't you just let her go?"

"Because she'll blab about the gold to that posse, that's why! Not to mention the fact that I just killed three people! All right then, she's *your* problem! Now get over there and take two of those horses. Make sure one of them has the shovels and ropes." When they hesitated, she said angrily, "*Now!* They'll be here soon!"

The two reluctantly went across the road and, with their hands still tied together, awkwardly untied the horses as Monica mounted her own horse. Bringing it up behind their horses, she laid the rifle across her lap.

She said amiably, "You know why this palomino didn't spook when I started shooting? Because it used to belong to outlaws, that's why. I could shoot you two now and he'd stand right where he was unless I said otherwise."

Farrell and Nancy gave each other worried looks.

Seeing this, Monica felt a rage grow within her. She said vindictively, "Don't worry, Hoge. I'll let her stay alive—as long as she behaves herself."

Wryly, Nancy replied, "Gee, thanks."

Too angry to reply directly to her, Monica spoke to Farrell. "I'm warning you, Hoge. One wrong move and I'll leave her worse than I did those others back there. Now you two stay ahead of me, but not too far ahead. Just go where I tell you..."

THEY WERE NOW miles away from Aubrey and headed toward the Missouri border.

The sun was almost directly overhead, and with it the cool spring morning warmed considerably, drying Nancy's wet clothes as she rode. Yet the warm temperatures did nothing to fill her belly. Both she and Farrell had not eaten since the other night, and both were feeling it down to their groaning stomachs.

Nancy said quietly, "Hoge, how long are we going to ride without food?"

With his tied hands holding the reins, Farrell said, "I don't know, Nancy. At this point, I could eat this horse and hers, and I might throw in yours for a snack."

"If I don't get anything in me soon I'm going to faint."

"And me right after you. Just hold on a while longer. I'm sure she's going to stop soon. I just feel it in my bones."

"When we get to a turn in the bend, do you think we could spur our horses?"

Farrell shook his head and said, "She'd cut us down before we got two feet. You saw her work back there. She's now killed four people. She has no hesitation to pull a trigger and that's the same kind of thing that our most esteemed gunfighters have. The ability to kill without a second thought."

Nancy said sullenly, "'Our most esteemed gunfighters.' Murderers are what they are. Just a group of very sick men who are too stupid to get a job."

Behind them, Monica said, "Hey, what's all this conversation all of a sudden?"

Farrell said sagely, "Just discussing a little history, that's all."

"History!"

"Yeah, Monica, history. You know, it makes the world go 'round."

"Let me tell you about history, amigo! There's the history that a group of men said they were going to make a country where everyone's created equal. Now, a little over a hundred years later, poor white trash like me still can't sit in a church with the 'respected citizens' of Aubrey. So what does a girl with a drunk for a father and whore for a mother do with her life? Why, she gets hold of a saloon on the so-called wrong side of town, that's what she does."

Farrell said, "I kind of wondered how you got to run the Silver Star."

"I know a thing or two about cards, Cousin. And if a deck is marked, all the better. I won the place from an old man named Bill Scatterwhite. He had a head for business, but didn't know cards from bad whiskey. He thought he did though, and that was my advantage. As he played, he got drunker and drunker, so drunk he couldn't tell a real card from a marked one. So I let him win until I turned the tide. He ended up losing everything but his gold eyetooth."

"What happened to him?"

"About a half hour after the game, he went up to his room and blew his brains out."

Nancy said bitterly, "I'm surprised you didn't yank the gold tooth out of his mouth while they were burying him."

Farrell winced at the comment.

Then, restraining her fury, Monica said, "You like to buck the tiger, don't you, honey?"

Nancy didn't bother to answer.

The sun was directly overhead now. As its warming rays penetrated their bodies, the three rode on for another hour, the only sound being the clopping sounds of their horses' hooves on the hard-packed road.

"Turn here."

Farrell and Nancy looked to the left and found a narrow trail going off into some dense aspens.

Farrell looked around and said, "I recall a ranch nearby."

"The old Browning farm," Monica said. "Long out of use."

Farrell nodded absently, but he knew otherwise. He was well aware that Nathaniel Browning's children were very much alive and that they had taken over the property from their late parents. A few weeks ago, he had even tried to find work there, but they didn't need any help at the time. Now it looked like he was returning to the area whether he wanted to or not.

Monica gestured with the Winchester. "Come on, folks. Ride."

They started to turn their horses when Nancy suddenly slid off hers and fell to the ground.

Farrell was dismounting a second after she fell.

Monica ordered, "Leave her there."

Ignoring her, Farrell got down on his knees and leaned over Nancy's prone figure. Her eyes were closed and her lips were slightly parted, indicating that her breathing was sparse. Farrell ran his tied-up hands through Nancy's hair and then stroked her face. He felt how cold her forehead was despite the valley's rising temperatures.

Monica commanded, "I said, leave her there!"

He said urgently, "She needs food."

"So do the wolves," she replied coldly. "Let them have her."

Farrell turned back and angrily faced her. "What kind of woman are you!"

Her tone held a withering sarcasm. "Oh, because I'm a woman I'm supposed to have compassion, am I?" Cruelly, she added, "This is some stupid thing you *men* made up to make us look like softheaded idiots! I've got about as much compassion in me as a damn coyote looking for rabbits, that's how compassionate I am!"

Farrell said bitterly, "You know, Monica, I'm startin' to see a resemblance."

Monica aimed her rifle. "Get out of the way and I'll put her out of her misery."

Farrell said through his teeth, "Then start shootin'."

Using his body to block Monica's aim, he sifted his tied-up hands under Nancy and lifted her up. After awkwardly carrying her to her horse, he put her on the saddle and pushed her booted feet through both stirrups. Then, after tightly winding her rawhide ropes around the pommel of her saddle, he remounted his own horse.

As Farrell led Nancy's horse onto the narrow trail, he kept a careful eye on her, making sure that she didn't slip off the saddle.

Monica watched them as she followed closely behind, her rifle at the ready.

After a few minutes, she said, "Kind of stuck on her, aren't you, Hoge?"

Farrell didn't answer. He just kept watching Nancy worriedly as she leaned forward on her saddle.

• • •

Through a parting in the trees they saw an ancient line shack ahead of them.

"There it is, Hoge," Monica announced grandly. "Our palace."

He asked sullenly, "Are we going to *eat*?"

"Just get over to the fence and tie your animals..."

After the horses were tied to a rotting fence that fronted the place, Monica pushed open the shack's worn cordwood door and entered while Farrell carried Nancy inside after her.

Farrell saw Garth seated at a table playing Solitaire, an open bottle of whiskey at his elbow.

"About time you showed up," he growled. "What'd ya do, come here by way of the Panhandle?"

Monica tensed at the remark, seeing it as a dig at her.

Holding in her anger, she said, "Ask lover-boy."

Garth watched as Farrell gently put Nancy onto an old armchair covered with a torn cotton blanket. Then the young man kneeled beside her and rubbed her hands to get some blood flowing.

"What the hell is *she* doing here?" Garth asked loudly.

Monica took off her Stetson and tossed it on an old mattress in the corner. Then she tartly replied, "She's just a stray we picked up."

Confused, Garth said, "But—but we left her back at the stage station! How'd she get all the way out here?"

Farrell turned to look back at them. Angrily, he said, "Could you just shut up for one minute and give her something to eat!"

Garth's face stiffened. Rising, he said, "Listen, Farrell, ya don't give *me* orders!" His hand reached back for his holstered pistol until he heard the Winchester's lever pulled down. He turned and saw Monica pointing the rifle at him.

"What kind of fast shuffle is this?"

Monica said, "Just keeping things calm, that's all, Charlie."

"I know where the gold is," he reminded her. "You'd kill me to save *him*?"

Monica shrugged. "Maybe I'll just wing ya. That way you could be alive and still lead us to the gold. Now you wouldn't want your gun arm to have a hole in it, would you?"

"You take an awful gamble with my patience, woman."

"I've been gambling all my life, Charlie. Why should this moment be any different?"

Finally, Farrell shouted at them, "For God sakes! Will you two stop arguing! Her pulse is getting weaker!"

Monica glared at him, but she made sure her voice didn't betray her rage.

With feigned patience, she coolly said, "You cook the food, okay, Charlie? I'm all in."

At that point, Garth's face was truly a scary sight.

It was almost nightfall.

The sharp glare of the sun pierced through the moth-eaten curtain hung over the western-side window, casting long shadows upon the dirt floor.

Farrell had revived Nancy long enough to feed her some venison and pieces of rabbit meat cooked on the giant cast-iron stove in the far corner and had her wash it down with water from an old pump they found out back. After the meal, the weary young woman fell asleep in the chair while Farrell sat on the floor beside her. It was close in the shack, and he had to remove his Stetson to cool off.

Seeing how weak Nancy was and Farrell's concern for her, Monica was confident that neither of them would make an attempt to get away; so she allowed herself a few hours of much-needed sleep in the corner mattress, her fingers curled around the rifle's stock as she dozed.

Garth was outside with his own rifle, hunting for the evening's meal.

In fact, it was his distant shot at a rabbit that woke Nancy up.

Farrell sat up attentively, his tied-up hands on the arm of the chair. Their captors apparently thought it best to let their hands remain tied.

As she groggily opened her eyes, Nancy gazed at Farrell and smiled.

"Howdy, stranger," she said weakly.

Farrell returned her smile.

"You were out for the longest time," he said. "I was torn between letting you rest and...and just hoping that you'd open your eyes again."

With her eyes searching his face, she asked, "You haven't slept yourself, have you?"

"I dozed here and there."

"And you haven't eaten?"

"They gave me some scraps of dead squirrel."

"I'd laugh if I wasn't so dead-tired."

"I'll laugh as soon as we get out of this mess."

Nancy glanced down at her tied-up hands.

"I see they kept these on us."

"Don't worry, I looked around. Seems the only knife within a mile of this place is in Garth's pocket." Farrell then looked down at his own bonds and said, "That boy Joshua did too good a job if you ask me."

Nancy said earnestly, "At least *he* got away. I'm glad he didn't end up like—" She stopped and sniffed back a tear.

Farrell took her hands in his.

"Don't worry, you're in good company. I think I'm gonna have nightmares all my days thinking about that massacre too."

Nancy turned her gaze toward Monica's sleeping figure. Her eyes burned with rage.

"That bitch! She's crazy as a loon."

"She's still sane enough to keep us here. Between her and Garth, I'm not sure *who's* wearing the pants around here."

Nancy sighed wearily. "We've been keeping good company, haven't we, Hoge?"

"Right now, it seems like that company is keeping *us*."

Nancy nodded. Then, after a moment, she looked at him and asked, "Is your real name Hoge?"

Farrell hesitated. After a moment, he replied, "Well, not exactly."

"*Not exactly*?"

"My real first name is..." He hesitated again.

"Yes? Go on, I'm on pins and needles."

"...My real name is Harv."

"Harv?"

"As in *Harvey*."

"Harvey, Harvey," she repeated lightly, then nodded. "I like the sound of that."

"Well, I *don't*!"

"So you call yourself 'Hoge.'"

"Yes!"

Nancy studied him, not saying anything for a moment. Then she said earnestly, "You're a good man, Harv Farrell. And this dumb Pinkerton shouldn't have dragged you into this mess."

He said sincerely, "Ma'am, I wouldn't want to be dragged into a heap of trouble by anyone else. Now let's take it easy and *both* get some sleep..."

Predictably, all they had gone through during the day had worn them down, and in minutes, they were both asleep; Nancy in the chair and Farrell stretching out on the old rug next to it, his Stetson over his eyes.

Lying on the mattress with her face turned away from them, Monica was awake. Tears rolled down her cheeks as her fingers tightened around the stock of the rifle.

SIX

So tired were the two young people that they both slept for the next thirteen hours. In fact, it was another rifle shot fired by Garth that woke both of them up.

As they stirred awake, Monica stood over them, her rifle cradled in her arms. She gave them the bitterest of smiles.

"Well, well," she said cuttingly, "the lovebirds are up."

Days ago, the remark would've embarrassed them, but this time, they didn't shy away from it. Having had a good night's rest, they both glared at her with a new defiance.

"That's right," said Nancy tersely, "we're up."

Monica scowled at them and then went to the door to let in Garth.

He entered the shack with a dead rabbit in his huge fist. Within minutes, he skinned it with his knife and it was cooked on the old stove for the morning's breakfast. The old shack had no plates or utensils, so they all sat around a rotting wooden table eating it with their fingers. Feeling generous, Garth had even cut apart their rawhide bonds.

The ex-guerrilla said, "Too bad you and Kansas missed last night's dinner. That was some bunny I cooked."

"I bet," said Farrell.

"But you two were dead to the world so me and Monica didn't have the heart to wake ya."

"Appreciate it."

"It also left more food for us."

Feeling his wrists for the first time that day, Farrell said, "Good to know the blood's still flowing."

"Yeah, but you're not getting any guns."

Farrell looked around the shack, taking note of its bare furnishings, but his eyes fell to the open liquor bottle on the floor beside the mattress.

"What'd you do, Garth? Stop by a saloon and pick up a bottle during your getaway?"

"No," said Monica, wiping her fingers on a slightly used handkerchief. "I got it for him. I also provided the rifles and ammunition."

"You said you hooked up with Garth. How'd you find him? Newspaper ad?"

Seated next to Farrell, Nancy suppressed a grin.

Monica said tartly, "As it turned out, that wasn't necessary."

Garth wiped his mouth with the sleeve of his shirt and said, "*I* found *her*. I survived for years being hunted by the whole Yankee army and *they* couldn't find me. You think a bunch of stupid sodbusters with horse-feed for brains are going to find me? I circled around town, covered my tracks and came right back. I sat there in that back storeroom and waited for her. When she came back, we had a nice talk about that little doin's at the jail." Then he looked at Monica and gave a little chortle.

Farrell's eyes went to Monica and he noticed her glum expression; he wondered what the "talk" consisted of. When she unconsciously used the fingers of her right hand to rub a red mark on her left wrist, he had a good idea what had happened.

Nancy ventured, "So you've joined forces."

Garth stopped and looked at her, amused. "Yeah, lady, I guess you could say that. But what gets me is what happened to bring you all the way out here."

Monica looked across at him and told him of Nancy's visit to Aubrey after the marshal and his men took Garth to jail.

Garth studied Nancy as he rubbed the days' old beard that had started to grow thick on his face.

"You did all that just to see that our boy Farrell doesn't get into any trouble?"

"What can I say?" asked Nancy lightly. "I'm a minister's daughter."

Garth was not fooled by Nancy's glib reply. "Yeah," he said wryly, "I'll bet you are..."

Farrell said, "Listen, folks. Do you really need us? I mean, we've gotten into enough trouble already here."

Garth shook his head, as if Farrell was just not getting it. "Don't you see? We're willing to give you a third split. Jesus Christ, man, we're talking about millions right in your lap. After I get to my contact with the Mex government and get the money for the gold shipment, you'll live free and easy for the rest of your days. By then, I don't care who knows about the gold because I'm taking off to the South Seas as soon as I collect. Go to one of those islands and live like a goddamn king or potentate or caliph or whoever runs the roost."

Nancy looked across the table and asked, "And what about you, Monica? What are you going to do with all that money?"

Monica's eyes narrowed as she looked at her. "Are you *really* interested, honey?"

"No," Nancy replied plainly, "I'm just making conversation."

Farrell practically cringed when he saw the rage in Monica's face. However, Garth saw it and broke into laughter. Monica angrily rose, grabbed her rifle and went outside the shack, slamming the door after her.

After drying his tears, Garth said, "Girl, I know you got a little cross with me at the swing station, but the way you talk to Queen Isabella over there..." He laughed again, trying to compose himself. "Well, I just gotta say, you sure do call a leopard by its spots, don't you?"

Nancy looked off briefly, as if she were getting bored just sitting there.

Then she faced Garth and leaned forward on the table, her expression serious.

"All right, Mr. Garth, I'll do that right now. I think we should face the truth here. The gold cache is rightfully yours; it's your secret, you know where it is, *you* have the ability to make us all rich. No one else here has that much power but you."

Garth sobered considerably and his eyes studied her as she talked.

"Yeah," he said cautiously, "and what does that mean?"

"So what I'm getting at is this. It's basically your gold cache, though Hoge will help you physically get to it. You both have a function, it makes sense, and you can't dispense with each other...but who needs Monica?"

Farrell stared at her as if she were another person.

Garth sat back and watched her, intrigued. He said, "Go on, honey, you've got the floor."

Nancy brought her hands together and bent the fingers into a kind of steeple; as her eyes were on them, she said slowly, "I would say that Monica was dispensable..."

Garth rubbed his bearded chin thoughtfully.

"So you're talking—"

Nancy suddenly hit the tabletop with the palms of her hands, making Farrell jump. She said, "I'm saying, do what you had done when you rode with Quantrill and captured enemies in your midst! What was the phrase you used? You...*paroled* them?"

Garth's eyes lit up and he smiled at a distant memory. He nodded and said, "That's right, gal. That's *exactly* what we did." Then he leaned forward and slyly asked, "But if Monica is *dispensable*, then what does that make *you*?"

Nancy smiled shyly and said, "Oh, I don't know about that, Mr. Garth. You need Hoge to help you get the gold, so he's an important part of the task at hand. And you wouldn't want to kill off his fiancée, would you?"

Both Farrell and Garth stared at her. Then she took Farrell's hand in hers and kissed it.

Garth's eyes went from one to the other. Satisfied, he said, "Yeah. Yeah, I could see that you too are fond of each other."

Farrell sat there, trying to get rid of the surprised look on his face.

"So when you gettin' hitched?"

Farrell replied without thinking, "Beats me."

"Uh," said Nancy quickly, "right after we get the gold."

Garth eyed both of them and laughed. Then he said, "You know, Hoge, we try to get away, but somehow they always find a way to hogtie us! Let's have a drink!" Then, after taking a swing from the bottle, he looked at Nancy and said earnestly, "And I'll give some *serious* thought to what you're sayin', ma'am."

"I think you'd better, or she might kill again."

Garth almost choked on his whiskey. After a few coughs, he asked, "What was that you said?"

"I said she'll kill again."

"You mean...she killed someone else besides the marshal?"

Nancy nodded grimly, and Farrell noticed that her glibness was all gone. In fact, she was dead serious now.

"On the main road outside Aubrey. She killed three people. Two posse members and Alma."

"Alma!" Baffled by this information, he asked, "How'd she get there?"

Nancy told him the whole story.

Garth sat back and shook his head. "Glory be. That white trash did all that?"

Again, Nancy nodded, her mouth a straight line.

"Well," he said, "I'm glad you told me."

"Just wanted you to watch your back."

"Well, I do appreciate it! Now, a little libation to forget our troubles..."

After Garth took a few swigs of the whiskey, he passed it to Farrell, who took a swig. Finally, he passed it to Nancy, who surprised her "fiancée" by taking to the drink enthusiastically.

Garth said loudly, "Minister's daughter! Hah!" Then he roared with laughter.

After a few minutes, he rose and said, "Well, youngin's, I'm afraid I'm going to have to take care of business." Then he touched the ivory butt of his holstered Colt and said, "And while I'm out there, I might... 'dispense' with our Miss Lawson!" He laughed again and then went outside, shutting the door behind him.

Finally alone with Nancy, Farrell turned on her immediately.

"Are you crazy? *Fiancée*! Why did you tell him that?"

"Because they need you—at least for now. They don't really need me. By hooking up with you in 'marriage,' I bought myself some time."

Farrell nodded, grudgingly accepting her explanation, but he wasn't satisfied yet.

"And what about him 'dispensing' with Monica? For God sakes, Nancy, you were prodding him to kill her!"

Nancy looked hard at him, her face a sudden mask of pain.

"Maybe I did," she said, emotion thick in her voice. "I had to set them against each other. And quite frankly, after that massacre we lived through, I'm not sure that provoking him to kill her is so wrong!"

Farrell stared at her oddly.

"This is not you talking."

"Oh really? Then tell me who it is! I don't see anyone else here, do you?"

"If you push him to kill her, that makes you an accessory!"

"Oh, Jesus, Hoge! The woman's a mass murderer!"

"So is *Garth*! That good friend of yours who you're pushing to do this deed!"

Nancy looked away for a moment, feeling her argument weakening.

He said softly, "Don't you see? We've *both* been rubbing elbows with trash over the past few days, now we're startin' to think like them!"

Nancy looked at him with sadness in her eyes.

"I know you're right," she said. "But we've still got to keep them at each other's throats. It's our only way to keep them off our backs."

Farrell studied her then, detecting something else was wrong.

"But that's not all, is it?"

Nancy looked at the dirt floor and shook her head.

"What else?"

She looked at him sympathetically. Then she said, "There was never any reward."

"There wasn't?"

She shook her head. "No. I...I tricked you into helping me."

Farrell shrugged. "Oh, hell. I kind of figured that."

Nancy stared at him. "You *did*?"

"Um-hm."

"Then why—"

Farrell stepped closer to her and tenderly lifted her

chin. He said gently, "I didn't stick with you because of *reward money...*"

She took his hand then, and kissed it for real.

GARTH STOOD beside the trunk of an aspen and did what he had to do. Then he buttoned up his fly and turned around in time to see Monica standing behind him, her Winchester under her arm.

"Finished?" she asked.

"Yeah...impressed with what you saw?"

"I've seen better."

"Not west of the Colorado you haven't." He started to step around her when her voice stopped him.

"That girl's a Pinkerton!"

Garth turned around and stared at her. "You sure?"

Monica nodded.

Garth said quietly, "Then Hoge must know it too. 'Specially since he's her fiancée."

Monica almost shouted. "*What*?"

Garth told her to shush, then glanced toward the shack.

She said through her teeth, "I don't believe it!"

"I'm not sure I do either now. But she hooked up with him from the beginning at the stage station. In fact, how do I know those two didn't know each other before they even got there separately? Maybe Hoge's a Pinkerton too and they acted like they didn't know each other so's they could trail me from two different directions."

Monica nodded and said, "Now you're using your

head. This whole shebang could be a setup by the government to hook you *and* the gold."

Garth stared at her, thinking.

"If that's true, we're gonna have to cut off the head of the snake, but fast!"

"I was hoping you'd say that."

"Too bad," Garth said with some regret. "I could really use another man to help me dig out that coach, then watch my back when I deal with the Mexes."

Monica said, "*I'll* watch your back. And being from the Panhandle, I picked up some Spanish. I could help with the translations."

Garth looked at her appreciatively and said, "True enough. But you can't swing a shovel like a man or pull a rope like one."

"So you find another sucker who'll help you, and after the whole deed is done, put him in the ground."

"I like the way you think."

"Gracias."

"But you'll kill when *I* say so, no other time. Savvy?"

"What's with you?"

He came close to her and his gray eyes shone in the sunlight. "We don't need no more massacres, like those three you gunned on the Aubrey road, get me?"

Monica's face contorted in rage.

"Those two told you!"

Garth nodded and said, "Guess it slipped your mind, huh?"

"I like that! *You're* telling *me* not to kill? Talk about the pot calling the kettle—"

"I don't give a damn about pots and kettles! And I don't care who you dry-gulch! But too many dead folks is gonna call the law down on us so fast, we can forget all about the gold. Comprende?"

Monica nodded glumly.

"Good! Now this'll seal the deal..." He threw his arms around her and pressed his lips against hers so hard that she felt them getting bruised. Her right hand was reaching for a knife scabbard she wore on her waist, but then her fingers trembled on the hilt, and gradually, they dropped off as she gave herself to him.

NANCY LIFTED the dirty canvas and looked through the small window which that faced the front of the shack.

"It's awfully quiet out there," she said, with some apprehension. "We would've heard a gunshot by now."

Farrell rose from off the floor behind the corner mattress.

"Garth's rifle isn't here."

Nancy turned back to face him. "It *must* be here! We didn't see him leave with it."

"What difference does it make? We could try for the horses, they're just outside the door."

Nancy shook her head and said, "They're *both* outside. I may not be able to see them, but I bet they've kept the front of this shack within their sights. The minute we start to untie a horse, they could open up on us."

Farrell came up to her. "But they *can't* see us go out the back."

Nancy said urgently, "It's taking a chance. One or the other could've circled around to the rear."

"Yes, it is taking a chance. But now we're alone, it's as good a chance as we'll have of getting away. How long do you think those two will tumble to what you're doing? Or for that matter, let us live?"

Nancy nodded. She said softly, "You've got a point, Harv."

Farrell frowned at her.

Nancy took his hand and squeezed it. She smiled at him and said, "All right, *Hoge*! But let's work fast!"

They turned toward the back window. Farrell ripped off the old curtain covering it and saw that the window was small, perhaps a foot long and twenty inches wide.

"Damn," he said. "Might be too small for me."

"I think you're thin enough."

"All right, but you go first."

Nancy reached over and put her hands on the sill. Then she jumped off the ground and put her head through the opening. As she swiveled her narrow hips through, her hair fell in her eyes and she grunted painfully; the edges of the sill weren't sanded down evenly and she worked hard to keep her hands from being punctured by splinters in the wood.

Finally, she made it through and with her outstretched hands before her, dropped to the ground outside. After she rolled to her feet, she got up quickly and reached out to help Farrell.

He pushed his head through the opening and then found himself caught as his midsection became stuck in the opening. He gritted his teeth and cursed as he tried to swivel his hips back and forth and get himself moving forward inch by inch.

"Hoge!" Nancy whispered hoarsely. "Take off your holster!"

Reaching back, he strained his fingers to loosen the belt buckle on his holster as Nancy kept a worried eye toward the front of the shack. After a few moments, the holster dropped to the floor inside the shack and Farrell found a new impetus to push himself through as Nancy took his hands and pulled. Gradually, he found himself on the outside, and she stood back as he dropped himself to the ground.

As she helped him up, Nancy asked, "Think they heard us?"

Farrell looked back and whispered, "I don't know. But let's not stop to find out. The Browning property is close by, due west of here. We'll try to get a couple horses there."

"Sounds good to me."

They moved deeper into the woods behind the shack, picking up speed with every step. Sometimes they found themselves holding each other's hands as they fled, each not wanting to ever lose track of the other...

It wasn't long before their captors were back at the line shack. Monica picked up Farrell's Stetson with one hand and the empty holster with the other.

She said tightly, "With those two left alone in here, you picked a hell of a time to get lovey-dovey..."

Garth put his hands on the waistband of his pants and jerked them up with emphasis. "I didn't notice you complainin'."

Ignoring that, she dropped the items to the floor and

said, "We've got to catch them, especially that girl. We can't let her get to a telegraph office and contact the Pinkertons."

"The horses are still outside, meanin' they didn't leave out the front, and anyway, no matter what we were doin', we would've heard them."

"The holster was by the window, so they traveled through the woods out back."

"Toward the Browning farm." Garth then reached behind the chair Nancy had slept on and pulled out his rifle. "Come on, let's catch 'em."

SEVEN

In less than a half hour, they pushed aside some low-hanging tree branches and found themselves facing a two-story frame house with a picket fence around it. They could also see, at some distance behind the house, a barn with a corral and outbuildings, with a wide area covered with fresh grass surrounding them. From where they stood, they could even glimpse the movements of horses in the corral.

Nancy scanned the area and said, "That's strange. Lawson said the place was abandoned."

Farrell said, "She and Garth probably weren't near this property for a while. Just because a line shack was abandoned doesn't mean the rest of the property isn't inhabited. A little while ago, I tried to find a job here, but they didn't need anyone at the time."

"You think they'll remember you?"

"Who remembers an unemployed drifter?"

She said softly, "If it were you, *I* would."

Farrell turned to look at her, and she returned his gaze, not flinching. He moved closer to her then and put his hands on her shoulders. Again, she didn't move away as she closed her eyes and waited.

The slam of the barn door made them jump and they turned to see a tall, lanky, middle-aged man walk from the barn to the house. Instinctively, they crouched in the bushes and watched.

Farrell said, "That's the foreman, Ozzie Swift. He's the one told me they didn't need anyone there."

"The place looks quiet. I don't see any cattle."

"It's a horse ranch. They breed some pretty good stock. Chance is some of their hands are out with a string delivering them to some other rancher along the border. You can make some good money selling horses."

"Well, while no one's around, let's see if we can get a couple..."

Scanning the area to see that they weren't being watched, they both ran over to the corral gate. Nancy stayed outside and kept an eye on the house as Farrell quietly pulled open the gate and went inside.

Farrell asked, "Have any breed in mind?"

"As long as it gets us to the nearest telegraph office in one piece, I don't care."

Farrell noticed a brown and white stallion standing close to the fence who looked up when he entered. Sensing this new visitor's kind nature, the horse came toward him eagerly, bobbing his huge head.

"I think he likes me."

Nancy smiled and said, more or less to herself, "He's got company, Harv."

Suddenly, both of them heard the lever come down on a Winchester. Startled, both of them turned and stared at the corner of the barn. Swift had just jumped out from behind the wall and was pointing his rifle at them.

Farrell instinctively reached for his holstered gun and then remembered that he didn't even have a holster.

Swift said, "Good thing you ain't wearin' a gun, cowboy, or you'd be pushin' up daisies about now."

Nancy cursed and reluctantly raised her hands.

Gesturing with the long barrel of the rifle, Swift said, "Okay, cowboy, get out of that corral and join your foul-talking lady friend." Farrell passed through the gate and closed it behind him, then raised his hands.

Swift looked at him oddly and said, "Haven't I seen you before?"

Farrell said awkwardly, "Ever been to Texas?"

"*Now* I remember! You were here a few weeks ago tryin' to find work. So when we turned you down, you figured to get back at us by stealing our horses, huh?"

Nancy said, "Listen, Mr. Swift, it's not what you think!"

"Know my name too, huh? Well, I don't know about you, lady, but when I see two folks figurin' to run off with our stock and I don't recall my boss getting paid for it, well, I damn well call that stealin'! Now get going inside. I want young Browning to get a look at you two before I ride for the marshal."

When they hesitated, Swift's voice grew harder as he stepped back and tightened his grip on the rifle. "I said, *inside*! They still hang horse thieves in Kansas. I'd be doin' the state a favor by killin' you right now and let your lady friend watch!"

With their hands still raised, they slowly marched over to the picket fence.

Entering the house, they both looked around curiously. Nancy immediately took note of the hand-woven rugs and the tastefully chosen furniture; of the paintings that hung on the walls that were distinctive, yet not too showy; and it was then that she deduced who was responsible for the decor.

She asked Swift, "There's a woman running the ranch, isn't there?"

Swift gruffly answered, "Miss Valerie Browning runs the place with her brother Seth, if that's any business of yours."

Farrell asked her, "How could you tell a woman has something to do with running the place?"

Nancy replied, "Look at the furniture, the placement of the rugs, where the paintings are hung. Someone actually gave some thought to how it would all look. When men run a ranch, they just choose a good couch to lay in when they get drunk and hang some old guns on the wall."

"Hey, I resent that!"

"That I can't help, Harv."

As Farrell scowled at her, Swift said, "Both of you, shut up! Just get in the study."

With Swift behind them, Farrell and Nancy passed the old, but well-kept, grandfather clock in the foyer and then looked up toward a carpeted stairway going to the second floor. Both of them took note of a wooden ramp paralleling the stairs. With Swift prodding them, they walked over to a pair of sliding doors with polished brass handles.

Swift ordered, "Pull 'em open."

Farrell did so. Inside the room, they saw two young

people, both of whom looked to be in their twenties, in the middle of a conversation. Seth was of medium height, had receding dark brown hair, and wore rimless spectacles. He wore a slightly rumpled dark suit and string tie. In fact, his appearance seemed far more appropriate to some university back east than the main house of a horse ranch. His sharp brown eyes shone brightly when he turned to face the new arrivals.

Standing near him was Valerie, who was his height, but slightly thinner in frame. Her hair was lighter than her brother's and tastefully pinned to the top of her head. She wore a blue blouse and matching skirt, and as she turned to face them, her bright blue eyes regarded both of their new visitors with interest.

Swift said, "Sorry to bother you, folks, but I just caught these two here trying to steal Chester from the corral."

"Really?" said Seth, frowning slightly. "Well, we can't have any of that."

Farrell noted that Seth sounded as if he were from the East.

Valerie took a step toward them and asked curiously, "Did you two really try to steal one of our horses?" Her cultured accent matched her brother's perfectly.

Before either of them could answer her, Swift said, "We turned him down for job a few weeks ago. Now he and his lady friend are gettin' back at us by stealin' our stock."

Valerie's blue eyes regarded Swift standing behind them. Farrell and Nancy didn't miss the sudden anger in her gaze.

"I asked *them*, Mr. Swift."

Swift frowned and said nothing.

Leaning toward them, she reached out and gently put her hand on Nancy's face. Still with her hands raised, the Pinkerton did nothing, just blinked her eyes slightly at the other woman's touch.

"Good God, Seth! She's got bruises on her face." Then she took a step back and looked at both of them with some horror. "Their clothes are torn and they both look like they've been through hell."

Seth stepped forward and said, "Then it's obvious that these two weren't attempting to steal our horses out of any malice, but because they desperately needed them." He faced them and asked, "Is that true?"

Both Farrell and Nancy nodded vigorously.

Valerie said, "I thought so!" Then she said to Swift, "Go back in the kitchen and tell Hattie to fix up some food."

"Absolutely!" said Seth.

Swift shifted his weight and his stare grew harder. When he spoke to the siblings, he sounded as if he were addressing children. "Now, listen, folks, honestly, I think you two have been too long back east. These jaspers are *horse thieves*! You don't coddle horse thieves out here!"

Seth glared at him, and the two captives noticed his rage for the first time. Angrily, he gestured toward Farrell's waist and asked, "And what kind of horse thief doesn't even bother wearing a gun, Mr. Swift! Both of them are hatless and their clothes are torn, even a blind man can tell that they've been in some kind of trouble. Besides, the Constitution of this country says a man is innocent until proven guilty!"

Swift rolled his eyes and said, more or less to himself, "Oh no, here we go again..."

Valerie said curtly, "That'll be quite enough, Mr. Swift! Now you have your orders."

Swift began to say, "But, folks, if you can let me—"

Seth said, "My sister said *Go*, Mr. Swift! Now tell Hattie to cook something and take that infernal weapon with you!"

Swift turned away, cursing under his breath and left the study to go back through the hallway on to the kitchen area in the rear of the house.

Valerie gently took Nancy's arm and led her over to the upholstered couch. Seating her, she then turned and went over to a small bar near the rear wall. "Do you want a drink?"

Nancy replied, "Maybe a glass of brandy."

Farrell said, "Just a glass for me too, please."

"Of course," she said, and started to make the drinks.

Seth saw that Farrell was still standing and quickly said, "Please, Mr. Farrell."

Farrell stopped and looked at him. "How do you know my name?"

"Oh, I remembered you. You told me you had experience with horses and you seemed eager for work, but I let Mr. Swift talk me out of it. That was stupid of me, I'll admit, and I can promise that it'll never happen again." Farrell nodded absently and took a seat next to Nancy.

As she handed them the drinks, Valerie said, "It's unfortunate that Mr. Swift is getting a little too cruel as he gets older. He's become quite trigger-happy, if you ask me."

"Yes," agreed Seth as he went to a shelf and reached for a humidor. "He's already shot down two, no, *three* men in three separate incidents, claiming that they were horse thieves, but for all I could see, these men were just in need of a good meal and a bath." He removed a cigar from the humidor and thumbed a match alight.

As he puffed on it to get it going, Valerie asked the two, "Why are you here?"

After they finished their drinks, Nancy told them as much of the story as she could without taking up too much time.

Seated in an opposite chair, Valerie said tightly, "The fiends!"

Gesturing with his glass, Farrell nodded and said, "I'm with ya there, ma'am. Fiends is just what they are."

Nancy said, "So you see, Mr. Browning, I have to get to a telegraph office to alert the nearest fort and also the Pinkertons."

"Of course, at once!" he said. Turning to his sister, he said, "Felipe's out back, have him hitch up the horses to the buggy."

Valerie nodded and started to leave. Before she could, though, Seth said, "You've both been through a horrible experience. And it's just a small example of how people around the world have treated each other throughout history."

Valerie turned back and playfully said, "Uh-oh, look out. My brother's about to become *Professor* Browning again."

Seth replied good-naturedly, "That'll be enough from you, big sister. Now get on your way."

She smiled and said, "Yes, Teacher..." Then she went out.

Seth turned to the two young people seated in the chair and asked, "More brandy?"

Both of them shook their heads.

Seth sat in the chair and flicked his cigar into an ashtray.

"Unfortunately," he said earnestly, "the kind of people you've just described have always been with us throughout history. Atilla the Hun, Ivan the Terrible, Torquemada, Quantrill. They'll be with us as long as we forget our humanity and excuse the deaths of helpless innocents as 'progress.' And it doesn't matter what the excuse for the killing is, whether it's for gold or the acquisition of land or the subjugation of others for some insane doctrine of some kind, the minute we allow this kind of thing to happen, humanity will be lost..."

The two of them stared at him. They were taken with his words, but didn't know how to respond. Preoccupied with their own problems, they had never heard anyone talk like this before.

Seth reddened and looked down at his shoes. Then he faced them and smiled shyly.

"I get carried away sometimes. You see, my sister was right. I taught history at a small college in upstate New York."

Nancy asked, "What brought you out here?"

"Our mother died some years ago and our father needed us to run the property. You see, our father suffered horribly through the war. Both of them did actually. We were only children back then and we didn't understand. You see, my family was from the north and both my parents were against the enslavement of the Negro. Unfortunately, this fervent belief in human dignity didn't sit well with some people...I'll never forget that day in April, 1863. Valerie and I were in Independence visiting with our kin when a group of men stormed this place. I'm not sure whether they were led by Quantrill or Bloody Bill Anderson, but either way, they did their worst."

Both of his listeners tensed, almost dreading what Seth would say next. They could see that the young man was having trouble continuing, and he spoke haltingly.

"They...they took our mother out...to that barn..." He stopped and swallowed hard, his face suddenly stiff and pale.

Nancy leaned forward and said softly, "It's all right, Mr. Browning."

Farrell agreed grimly, "We get the idea."

Seth sniffed back a tear and said, "My father can't walk. Two of these men crippled him many years ago."

Farrell said, "I thought both of your parents were dead."

"My father *is* dead, Mr. Farrell." Seth touched the left side of his chest and said, "He is dead in here. My mother lingered for a while, but the violence she suffered was just too much for her. She got a heart attack and died just three years afterward. My father is upstairs, his old, tired body stuck in a wheelchair for the rest of his days. Sometimes Valerie and I just sit next to him and watch him and hope that something in our youth and energy will bring him back to us. He had a stroke several years ago; he can move his arms and hands a little, but he can never speak again.

"You know, I can understand a person's preoccupation with making a living and getting ahead, but it would also be good if people remembered that there are those in the world who are still victims of man's cruelty, and that those who don't remember history will most certainly repeat it."

Without realizing it, Nancy reached down at her side, found Farrell's hand and squeezed it till it hurt.

The sound of a rifle shot followed by a woman's scream sounded from the kitchen area beyond the stairway; then the chaotic sounds of footsteps moving haphazardly from the corridor outside the kitchen mixed with that of harsh voices shouting orders.

Seth sprang from his chair and ran over to his desk. Yanking a drawer open, he pulled out a Colt and started to raise it until Farrell leaped off the couch and grabbed his wrist. Looking him in the eye, Farrell took the gun from him and said quietly, "You've suffered enough, Seth. This is gonna be *my* show."

Meeting his gaze, Seth nodded and said, "Very well, Mr. Farrell."

Quickly, Farrell stuffed the pistol into the rear waistband of his pants.

Nancy rose off the couch and faced the archway, dread growing within her.

In the next moment, Valerie was shoved into the room by Monica, who was brandishing her Winchester. Garth followed her, leveling his rifle at those already in the room.

Valerie ran into her brother's arms and then turned back, giving a hateful look to Monica.

"She shot Mr. Swift!" she cried, her voice trembling.

"Wrong, honey," Monica replied venomously. "I *killed* Mr. Swift!"

Valerie continued, pointing toward Garth, "And

that one struck Hattie across the jaw with the butt of his rifle! I don't know if he killed her!"

Ignoring the accusation, Garth said, "Thought this place was full of spiders and weeds by now, guess I was wrong...I'm glad you folks found our friends. Now if you don't mind, we'll be taking them with us for a little ride."

Angrily, Seth said, "You're not taking them anywhere, certainly not to shoot them down in cold blood."

Garth looked at him oddly. "I don't get it," he said. "These folks are strangers to you, why should you care about what happens to them?"

Seth answered, "Maybe that's why I do care, Mr. Garth. Because they're strangers, and no one expects us to care about them."

"You know my name? What else did they tell you?"

Seth glared at him, controlling his rage.

"I know *all* about you, Mr. Garth, and this filthy murderess as well. I know of your being wanted by the federal government for your war crimes and I also know of your hidden gold!"

Nancy cried, "Seth!"

"It's all right, Miss Belmont. I don't care if they know." Then he stared at both Garth and Monica and said, "You've murdered everyone who's known about your hidden gold, but the crimes you've committed are finally seeing the light of day. Treasure can remain buried for centuries, but atrocities always come out into the open sooner or later."

"Get *him*!" said Garth, smiling.

Monica growled, "I'm still wondering what part of

his body to shoot first for that 'filthy murderess' remark."

"Nevertheless," Seth continued, "you can't murder Mr. Farrell and Miss Belmont. Because if you do, you'll have to kill *me* as well."

Her voice thick with emotion, Valerie added, "Wrong, Seth. They'll have to kill *us* first!"

Nancy cried, "Neither of you has to do this!"

Seth turned to Valerie and said lightly, "Oh, I don't know. Sis, what was that quote father taught us? Something about being Our Brother's Keeper?"

Valerie replied sincerely, "The words escape me right now, Seth, but I agree with you completely."

Monica jacked down the lever of the Winchester and aimed first at Seth.

"Oh, this is going to be a pleasure!"

Farrell was reaching into his rear waistband for the gun when a sound came from the hallway.

Garth and Monica looked at each other.

"Who else is here?" Garth demanded to know. No one answered him.

"Better find out," said Monica. "I'll cover them."

Garth had a last look at them and then left the study, turning toward the stairway.

Farrell leaned toward Nancy and whispered to her, "When I shout, get yourself close to the Brownings and push 'em to the ground."

Nancy whispered back, "Be careful, Harv."

Farrell replied, "You know, I'm starting to like that name."

Curious about what was happening to Garth, Monica backed out of the study while still keeping them covered with the rifle.

Before she had a chance to call up to him, Garth shouted down from the second floor.

"Don't worry!" he called down. "Just an old man in a wheelchair who can't talk. He won't give us trouble." He started to come down the stairs.

As Monica was turning to face the study again, Farrell wrapped his fingers tightly around the butt of the gun and started to lift it from his rear waistband.

Suddenly, there was the sound of a rifle firing from the direction of the kitchen corridor and Monica was thrust forward, her own rifle flying out of her hands.

Farrell cried, "Now!"

Nancy flung herself into both siblings and shoved them to the floor, her arms protectively wrapped around them.

Farrell drew the gun and went for the double doors. Before he got to them, he heard a shot fired from Garth's rifle and quickly dropped to the ground. Looking up, he caught sight of Monica. He saw her hands thrust up behind her back as she staggered out into the hallway. Her Stetson had fallen off and her face was deathly pale; only her mouth, once full and wide and desirable, was now full of blood.

Garth had by now descended the stairs and fired into the room, the slug barely missing Nancy, who was covering the Browning siblings with her own body. The slug ripped the carpet near them.

To thwart Garth's aim, Farrell quickly leaped up and put his hand on the inside brass handle of one of the doors and shoved it closed, instantly pulling the opposite door shut as well with a loud slam.

Garth got to the doors just as they closed. When he put his hand on the brass handle to yank them open,

Farrell heard the movement and fired a bullet through the door where he thought Garth was standing. But the shot was quick and fired too high, causing Garth to duck behind the hallway wall. Cursing, the ex-Reb turned around and looked down at the body of Ozzie Swift, his still-smoking rifle on the floor beside him.

Monica was gritting her teeth in pain as she fought to stay on her feet. She clutched the wall and stared at Garth; her eyes showing fear and desperation for the first time.

Indicating the dead body at their feet, Garth sneered, "So you killed him, huh? You killed him good enough for him to get back on his feet and kill *you*, that's what you did, ya dumb bitch!"

With her last ounce of strength, she threw herself onto Garth and reached up to tightly grasp his shirt.

"Charlie!" she said, panting. "Don't leave me! Take me with you to get the gold!"

Garth gazed down at her and shook his head. "I warned you not to be so trigger-happy..." As one hand held the rifle, his other slid into his pocket.

"Sorry, sweetheart. But there's no gold where you're goin'..."

With one quick movement, he cut her throat with his razor-sharp knife and then shoved her off of him. Her eyes bulged with shock as her fingers reached up to her bleeding throat. By the time Garth ran out the front door, Monica had fallen to the floor and, after her body jumped and writhed in convulsions, she finally died.

Inside the closed study, they heard the slam of the front door as Garth fled the house.

Farrell asked urgently, "Everyone all right?"

Rising from the floor, Valerie said, "We're all very lucky."

When they heard Garth's horse whinny and hoof beats on the ground outside, Seth said, "We'd better take after him."

Farrell said earnestly, "No, Seth. I said it before, this is *my* show."

Nancy said, "I'm coming with you!"

"There's that woman in the kitchen to look after." Then he faced the siblings and said, "Make sure she doesn't follow me."

Standing behind Nancy, Valerie put her hands gently on her shoulders and said, "Don't worry, Mr. Farrell."

Seth added, "She'll be safe with us."

As Nancy turned around to argue with them, Farrell ran over to the sliding doors and pulled them open. Rushing into the foyer, he looked down and saw the bodies of Ozzie Swift and Monica. He lingered briefly as he looked down at the dead woman, but forced his gaze away. Picking up the dead foreman's rifle, he headed for the front door and threw it open.

Farrell got to the picket fence just in time to see the trail of dust rising in the east road. He ran over to Monica's horse, untied the reins from the fence and leaped into the saddle. The animal was not used to Farrell's smell and fought him briefly, but the Texan quickly took charge and used his spurs to jab into the horse's flanks. The animal whinnied fiercely, but finally obeyed, turning into the east road.

Farrell saw the figure ahead of him getting farther and farther away, forcing him to jab his spurs again.

The horse picked up speed and the angry clouds of dust rose in their wake as they headed for the Missouri border.

EIGHT

As he sped after his quarry, Farrell caught sight of him turning a bend in the road and disappearing around the foot of a craggy hillside. At first he thought that Garth was planning some kind of ambush, but then he saw him emerge from a hollow of trees far ahead of him and continue his journey down the road. It was as if Garth had attempted to veer off and make a run for it deep into the woods, but was blocked off from escape by the row of foothills which lined the side of the road.

As the two barreled down the Independence-Lone Jack road, Farrell noticed that the distance between them was narrowing. Something was definitely wrong with Garth's horse. Perhaps his mount was not used to hard riding, or perhaps the ex-guerrilla was pushing the animal too much, but either way, Farrell saw that it stumbled at least twice. He could imagine the foam developing on the horse's coat, and the labored breathing, the animal trying as he could to outdistance the more durable gelding pursuing it.

Then he realized that Fred Parker had specifically demanded that Farrell give Garth a certain horse from a certain stall. It was obviously the stationmaster's way of getting even with Garth for punching him. He purposely had Farrell give him a horse that tired easily; a nag that was adequate for an ordinary ride, but one that didn't hold up when pressed into a desperate chase; and Fred just *knew* that the ex-guerrilla would be making that final fast getaway from one of his crimes.

As the gap narrowed, Farrell thought of drawing the rifle from the saddle boot and firing at Garth, but he knew that an accurate shot fired from the back of one speeding horse to another was nigh impossible. He certainly didn't hold with any of that eastern-based pulp western blather that a lawman pursuing an outlaw on horseback can accurately shoot him off his horse. Even with a rifle, the idea of hitting a moving target from horseback while speeding down some oft-used trail was absolutely ridiculous.

He saw Garth speed past what looked like a large sign on the right. He vaguely recalled the sign when he and Garth had headed in the opposite direction and hadn't noticed the words on it before. Now, however, as he started to pass it, there was no mistaking the words: *YOU ARE NOW ENTERING MISSOURI*.

Keeping up a steady pace, Farrell crossed the Kansas-Missouri border, but as he stared far ahead of him, he saw that Garth's animal was definitely slowing down.

Suddenly, he heard booming sounds in the distance, three of them, one after the other. At first he thought it was thunder; and as he rode, he looked up and searched for storm clouds, but all he could see was a clear blue sky.

It would be another ten minutes of hard riding before Farrell saw the horse ahead of him openly rebel, fighting Garth's attempts to spur it on by veering all over the road. With his horse skittering back and forth, Garth soon found himself fighting to control the animal with little room for him to maneuver. Both rider and horse were now at the base of a mountain, with a wall of sheer rock directly behind them.

Now, while horse and rider were in more or less a stationary position, Farrell pulled the rifle out of the saddle boot and pulled on the reins, cautiously slowing his own horse to within a quarter mile of his quarry.

As if he sensed what Farrell was doing, Garth suddenly pulled his own rifle from the saddle boot and turned it toward Farrell.

Bringing his horse to a complete stop, Farrell raised the rifle to his shoulder and aimed it at the man ahead.

Then, before either man could pull a trigger, a loud explosion shook the area and a sudden rumble of earth was heard from above.

For Garth's horse, the explosion was the last straw. The frightened animal reared back and threw its rider to the ground. Then, as the ex-guerrilla hit the dirt heavily, the horse sped off down the road and disappeared around a bend.

Stunned, Garth rose slowly and had just enough time to look up and see tons of rock and loosened earth coming down. Farrell yanked the reins of his horse, turning it back down the road. He needn't have bothered; the animal quickly understood the danger and did exactly what its rider wanted, spinning around and racing back in the direction it had come from.

Then, from a safe distance, Farrell stopped the horse and turned around just in time to see Garth, now reduced to a small, pitiable figure still holding a rifle, screaming at the top of his lungs as the whole side of a mountain rained boulders and tons of earth down on him. Farrell winced as he saw the ex-guerrilla struck down by the falling debris and buried under it within seconds.

And then, just as quickly, the landslide stopped. Half the road was buried under the fallen hillside and angry clouds of dirt rose in the air.

Curiously, Farrell walked the spooked horse forward, wondering why there had been an explosion in the first place. After he got to the spot where Garth had stood, he sat his horse and looked the ground over.

Then he saw it.

As he fanned away the dust stinging his eyes, he caught sight of a thick-fingered and calloused hand, now completely covered with blood, sticking out of the topsoil, and not moving.

"What are you doin' here?" asked an unfamiliar voice roughly.

Two men came from across the road. They were dressed in shoddy overalls and dust-covered hats. To Farrell, they both looked like they couldn't add up two and two between them. Seeing that they were both carrying rifles and that they were about to raise them, Farrell raised his own weapon and pointed it at them levelly.

"Put 'em down, gents."

The two men glanced at each other, then reluctantly dropped the long guns to the ground.

"Now," Farrell asked, "where'd that explosion come from?"

The taller of the two said, "You can't blame us, Mister. Frank and me don't cotton to all this diggin', so we just got a couple sticks of dynamite and figured we'd blast it out 'afore the rest of the town got wise."

"Blast *what* out?"

The other man shook his head derisively and said, "The *gold*, ya damn fool! Ain't ya heard?"

Farrell blinked his eyes through the dust and gave them a wry smile.

"Yeah," he said softly, "I heard..."

THE CAVALRY PATROL rode up to them at a trot. It was a squad of eight men, led by a fresh-faced lieutenant and a sergeant who was about fifteen years older. The young officer raised his white-gloved hand and the troops halted before Farrell and the two men in the road.

The soldiers sat their horses and gawked at the fallen hillside, much of which was lying across the road. Seeing a few soldiers close in around the two sodbusters, Farrell lowered his rifle.

The lieutenant touched the brim of his campaign hat and said, "Mr. Farrell, I presume?"

Farrell looked at him oddly and said, "How'd you know who I was?"

The young officer replied, "We received an emergency telegraph message from the Pinkerton agency in

Chicago. One of their operatives, a young lady by the name of Nancy Belmont, wired Pinkerton headquarters and they in turn contacted Fort Benson to look out for you and an ex-Confederate guerrilla by the name of Charles Taggert, alias Charles Garth. We understand that you were chasing him straight from the Kansas border country, which, considering Mr. Taggert's crimes in that region, I find ironic...where is Mr. Taggert?"

Grimly, Farrell gestured behind the troopers to the hand sticking out of the ground. All of them, including the lieutenant, turned around and spotted it.

The young officer turned back to Farrell. Hiding his own disgust behind a veneer of official protocol, he said curtly, "I see..." Then his eyes went to the two men standing among the soldiers with their hands raised. "And these two men you held your rifle on?"

Farrell said, "They blew up the mountain."

The two men didn't deny it. They saw that Farrell had some kind of favored status among the soldiers and, instead of arguing, they both smiled up at the lieutenant as if he was some kind of benevolent father figure offering them candy.

Instead of returning the smile, the young officer sternly said, "We've stopped other men in this vicinity who claimed they were digging for *Quantrill's gold.* This rumor of buried Confederate gold is nothing more than a damnable lie spread by ex-Confederate guerrillas and other internal enemies to sow discord and anarchy among the populace."

Farrell made no comment. Instead he just watched the lieutenant's face closely for any hint that the young man himself didn't believe his own speech. Ultimately, he decided that the lieutenant was good, *very* good. Hell, he almost believed it himself.

Leaning on the pommel, the lieutenant eyed the two miscreants and added, "Bringing half a mountain down across a major thoroughfare and impeding commerce and the travel of ordinary citizens is a matter we don't take lightly, gentlemen. Sergeant, put these men under arrest."

The two sodbusters suddenly looked scared as the big sergeant and two other soldiers dismounted and came over to them.

Farrell said, "I wish you wouldn't throw the book at 'em, Lieutenant. I'm sure they're just two ordinary folks bitten by gold fever." He paused, reflecting on his own involvement. "It can happen to any of us," he added.

The two sodbusters, still with their hands raised, both nodded stupidly.

The lieutenant said, "I'll consider that, Mr. Farrell. But they used dynamite near a public road." With his head, he indicated where Garth's body was. "You see the results of their hunger for gold. Mr. Taggert may have deserved such a fate, but it wasn't their place to decide it, even if they didn't consciously intend it.

"In the meantime, you'll be escorted just a few miles east of here to Fort Benson, where you'll give us all the details about this affair to our commanding officer."

A RUDDY-FACED OFFICER named Major Harley leaned back in his chair, his big hands clasped together in his lap as he contemplated Farrell's story. His adjutant was sitting at another desk, furiously writing everything down in an official-looking journal.

The major lightly fingered his dark brown handlebar mustache and said, "That's some story, Mr. Farrell."

The soldiers had given Farrell a private's blouse to replace his own torn-up shirt. Sipping from a mug of hot coffee, the Texan asked, "Don't you believe me?"

"Oh, yes! Yes, I do! Unfortunately, having seen several examples of man's greed and callousness up close, I definitely believe you."

"I'm glad," said Farrell, idly watching the steam curl up from the mug. "I fell for all of it as well. The search for gold, *somebody else's* gold." He looked up at the major. "What'll happen to it now?"

The major said, "We're still combing the area for it. It shouldn't be too hard for our troops to find a buried stagecoach eventually. There's nothing we can do about the gold rumor, and we certainly can't stop people from digging up the surrounding hills, but we'll certainly keep an eye on things and make sure that, if or when someone does find it, it gets returned immediately to the federal treasury. Unfortunately, we can't bring back to life the many victims who died in this affair, but at least we can make sure that it never happens again."

Farrell looked him in the eye and asked, "Knowing how folks can be, how can you make sure it doesn't happen again?"

The major gave a wry little smile and shrugged. "We're *not* sure, Mr. Farrell. We'll never be sure. Like everything else, we just have to be vigilant."

"I guess so."

Farrell looked down at the steaming mug in his hands. His discomfort was obvious.

Finally, after a long pause, he said, "I thought I was going to share in a pot of gold, and all I got for it were horrible sights I'll never forget. Major, I've never been in a war, and I'm not Two-Gun Tex who can shoot off the eyebrows of a jackrabbit at twenty paces. I'm just an ordinary guy who wants to stay out of trouble. But... never in my life have I seen so many people die as I have in the past two days..." There was a catch in his throat. As he stared off at an imaginary spot across the room, his mind went back over those days, isolating the violent acts, and remembering only one thing about them.

His voice was so soft then, it sounded like a whisper. "And I didn't do anything to prevent it..."

There was a pause as Major Harley took all this in.

Then he said, "You and Miss Belmont prevented the Brownings from getting killed."

"Yes, but—"

"Listen, Mr. Farrell," the major said. "I've known men who have seen atrocities up close. Some have survived the war, some have been further out west and seen Indian butchery, and some have even seen the results of the terrorist acts committed by Quantrill and Anderson. They've seen their friends killed before their eyes; but whatever it was, a bullet, cannon fire, an artillery bombardment, it missed *them*. These men, good men too, good soldiers, were tormented by what they'd seen. They ask themselves, 'Why did these people die, but I didn't?'"

Farrell leaned forward and asked anxiously, "How do they deal with it?"

The major answered simply, "They live. That's what they do. They continue to hold on to life. They *have* to, Mr. Farrell. They keep busy, they find love, they move on. But they *live*! There is no other choice. They *have* to live, not only for their own sakes, but because it would be the ultimate defiance to all the Quantrills of the world. To prove that whatever the butchers try to do...*it didn't work...*"

When Harley mentioned the phrase "they find love," Farrell thought of Nancy, and he wondered how she was. He hadn't seen her since he'd left the Browning spread. The army fed him, but they didn't give him a chance to communicate with anyone else.

"What about Nancy?" he asked. "I know she was also shaken up by what we went through."

"Lieutenant Finley, that's the young officer who met you on the road with his men, has already gotten Miss Belmont's report on what happened." He rose and said, "We're finished here, Mr. Farrell. Please consider what I've said."

He and Farrell shook hands.

"I *will*, Major."

"By the way, your friends are waiting outside."

After Farrell left the major's quarters, he saw them across the parade ground. Nancy, Seth and Valerie were leaving the commissary, where orders had been given to feed them on their arrival.

Nancy was wearing a plain sky-blue dress that seemed slightly tight on her, accentuating her breasts and shoulders. After she stepped off the boardwalk, she looked up and saw him. Then both of them ran across the grounds and, with little hesitation, plunged into each other's arms. They both stood there in the middle of the fort embracing tightly for several moments. Then, as if it was the most natural thing in the world, they kissed each other long and passionately. Soldiers passed by on the surrounding boardwalks and watched the pair, amused by their lack of restraint in such official surroundings.

After the kiss, Farrell looked her up and down. "Where'd you get—"

Anticipating his question, Nancy explained lightly, "It's one of Valerie's dresses. As you can see, I'm slightly taller than her."

"You look beautiful in it."

They were still in each other's arms when Seth and Valerie came up to them. The siblings grinned at each other and Seth gave his sister a wink.

Valerie cleared her throat.

Suddenly noticing that there were others around them, the couple turned to look at them, but still held onto each other.

"I'm sorry to interrupt," said Valerie, "but my brother has something to say." Then, after glancing at him, she playfully added, "*Again*."

Seth frowned at his sister briefly. Then he faced the two young people and said, "Mr. Farrell, I'll get right down to business. I need a foreman."

Farrell practically gaped at him. "What?"

"If you're half as good with horseflesh as you claimed you were during our last interview, I want you as our foreman."

Smiling, Nancy turned to Seth and said, "He'll take it!"

Farrell stared at her, pausing.

Seth asked, "Is that true, Mr. Farrell? Are you taking the job?"

Farrell looked into Nancy's eyes. Then, still gazing at her, he took her hand and kissed it.

Turning back to the siblings, he said, "My fiancée knows best."

Then Nancy asked hesitantly, "You don't mind if your foreman has a wife, do you?"

Valerie replied, "The house Mr. Swift lived in is big enough for two people, and I can't think of anyone more deserving of it."

As the four of them walked across the parade ground to where soldiers had parked the Brownings' horse and buggy, Major Harley stood in front of his open door and watched them go.

He thought hard about Farrell's question and wondered whether the hurt and pain caused by men like Quantrill would ever truly disappear. From his experience on the frontier, he knew that surviving an atrocity, with its painful memories and lingering guilt, was a herculean task no human being should have to face.

But as he watched the four happy young people get into the buggy and then pass through the front gates, he knew that even the wounded have a right to the future...

A LOOK AT: THE OUTLAWS HENNESSEY

BY BOB HERZBERG

Outlaw violence and swift Western justice are about to collide...

When farm boys Jed Tully and Ty Brody attempt to seek retribution against a greedy merchant by robbing his store one fateful night, they stumble upon a scene of chaos: the store already looted and its owner slain by the infamous Hennessey gang.

Framed for the robbery and hunted for murder, Jed and Ty find themselves forced to flee from the law's grasp and seek refuge within the ranks of the very gang they hoped to defy. The Hennesseys' brutality, entanglement with corrupt authorities, and internal strife shatter the innocence of the two youths, plunging them into a maelstrom of violence and moral ambiguity.

As they grapple with their newfound reality, Jed and Ty are faced with a daunting question. Can they retain their humanity amidst the chaos and muster the courage to confront the Hennessey gang, whose reign of terror threatens not only their own lives but the safety of their entire community?

AVAILABLE NOW

THANK YOU

Thank you for taking the time to read *Bloody Trails: A Western Double*. If you enjoyed it, please consider telling your friends or posting a short review. Word of mouth is an author's best friend and much appreciated. Thank you.

Bob Herzberg

ABOUT THE AUTHOR

BOB HERZBERG was born in Brooklyn, N.Y. in 1956. He had graduated from Erasmus Hall High School and went on to take a variety of jobs, from truck driver to warehouse manager to salesman. He always wanted to act in plays and do comedy and soon started performing in community theaters and colleges around New York. By the 1990s, Bob had performed standup comedy, improv and murder mystery/dinner theater at clubs in both N.Y. and Hollywood. Around the same time, he wrote and co-starred in *The Melnicks* series on local TV, which had been aired on both coasts. In 2006, he started writing western novels and mysteries. He is a member of Western Writers of America, International Thriller Writers and the Dramatists' Guild. In the past six years he has had four books published: *Shooting Scripts, From Pulp Western to Film,* which is about western authors and the films made from their works; *The FBI & the Movies*, which focuses on films with FBI characters and the Bureau's influence on these productions; *Savages & Saints: the Changing Image of American Indian in Westerns*, which details the Indian Wars and the films made about them; and *The Left Side of the Screen* which focuses on Communists and Liberals in Hollywood during the years 1929-2009. In 2008, he appeared on TV-Land's *Myths & Scandals* in a sequence about the FBI; in 2013, he appeared as a commentator on the 20th anniversary Blu-ray edition of *The Fugitive.* Bob latest, *Revolutionary Mexico on Film, 1914-2014,* will be released in 2015. He's been happily married to the lovely actress/poet Colleen Hayden. One day they hope to live out west.

www.ingramcontent.com/pod-product-compliance
Lightning Source LLC
LaVergne TN
LVHW040215110826
845146LV00005B/1293

* 9 7 9 8 8 9 5 6 7 8 3 2 9 *